How to Be Popular

HOW
TO BE
Popular

MEG CABOT

HOW TO BE Popular

HARPERTEMPEST

An Imprint of HarperCollins*Publishers*

HarperTempest is an imprint of HarperCollins Publishers.

www.harperteen.com

Library of Congress Cataloging-in-Publication Data
Cabot, Meg.
    How to be popular / Meg Cabot.— 1st ed.
        p.   cm.
    Summary: Sixteen-year-old Steph Landry finds an old book on
how to be popular and decides to change her social status by fol-
lowing its advice, much to the bafflement of her two best friends.
    ISBN-13: 978-0-06-088012-5 (trade bdg.)
    ISBN-10: 0-06-088012-0 (trade bdg.)
    ISBN-13: 978-0-06-088013-2 (lib. bdg.)
    ISBN-10: 0-06-088013-9 (lib. bdg.)
    [1. Popularity—Fiction. 2. High schools—Fiction. 3. Schools—
Fiction.] I. Title.
PZ7.C11165Ho 2006   2006000367
[Fic]—dc22

Typography by Sasha Illingworth
1 2 3 4 5 6 7 8 9 10

First Edition

In memory of my grandfather,
Bruce C. Mounsey

Acknowledgments

Many thanks to Beth Ader, Jennifer Brown,
Barb Cabot, Michele Jaffe, Laura Langlie, Abigail
McAden, and especially Benjamin Egnatz

HOW
TO BE
Popular

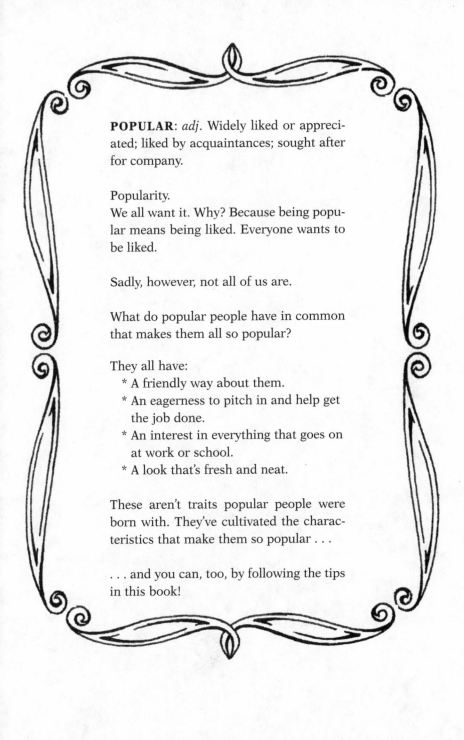

POPULAR: *adj.* Widely liked or appreciated; liked by acquaintances; sought after for company.

Popularity.
We all want it. Why? Because being popular means being liked. Everyone wants to be liked.

Sadly, however, not all of us are.

What do popular people have in common that makes them all so popular?

They all have:
    * A friendly way about them.
    * An eagerness to pitch in and help get the job done.
    * An interest in everything that goes on at work or school.
    * A look that's fresh and neat.

These aren't traits popular people were born with. They've cultivated the characteristics that make them so popular . . .

. . . and you can, too, by following the tips in this book!

 *One*

T-MINUS TWO DAYS AND COUNTING
SATURDAY, AUGUST 26, 7 P.M.

I should have known from the way the woman kept looking at my name tag that she was going to ask.

"Steph Landry," she said as she pulled out her wallet. "Now, how do I know that name?"

"Gosh, ma'am," I said. "I don't know." Except that, even though I had never seen this woman before in my life, I had a pretty good idea how she might have heard of me.

"I know," the lady said, snapping her fingers, then pointing at me. "You're on the Bloomville High School women's soccer team!"

"No, ma'am," I said to her. "I'm not."

"You weren't on the court of the Greene County Fair Queen, were you?"

But you could tell, even as the words were coming

out of her mouth, she knew she was wrong again. I don't have Indiana county fair queen hair—i.e., my hair is short, not long; brown, not blonde; and curly, not straight. Nor do I have an Indiana county fair queen bod—i.e., I'm kinda on the short side, and if I don't exercise regularly, my butt kind of . . . expands.

Obviously I do what I can with what God gave me, but I won't be landing on *America's Next Top Model* anytime soon, much less the court of any fair queen.

"No, ma'am," I said.

The thing is, I really didn't want to get into it with her. Who would?

But she wouldn't let it go.

"Goodness. I just know I know your name from somewhere," the woman said, handing me her credit card to pay for her purchases. "You sure I didn't read about you in the paper?"

"Pretty sure, ma'am," I said. God, that would be just what I need. For the whole thing to have shown up in the paper.

Fortunately, though, I haven't been in the paper since my birth announcement. Why would I? I'm not particularly talented, musically or otherwise.

And while I'm in mostly AP classes, that's not because I'm an honor student or anything. That's just because if you grow up in Greene County knowing that lemon Joy goes in your dishwasher and not your iced tea, you get put in AP classes.

It's actually sort of surprising how many people in

Greene County make that mistake. With the lemon Joy, I mean. According to my friend Jason's dad, who is a doctor over at Bloomville Hospital.

"It's probably," I said to the woman as I ran her credit card through the scanner, "because my parents own this store."

Which I know doesn't sound like much. But Courthouse Square Books *is* the only independently owned bookstore in Bloomville. If you don't include Doc Sawyer's Adult Books and Sexual Aids, out by the overpass. Which I don't.

"No," the woman said, shaking her head. "That's not it, either."

I could understand her frustration. What's especially upsetting about it—if you think about it (which I try not to, except when things like this happen)—is that Lauren and I, up until the end of fifth grade, had been friends. Not close friends, maybe. It's hard to be close friends with the most popular girl in school, since she's got such a busy social calendar.

But certainly close enough that she'd been over to my house (okay, well, once. And she didn't exactly have the best time. I blame my father, who was baking a batch of homemade granola at the time. The smell of burnt oatmeal WAS kind of overpowering) and I'd been over to hers (just once . . . her mom had been away getting her nails done, but her dad had been home and had knocked on Lauren's door to say that the explosion noises I was making during our game of Navy Seal Barbie were a little too loud. Also that he'd never heard of Navy Seal Barbie, and wanted to know what was so wrong with playing Quiet Nurse Barbie).

"Well," I said to the customer, "maybe I just . . . you know. Have one of those names that sounds familiar."

Yeah. Wonder why. Lauren's the one who coined the term "Don't pull a Steph Landry." Out of revenge.

It's amazing how fast it caught on, too. Now if anyone in school does anything remotely crack-headed or dorky, people are all, "Don't pull a Steph!" or "That was so Steph!" or "Don't be such a Steph!"

And I'm the Steph they're talking about.

Nice.

"Maybe that's it," the woman said doubtfully. "Gosh, this is going to bug me all night. I just know it."

Her credit card was approved. I tore off the slip for her to sign and started bagging her purchases. Maybe I could tell her that the reason she might know me is because of my grandfather. Why not? He's currently one of the most talked about—and richest—men in southern Indiana, ever since he sold some farmland he owned along the proposed route of the new I-69 ("connecting Mexico to Canada via a highway 'corridor'" through Indiana, among other states) for the construction of a Super Sav-Mart, which opened last weekend.

Which means he's been in the local paper a lot, especially since he spent a chunk of his money building an observatory that he plans to donate to the city.

Because every small town in southern Indiana needs an observatory.

Not.

It also means my mother isn't speaking to him, because the Super Sav-Mart, with its reduced prices, is probably going to put all of the shops along the square, including Courthouse Square Books, out of business.

But I knew the customer would never fall for it. Grandpa's last name isn't even the same as mine. He was afflicted from birth with the unfortunate moniker of Emile Kazoulis . . . although he's done pretty well for himself, despite this handicap.

I was just going to have to face the fact that, just like the red Super Big Gulp that wouldn't come out of Lauren's white denim D&G skirt—even though my dad tried. He used Shout and everything, and when it didn't work, finally went out and got her a brand-new skirt—my name was going to be forever stained on people's memories.

And not in a good way.

"Oh well," the lady said, taking her bag and her receipt. "I guess it's just one of those things."

"I guess it is," I said to her. Not without some relief. Because she was leaving. Finally.

But my relief turned out to be short-lived. Because a second later the bells over the front door to the shop tinkled, and Lauren Moffat herself—wearing the same white Lilly Pulitzer low-rise capris I'd tried on at the mall the other day, but had been unable to purchase due to the fact that they cost the equivalent of twenty-five hours of work behind the cash register at Courthouse Square Books—was coming into the store, holding a Tasti D-Lite

e Penguin, and going, "Mom. Would you hurry
e been waiting for you for, like, ever."

d I realized, belatedly, who I'd been talking to.

Vhatever. I can't be expected to read the name on
y credit card someone hands me. Besides, there are
e hundreds of Moffats here in Bloomville.

"Oh, Lauren, you'll know," Mrs. Moffat said to her
daughter. "How do I know the name Steph Landry?"

"Um, maybe because she's the one who spilled that
Big Red Super Big Gulp on my white D&G skirt in front
of everyone in the caf that day in the sixth grade?"
Lauren replied with a snort.

And she's never forgiven me for it. Much less let anyone forget about it.

Mrs. Moffat flung a horrified look at me over the
padded shoulder of her Quacker Factory sweater set.

"Oh," she said. "Dear. Lauren, I—"

Which was when Lauren finally noticed me, standing
behind the cash register.

"God, Mom," she said, giggling, as she pushed open
the door to slip back out into the evening heat. "Way to
pull a Steph Landry."

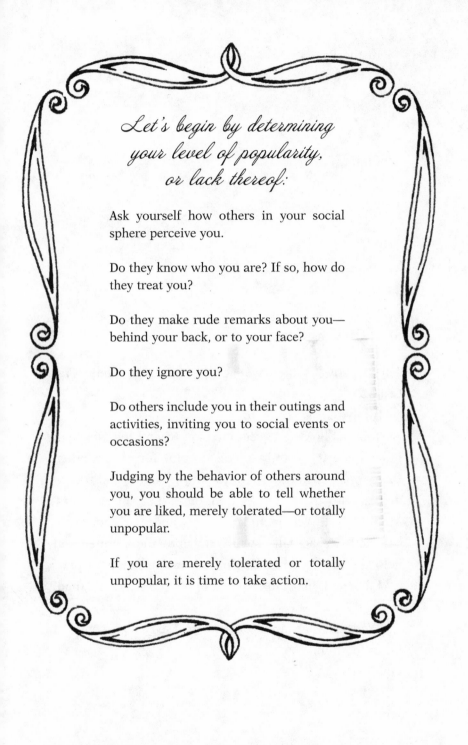

*Let's begin by determining
your level of popularity,
or lack thereof:*

Ask yourself how others in your social sphere perceive you.

Do they know who you are? If so, how do they treat you?

Do they make rude remarks about you—behind your back, or to your face?

Do they ignore you?

Do others include you in their outings and activities, inviting you to social events or occasions?

Judging by the behavior of others around you, you should be able to tell whether you are liked, merely tolerated—or totally unpopular.

If you are merely tolerated or totally unpopular, it is time to take action.

 *Two*

This is how Jason has been greeting me lately: "Yo, Crazytop!"

And yes, it *is* annoying.

Too bad he doesn't seem to care when I tell him that.

"What's the criminal master plot for the evening, Crazytop?" Jason wanted to know as he and Becca drifted into the store an hour after Lauren and Mrs. Moffat left it. Well, technically, only Becca drifted. Jason barreled. He actually swung up onto the counter and helped himself to a Lindt truffle from the candy display.

Like he didn't think this was going to make me mad, or anything.

"You eat that, and you owe me sixty-nine cents," I informed him.

He dug a dollar out of the front pocket of his jeans and slapped it down onto the countertop. "Keep the change," he said.

Then he plucked another Lindt from the display jar and tossed it to Becca.

Who was so surprised when the Lindt chocolate truffle came at her out of nowhere, she didn't think to catch it, so it smacked her in the collarbone, fell to the floor, and rolled under the display cabinet.

So then Becca was scrambling around on the A-B-C alphabet carpet, trying to find the lost truffle, and going, "Hey, there're a lot of dust bunnies down here. You guys ever think of vacuuming this place, or what?"

"Now you owe me thirty-eight cents," I said to Jason.

"I'm good for it." He *always* says this. "How long until you can shake this cracker box?"

He always asks this, too. When he knows the answer perfectly well.

"We close at nine. You know we close at nine. We've been closing at nine every night since this place opened, which, I might add, was before we were born."

"Whatever you say, Crazytop."

Then he helped himself to another Lindt.

It's truly remarkable how much he can eat without getting fat. I have two of those Lindt balls a day, and by the end of the month, my jeans don't fit anymore. Jason can eat like twenty a day and still have plenty of room in his (non-stretch) Levi's.

I guess it's a guy thing. Also, a growing thing. Jason

and I were almost the exact same height and weight all through grade- and middle school, and the first part of high school, even. And while he could beat me at chin-ups and anything involving throwing a ball, I regularly kicked his butt at leg-wrestling and Stratego.

Then last summer he went off to Europe with his grandmother to see all the sites in her favorite book, *The Da Vinci Code,* and when he came back, he was six inches taller than when he had left. Also, kind of hot.

Not Mark Finley hot, of course, Mark Finley being the hottest guy at Bloomville High. But still. That's a very disturbing thing to realize about your best friend, even if he *is* a guy—that he's gotten hot.

Especially since he's still trying to gain enough weight to catch up with his height. (I know. He has to *gain* weight.)

The only thing I can beat him at now is leg-wrestling. He even figured out how to cream me at Stratego.

And I think the only reason I can beat him at leg-wrestling is just because lying next to a girl on the floor gets him a little flustered.

I have to admit, since he got back from Europe, lying next to him on the floor—or in the grass on The Hill where we go a lot to look at the stars—gets me a little flustered, too.

But not enough to keep me from being able to flip him right over. It's important not to let hormones get in the way of a perfectly good friendship. Also to keep your mind on the task at hand.

"Stop calling me Crazytop," I said to him.

"If the name fits," Jason said.

"Shoe," I said. "The expression is, 'If the *shoe* fits. . . .'"

Which caused Becca, having found the missing Lindt ball at last, to come up and go, "I love the name Crazytop," all wistfully, while picking dust bunnies from her curly blond hair.

"Yeah," I said grouchily. "Well, that can be your nickname from now on, then."

But of course Jason had to be all, "Excuse me, but not all of us can be criminal masterminds like Crazytop here."

"If you break that display glass," I warned Jason, because he was still sitting on the counter, swinging his feet in front of the glass display case beneath it, "I'm making you take all those dolls home with you."

Because behind the glass are about thirty Madame Alexander dolls, most of whom are based on fictional characters from books, like Marmee and Jo from *Little Women* and Heidi from *Heidi*.

Can I just point out that it was my idea to put the dolls behind glass, after I figured out we were losing about a doll a week to doll collectors, who are notoriously light-fingered when it comes to Madame Alexander, and who carry very roomy tote bags—generally with cats on them—into shops like ours for the sole purpose of adding to their collections without the pesky burden of actually having to pay for the dolls?

Jason says the dolls terrify him. He says that sometimes

he has nightmares in which they are coming after him with their tiny plastic fingers and bright blue unblinking eyes.

Jason stopped swinging his feet.

"My goodness. I didn't realize it had gotten so late." My mom came out of the back office, her stomach, as usual, leading the way. I truly believe my parents are going for the state record in child producing. Mom's about to pop out their sixth child—my soon-to-be new baby brother or sister—in sixteen years. When this latest kid is born, ours will be the largest family in town, not counting the Grubbs, who have eight children, but whose mobile home isn't technically situated in Bloomville, as it straddles the Greene–Bloomville county line.

Although actually I think some of the younger Grubbs got taken away after child services found out their dad was mixing up batches of "lemonade" for them with bottles of lemon Joy.

"Hi, Mrs. Landry," Jason and Becca said.

"Oh, hello, Jason, Becca." My mom smiled glowingly at them. She's been doing that a lot lately. Glowing, I mean. Except when Grandpa's around, of course. Then she glowers. "And what are you kids planning on doing with your last free Saturday night before school starts? Is someone having a party?"

That's the kind of fantasy world my mom lives in. The kind where my friends and I get invited to fun back-to-school parties. It's like she's never heard of the Big Red Super Big Gulp incident. I mean, she was THERE when it happened. It's her fault I had the Super Big Gulp in the first place, on account of her feeling so sorry for me after having taken me to get my braces tightened, she surprised me with a Super Big Gulp to drink in the car on the way back to Bloomville Junior High. What kind of parent lets a sixth grader bring a Super Big Gulp to *school*?

Which is just more evidence to my theory that my parents have no idea what they're doing. I know a lot of people feel this way about their parents, but in my case, it's really true. I realized it was true the time Mom took us on a trip to a publishing trade show in New York City, and my parents spent the entire weekend alternately lost or just stepping out in front of the cars, expecting them to stop, because people stop for you when you step out in front of them in Bloomville.

In New York City, not so much.

It would have been okay if it had just been my parents and me. But we had my then-five-year-old brother Pete with us, and my little sister Catie, who was in a stroller, and my youngest brother, Robbie, who was just a baby and still in a Snugli (Sara wasn't born yet). It wasn't just me and my parents. There were little children involved!

After about the fifth time they tried to just mosey on out in front of a moving crosstown bus, I realized my parents are insane and not to be trusted under any circumstances.

And I was only *seven*.

This realization was cemented as I entered puberty

and my parents began to say things to me like, "Look, we've never been the parent of a teenage girl before. We don't know if we're doing the right thing. But we're doing the best we can." This is not something you want to hear from your parents under any circumstances. You want to feel like your parents are in control, that they know what they're doing.

Yeah. With my parents? Not so much.

The worst was the summer between sixth and seventh grades, when they made me go to Girl Scout Camp. All I wanted to do was stay home and work in the store. I am not what you'd call a big fan of nature, being basically a human chigger-and-mosquito magnet.

Then, to make matters worse, I found out Lauren Moffat was going to be one of my cabin mates. When I very calmly and maturely told the head counselor that this wouldn't work because of Lauren's extreme hatred of me, thanks to the Super Big Gulp incident, the camp counselor lady said, all heartily, "Oh, we'll see about that," and my mom actually APOLOGIZED for me, saying I have a hard time making friends.

"We'll change that," the counselor lady said, all confidently. And made me stay in Lauren's cabin.

Until two days later when I hadn't eaten a thing—too nauseated—or gone to the bathroom—since every time I tried to go, Lauren or another one of her "bunk" mates appeared outside the outhouse-style toilet and hissed, "Hey . . . don't pull a Steph in there."

That was when the counselor moved me to a cabin

with other rejects such as myself, and I ended up having a passably good time.

Obviously, given the above—I'm not even including the fact that my mom knows next to nothing about book-keeping or accounting and yet owns her own business, or that my father thinks there is a huge market out there somewhere for his unpublished book series about an Indiana high school basketball coach who solves crimes—my parents are not to be trusted.

Nor are they to be told anything personal involving my life, except on a need-to-know basis.

"No, no parties, Mrs. Landry," was how Jason replied to my mom's question about our evening plans. I've been coaching him as to how to handle my parents, because Jason's grandma is marrying my mom's dad, which makes him my mom's stepcousin. I think. "We're just going to drive up and down Main Street."

He said it like it was nothing—*I think we're just going to drive up and down Main Street.* But it was far from noth-ing. Because Jason is the first one of us to have gotten his own car—he'd been saving up all summer to buy his grandmother's housekeeper's 1974 BMW 2002tii—and this is the first Saturday night he's had possession of it.

It will also be the first Saturday night in our com-bined histories that Jason, Becca, and I do not spend lying in the grass stargazing on The Hill, or sitting on The Wall outside the Penguin, which is where everyone in our town—who does not have access to a car—sits on Saturday night, watching the rich kids (the ones who got cars for their sixteenth birthdays, as opposed to iBooks, like the rest of us) cruise up and down Main Street, the cleverly named main drag through downtown Bloomville.

Main Street starts at Bloomville Creek Park—where Grandpa's observatory is almost finished being constructed—and goes in this straight line past all the chain stores, which managed to drive the locally owned clothing shops out of business (the same way Mom thinks the Super Sav-Mart and its massively discounted book department is going to shut us down), up to the courthouse. The courthouse—a large limestone building with a white dome that has a spire sticking through the middle of it with a weather vane shaped like a fish on the tip, although no one knows why they chose a fish, since we're a land-locked county—is where everyone turns around and heads back down to Bloomville Creek Park for another lap.

"Oh." Mom looked disappointed. Well, and why shouldn't she? What parent wants to hear that her child is going to spend her last Saturday night of summer vacation driving up and down the main drag? *She* doesn't know how much better this is than sitting there watching other people do it.

Although Mom's idea of fun is putting the kids to bed and watching *Law and Order* with a big bowl of Ben and Jerry's Vanilla Heath Bar Crunch. So her judgment must obviously be called into question.

"How much longer you gonna be, huh, Crazytop?" Jason asked. I was reaching for the cash drawer, to start counting out the day's receipts. I knew that if they didn't tally to be equal to or greater than this day's receipts from last year, my mom was going to have a coronary.

"I wish someone would give *me* a criminal mastermind nickname," Becca hinted—not very subtly—with a sigh.

"Sorry, Bex," Jason said. "You don't have the recognizable facial characteristic—such as a huge chin, or a large amount of real estate between the eyes—that would merit the bestowing of a criminal mastermind nickname, such as Lockjaw or Walleye. Whereas Crazytop here . . . well, just look at her."

Sixty-seven, sixty-eight, sixty-nine, seventy singles.

"At least I can blow-dry my hair straight," I pointed out. "Which is more than I can say for your nose, Hawkface."

"Stephanie!" my mom cried, appalled that I would make fun of Jason's long, slightly too-large nose to his face.

"It's okay, Mrs. Landry," Jason said with a mock heavy-hearted sigh. "I know I'm hideous. Avert your gazes, all of you."

I rolled my eyes, because Jason is so very far from hideous—as I know, only too well—and lifted the cash drawer out of the register, then walked to the back of the store to lock it up in the safe in my mom's office overnight. I didn't mention to her that we're a hundred dollars shy of last year's day's total, and fortunately, she was too freaked out by my being so mean to Jason to ask.

Like she hasn't heard him call me Crazytop approximately nine million times. She thinks it's "cute."

Mom's never met Mark Finley, so obviously she doesn't really know what cute is.

On the way to the back, I noticed that Mr. Huff, one of our regulars, was engrossed in the latest Chilton's for Mustangs. His three children, of whom he has custody on weekends, were busy wrecking the Brio train set we put out for kids to play with while their parents shop.

"Hey, guys," I said to the little Huffs, who were ramming the train's caboose up an Arwen action figure's dress. "We have to close now. Sorry."

The kids groaned. Their dad clearly doesn't have as many cool toys at his house to play with as we did at the store.

Mr. Huff looked up, surprised. "Is it really closing time?" he asked, and looked at his watch. "Oh, wow, look at that."

"Way to pull a Steph Landry, Dad," eight-year-old Kevin Huff said with a laugh.

I just stood there, staring at the kid as he grinned toothily back at me. It was clear he had no idea what he'd just said. Or who he'd said it in front of.

The thing is, though, it's okay. Because I've got The Book now.

And The Book is going to save me.

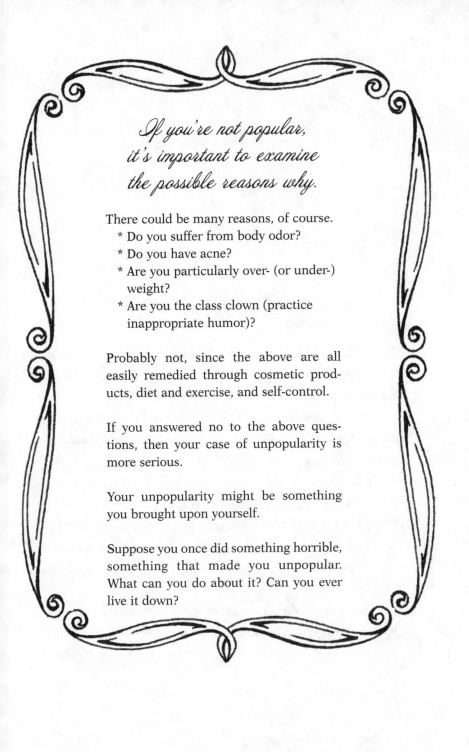

*If you're not popular,
it's important to examine
the possible reasons why.*

There could be many reasons, of course.
* Do you suffer from body odor?
* Do you have acne?
* Are you particularly over- (or under-) weight?
* Are you the class clown (practice inappropriate humor)?

Probably not, since the above are all easily remedied through cosmetic products, diet and exercise, and self-control.

If you answered no to the above questions, then your case of unpopularity is more serious.

Your unpopularity might be something you brought upon yourself.

Suppose you once did something horrible, something that made you unpopular. What can you do about it? Can you ever live it down?

 *Three*

STILL T-MINUS TWO DAYS AND COUNTING
SATURDAY, AUGUST 26, 10:20 P.M.

I don't know why I haven't told Jason and Becca. About The Book, I mean. I'm not embarrassed about it—well, not much, anyway.

And it's not like I stole it, or anything. I fully asked Jason's grandmother if I could have it the day I found it in that old box in the Hollenbachs' attic, which we were cleaning out so Jason could turn it into his Ryan Atwood pool house/Greg Brady bachelor pad (which, considering he is an only child, makes no sense. Except for the fact that it was easier to turn the attic into his new bedroom than strip the race car wallpaper off the walls of his old room).

And okay, I didn't pull out The Book itself and ask Kitty—Mrs. Hollenbach, Jason's grandmother, who asked us to call her by her first name, so as not to confuse her with the other Mrs. Hollenbach, her daughter-in-law Judy, Jason's mother—if I could specifically have IT. I just asked if I could have the BOX, which contained The Book as well as some old clothes and a couple of very steamy romance novels from the eighties—which, I must say, have caused me to look at Kitty in a new light, considering the heroine in one of them turned out to like having sex "Turkish-style," which in the book did NOT mean "while wearing a fez."

But Kitty just glanced into the box and went, "Oh, of course, dear. Though I can't imagine what you'd want with those old things."

If only she knew.

Anyway, so I haven't told them. I don't think I'm going to, either. Because, truth?

They'll just laugh.

And I don't think I could handle that. Thanks to Lauren Moffat, I've had five years of people laughing at—not with—me. I don't think I can take any more.

Anyway, it turns out driving up and down Main Street? It's not as fun as sitting around, *watching* people drive up and down Main Street.

And making fun of them behind their backs while they do so.

I can't believe that all summer, I've been longing to be *inside* a car instead of *outside* of one, watching the action on Main Street. When it turns out it's so much better back on The Wall. I mean, from The Wall you can see Darlene Staggs open the passenger door of that night's boyfriend's pickup, and barf up all the Mike's Hard Lemonade she ingested while sunning herself over at the lake that afternoon.

From The Wall you can hear Bebe Johnson's little chipmunk voice as she sings along with Ashlee Simpson on the radio.

From The Wall you can see Mark Finley adjust his rearview mirror so that he can see his own reflection and gently fluff up his bangs.

You can't do any of that stuff from the backseat of Jason's new car.

And I had to be in the backseat, because Becca gets carsick when she sits in the back. So she was in the front seat, next to Jason. Which meant I couldn't actually see anything much, except their heads. So when Jason went, "Whoa, did you see that? Alyssa Krueger just took a spill in the middle of the street trying to race in platform espadrilles from Shane Mullen's SUV to Craig Wright's Jeep," I missed the whole thing.

"Did she rip her pants?" I asked eagerly.

But neither Jason nor Becca were able to confirm pant-rippage had occurred.

If we'd been sitting on The Wall, I'd have seen the whole thing.

Plus, while I understand that Jason is excited about his new car and all, I think he's kind of gone overboard with the whole thing. Now when he sees another BMW, he practices this thing he calls BMW Courtesy, which means he lets other BMWs cut in front of him—especially if they are a Series 7, the king BMW of them all, or the convertible 645Ci. Which I find personally egregious, because that's what Lauren Moffat drives, on account of her father owning the local BMW dealership.

"Oh no, you did not just do that," I said when I saw Jason let a blonde in a red convertible cut in front of us up by the Hoosier Sweet Shoppe on the Square. "Tell me you did *not* just let Lauren Moffat in."

"BMW Courtesy, Crazytop," Jason said. "What can I say? She drives a superior model. I *have* to let her in. It's a moral obligation."

Sometimes I think Jason must be the biggest freak in Greene County. Bigger than me, even. Or Becca. And that's saying something, considering Becca spent most of her life on a farm with virtually no contact with children her own age, except at school where no one but me would speak to her on account of the fact that she wore overalls and fell asleep every day in fifth grade social studies. People would always try to wake her up, but I was like, "Leave her alone! She obviously needs a little nap."

I always thought Becca must have a very unsatisfactory home life, until I found out it was just because she had to get up at four every morning in order to catch the bus to school, since she lived so far out in the country.

It took careful negotiation to get her to ditch the OshKosh B'Goshes. The sleeping-through-class thing didn't get solved until last year, when the government bought out her parents' farm to put I-69 through it, and the Taylors bought the Snyders' old house down the street from ours with the money.

Now that Becca can sleep in until seven, she's wide awake in class. Even Health, which you don't necessarily have to stay awake for.

It figures these two people would be my best friends. I mean, not that I don't feel lucky to have them in my life (well, okay, maybe not Jason, the way he's been acting lately). Because we've had some major laughs together. And those nights we've spent, stretched out on our backs on The Hill, watching the sky above turn pink, then purple, then finally the darkest blue as the stars came out one by one, while we talked about what we'd do if a giant meteor—like those in the Leonid shower—came hurtling at us at a million miles an hour (Becca: Ask the Lord to forgive her sins. Jason: Kiss his ass good-bye. Me: Roll the heck out of the way).

But still. Becca and Jason are not what you'd call normal.

Take what we were listening to as we drove around in Jason's car: a compilation Jason made of what he considered the greatest music of the 1970s. Since his car was from that era, he thought it only fitting that we should listen to the songs that were hits in that decade. Tonight we were listening to his favorite year . . . 1977—the Sex Pistols' "God Save the Queen" and the *Star Wars: A New Hope* soundtrack, complete with Cantina scene.

Seriously. There's nothing like cruising up and down Main Street to the sound of an alien space band.

It was while we were stopped at the light in front of the art supply store that I saw Mark Finley pull up to the corner of Main Street and Elm in his purple-and-white four-by-four and honk.

And my heart, as it always does whenever I see Mark Finley, did a somersault in my chest.

Lauren, who was in her convertible in front of us, got all excited and honked and waved back. Not at us. At Mark.

It was hard to see what Mark did next, because Jason was making obscene gestures at him . . . from below the dashboard, so Mark would be sure not to see him, since you don't really go around making obscene gestures at the school quarterback if you want to live to see the first day of eleventh grade.

"Look, Steph," Jason said. "It's your boyfriend."

This caused Becca to laugh uproariously. Only she was trying to hide it, so as not to hurt my feelings. So all that came out was a snorting noise.

"Has he seen your new crazy hairdo?" Jason wanted to know. "I bet when he does, he'll forget all about Little Miss Moffat and make a beeline for your tuffet, instead."

I didn't say anything. Because the truth is, even though Jason doesn't know what he's talking about, that's EXACTLY what's going to happen. Mark Finley is totally going to realize that he and I belong together. He *has* to.

Anyway, driving up and down Main Street turned out to be a bust. Not just to me, either. After about the third turn, Jason went, "I feel like ass. Who wants coffee?"

I didn't, but I knew what he meant about feeling like ass. I mean, driving up and down a street—even a street on which every single person you know, practically, is also driving up and down—is boring.

And the good thing about the Coffee Pot is that if you get a seat on the upstairs balcony, you can still see what's happening on Main Street, because that's where the Pot is located. It's across the street from The Wall, behind which the Goths and Burners gather to kick their little leather beanbag hacky sacks in the red glow of their clove cigarettes.

No sooner had we snagged our balcony table than Jason elbowed me and pointed over the railing.

"Ken and Barbie alert, at two o'clock," he said.

I looked down and saw Lauren Moffat and life mate, Mark Finley, heading toward the outdoor ATM directly beneath us. It's really incredible to me that someone as nice as Mark could be with someone as evil as Lauren. I mean, Mark is almost universally liked (except by Jason, who harbors an irrational disdain for just about everyone except for his best guy friend, Stuckey, who might possibly be one of the most boring human beings on the face of the earth; Becca; and me—when we're not fighting, anyway). Mark's been voted president of his class every year since, um, forever, because of his niceness. Whereas Lauren—

Well, let's put it this way: Mark can only like Lauren because of her looks. Two such beautiful people—because of course Mark isn't just nice; he's Brad Pitt handsome, too—sort of *have* to be together, I guess. Even if one of them is a spawn of Satan.

And Mark and Lauren—they're *definitely* together. Mark's arm was around Lauren's shoulders, and her fingers were slipped through his. The two of them were totally canoodling, oblivious to the fact that there might be people sitting above them who didn't necessarily want to witness them kissing. Although obviously I was the only one to whom the sight of Mark kissing Lauren was like a red-hot poker through the heart. Becca and Jason just don't like seeing people putting their tongues in other people's mouths, on account of the grossness factor.

"Ugh," Becca said, averting her gaze.

"I'm blind now," Jason declared. "They've blinded me with their disgusting PDA."

I craned my neck to see over the side of the railing. But the two of them had ducked beneath us so Mark could use the cash machine. All I could see was some of Lauren's hair.

"Why do they have to do that?" Jason wanted to know. "Make out in public like that? Are they trying to rub it in that they have a special someone, and the rest of us don't? Is that what they're trying to do?"

"I don't think they do it on purpose," Becca said. "I mean, it's still gross. But I think it's just that they can't resist each other."

"See, I don't believe that," Jason said. "I think they do it on purpose to make the rest of us feel bad for not having found our soul mate yet. Like high school is really the place where you'd want to find your soul mate."

"What's wrong with finding your soul mate in high school?" Becca wanted to know. "I mean, maybe that's the only chance you'll ever have to meet your soul mate. If you blow it off, just because you don't want to meet your soul mate in high school, you may never meet your soul mate at all, and wander lonely as a cloud for the rest of your life."

"I don't believe we HAVE only one soul mate," Jason said. "I think we're given multiple chances to meet multiple soul mates. Sure, you could meet a soul mate in high school. But that doesn't mean if you don't act on it, you'll never meet anyone else. You will, just at a time that's more convenient for you."

"What's so inconvenient about meeting your soul mate in high school?" Becca asked.

"Let me see," Jason said, rubbing his chin like he had to think about it. "How about . . . you still live with your parents? Where are you and your soul mate supposed to go, you know, to get it on?"

Becca thought about it and said, "Your car."

"See, that's B.S.," Jason said. Only he didn't just say the initials. "What's romantic about that? Forget about it."

"So you're saying nobody should date in high school?" Becca asked. "Because it's not romantic to make out in a car?"

"Sure, you can date," Jason said. "Go to the movies

and hang out and stuff. But don't, you know. Fall in love."

"What?" Becca looked appalled. *"Ever?"*

"Not with somebody you go to school with," Jason said. "I mean, come on. You don't want to spit where you eat, do you?"

Only he didn't say spit.

"Ew," Becca said.

"I'm serious," Jason said. "You date someone in school, what happens if you break up? You have to see them every day anyway. How's that going to be? Super tense. Who needs it? School sucks enough without throwing THAT into the mix."

"So you're saying"—Becca needed some clarification—"that you've never thought about dating—never had a crush on—anybody in school? Not anybody?"

"Exactly," Jason said. "And I never will."

Becca looked like she didn't believe him, but I knew he was telling the truth—knew it from firsthand experience, when, back in the fifth grade, a new teacher who didn't know any better let us sit next to each other in class, and Jason proceeded to pinch, poke, and tease me until I couldn't bear it anymore. When I consulted with my grandfather concerning how I ought to handle the situation—whether I ought to pinch Jason back, or tell on him—Grandpa said, "Stephanie, when boys tease girls, it's always because they're a little bit in love with them."

But when I had—unwisely, I now realized—repeated

this to Jason (the very next time he pretended to wipe a booger on my chair just before I sat down on it), he became so angry that he didn't speak to me for the rest of the year. No more G.I. Joe meets Spelunker Barbie. No more games of Stratego. No more bike races or leg-wrestling. Instead, he hung out with his stupid friend Stuckey, leaving me to have to befriend Sleeping Beauty (aka Becca).

He didn't warm up to me again until the sixth grade, right after the Super Big Gulp incident, when Lauren's campaign of terror against me reached its peak, and he couldn't help but feel sorry for me, sitting alone in the cafeteria, and he finally started having lunch with me again.

Jason doesn't believe in in-school romance. In a BIG way.

"Because otherwise," he went on, at the café table, "you'll be like those two morons down there. Speaking of which, Crazytop? May I ask what you're doing?"

I stopped shaking the sugar packets I'd torn open over the balcony railing and looked at Jason innocently. "Nothing."

"Clearly," Jason said, "you are not doing nothing. You are most definitely doing something. What it looks like you're doing is pouring packets of sugar on Lauren Moffat's head."

"Shhh," I said. "It's snowing. But only on Lauren." I shook more sugar out of the packets. "'Merry Christmas, Mr. Potter,'" I called softly down to Lauren in my best

Jimmy Stewart imitation. "'Merry Christmas, you old Building and Loan.'"

Jason started cracking up, and I had to hush him as Becca saw my sugar supply running low and hastened to hand me more packets.

"Stop laughing so loud," I said to Jason. "You'll spoil this beautiful moment for them." I sprinkled more sugar over the side of the balcony. "'Merry Christmas to all, and to all a good night.'"

"Hey!" Lauren Moffat's voice, sounding noticeably irritated, floated up to us. "What—ew! What's in my hair?"

We all three ducked beneath our table so Lauren couldn't see us if she realized what was happening and looked up. I could see her between the slits of the fencing around the balcony, but I knew she couldn't see me. She was shaking out her hair. Becca, crouching across from me, had to put her hands across her mouth to keep from giggling. Jason looked like he was about to pee in his pants, he was trying so hard not to laugh.

"What's the matter, babe?" Mark came out from beneath the balcony, putting his wallet into his back pocket.

"There's something—sand or something—in my hair," Lauren said, still fluffing out her hair—which you could tell she didn't want to do, since she'd flat-ironed it so straight.

Mark leaned closer to examine Lauren's hair. "Looks okay to me," he said. Which just made us laugh harder, until tears were streaming out of the corners of our eyes.

"Well," Lauren said with one last shake of her perfectly straight locks, "I guess you're right. Come on. Let's go."

It was only when they'd rounded the corner toward the Penguin that we finally sat up, laughing semi-hysterically.

"Oh my God, did you see her face?" Becca asked between guffaws. "'There's something in my hair!'"

"That was fantastic, Crazytop," Jason said, wiping tears of laughter from his eyes. "Best master plan yet."

Except that it wasn't. Not by a long shot. He didn't have the slightest idea.

"Can I get you guys the usual?" That's what Kirsten, our waitress, wanted to know, coming up to wipe down our table—she'd apparently noticed all the sugar I'd spilled on it.

Usually when Kirsten is our waitress, Jason drops his napkin or something and has to crawl around looking for it. Because he feels about Kirsten the same way I feel about Mark: He thinks she's perfection. And maybe she is. Who am I to judge? Kirsten, who is from Sweden, is working her way through college on the tips she earns at the Coffee Pot. And yet she still manages to maintain her blond highlights, which is just one of the many reasons Jason has spent night after night lying on The Hill, composing haikus in her honor. He gets especially poetic about her when Kirsten wears a men's white button-down shirt with the ends tied just under her ribs, and no bra.

Personally, I think Kirsten is nice, and all, but I don't

think she's good enough for Jason. I would never admit this to HIM, of course. But I've noticed she has really dry skin around her elbows. She should totally invest in some lotion.

But tonight, for some reason, Jason didn't appear to notice Kirsten. He was too busy asking how Monday morning was going to work (not the part about how I was going to change the social structure at Bloomville High with the help of his grandmother's book—Jason and Becca don't know about that. Obviously). We were discussing what time we'd actually have to leave the house for school now that Jason has a car—a glorious eight A.M., to get us there by first bell, at eight ten, as opposed to the hideous seven thirty, which is when the bus shows up in our neighborhood.

"Can you imagine their faces when we pull up?" Becca was saying as Kirsten came over with our order. "I mean, in the student parking lot?"

"Especially if we're listening to Andy Gibb," I pointed out.

"The A-crowd," Jason said, "can eat me."

"What is the A-crowd?" Kirsten asked.

"You know," Becca explained as she stirred more Equal into her decaf. Becca's got weight issues on account of how when she lived on the farm, her parents had to drive her everywhere because there was nothing within walking distance of their house. Now that she lives in town, her parents still drive her everywhere, because they want to show off their new Cadillac, which they also bought with the I-69 money. "The popular people."

Kirsten looked confused. "You are not popular?"

This caused uproarious laughter on our part. Which was okay, because we can talk openly about our lack of popularity at the Pot, as we are the only people from Bloomville High who go there. It's kind of a hippyish place where they hold regular poetry readings and have loose teas in these giant plastic containers.

And besides, not that many teens in Greene County drink coffee (even half coffee, half milk, and a lot of sugar, like I drink), preferring Blizzerds (spelled that way so as not to get sued by Dairy Queen for copyright infringement) from Penguin.

"But you guys are so nice," Kirsten said when our laughter had died down. "I don't understand. Aren't the most popular kids in your school the ones who are nicest? Because that's how it was in my school, back in Sweden."

Seriously, that practically brought tears to my eyes. I never heard anything quite so sweet. *Aren't the most popular kids the ones who are nicest?* Sweden must be the best place to live. Because out here, in the cruel Midwest, popularity has nothing whatsoever to do with niceness. Unless you're Mark Finley, of course.

"Come on. You guys are kidding me," Kirsten said with a smile that revealed her crooked eyeteeth—eyeteeth about which Jason has waxed particularly eloquent in his haikus. "You are popular. I know it."

Which is when Jason stopped laughing long enough

to go, "Wait, wait . . . so, Kirsten, you're saying you've never heard of Steph Landry?"

Kirsten blinked at me with her big brown eyes. "But that is you. Are you famous, or something, Steph?"

"Or something," I said uncomfortably.

That's the thing. Kirsten's probably the only person in Greene County who hasn't heard of me.

Good thing I have Jason around to set her straight.

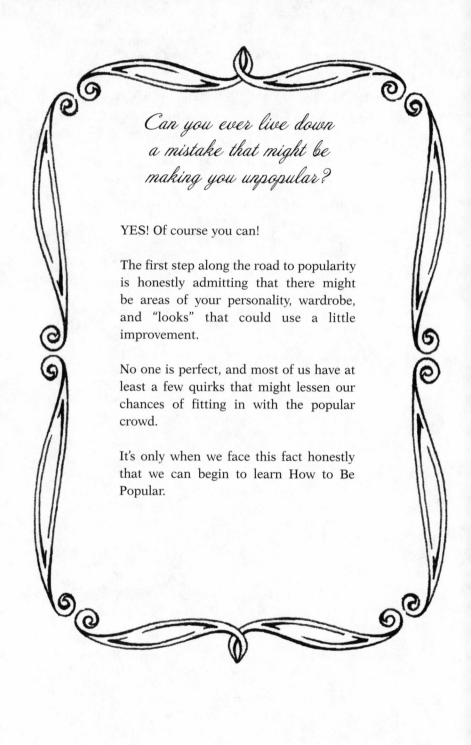

*Can you ever live down
a mistake that might be
making you unpopular?*

YES! Of course you can!

The first step along the road to popularity is honestly admitting that there might be areas of your personality, wardrobe, and "looks" that could use a little improvement.

No one is perfect, and most of us have at least a few quirks that might lessen our chances of fitting in with the popular crowd.

It's only when we face this fact honestly that we can begin to learn How to Be Popular.

 # Four

I should hate him. But I don't. It's hard to hate someone who looks that good with his shirt off.

I can't believe I just thought that. I can't believe I'm sitting here DOING this, when I swore I wouldn't. Anymore.

Well, it's his fault anyway, for not lowering his blinds.

The thing is, what are you supposed to do when you know something is wrong, but you just can't stop doing it?

Of course, I guess I could stop if I really wanted to. But, um. I don't want to. Obviously.

Really, if you think about it, it's just research. On guys. My interest in seeing Jason undressed is purely scientific. Which is why I use the binoculars I sent away to Bazooka Joe for when I was eleven. (Sixty Bazooka bubble gum wrappers, plus four ninety-five, for shipping and handling. They actually do work. Sort of.) I mean, someone has to observe guys in their natural habitat and figure out what makes them tick. Especially when they're naked.

But I really do feel guilty about it. Especially about the binoculars.

Just not guilty enough to stop.

Plus, you know, if you ask me, he sort of deserves it—especially tonight, after telling Kirsten the Super Big Gulp story. Like she needed to know about that.

Then afterward he had the nerve to be all, "Hey, let's go to The Hill." Like I was really going to go stargazing with the guy who outed me to the one resident of our town who didn't know about pulling a Steph Landry.

Not to mention I didn't have my Off! with me and I am not likely to lie on the grass and be eaten alive by chiggers just in order to see a few shooting stars. I mean, this is why Grandpa built the observatory, for God's sake.

So the guilt? Not so much. Certainly not enough to go to confession about it or anything.

Especially since, even if I did go to confession about it, Father Chuck will say something to my mother—I just know it. And then she'll tell Kitty. And Kitty will tell her son, Dr. Hollenbach, who'll tell Jason (or, at the very least, he'll tell Jason to put his blinds down). And then I won't get to see him anymore. Naked, I mean.

And that would totally suck.

Plus, you can't tell me that what I'm doing is all THAT

wrong. Guys have been doing it to girls for hundreds—maybe thousands—of years. For as long as there've been windows and people changing in front of them—people who didn't put down their blinds, anyway—there've been other people looking in those windows.

It's about time we girls had a little payback, is all I'm saying.

And as much as it grieves me to report it, Jason regularly provides some fine, fine payback. I don't know what he ate when he was in Europe, but he came back looking so hot! He didn't have those biceps before he left. No way did he have those abs.

Or maybe he did and I just never noticed.

Of course, it's not like, before he left, I was seeing Jason naked on a regular basis, either. It wasn't until he moved into the attic, which happens to have a window I can see right into from our upstairs bathroom window, that I noticed I could see him.

And people in my family wonder what I'm doing in the bathroom for so long. Like my little brother Pete, who just banged on the door.

"What are you doing in there?" he wanted to know. "You've been in there an hour!"

My big mistake was opening the door.

"What do you want?" I asked. "Why aren't you in bed?"

"Because I gotta pee," Pete said, barging past me and whipping it out. "Whadduya think?"

"Ew," I said. I seriously doubt Lauren Moffat has to

put up with her little brothers peeing in front of her in her own home.

Of course, Lauren probably has her own bathroom. She doesn't have to share it with her four—soon-to-be five—siblings.

"I told you I gotta go," Pete said, clearly not caring about the psychological scars his being full-frontal in front of me could cause. He looked around, then went, "Hey. Why are you sitting here in the dark?"

"I'm not," I said. Even though the light in the bathroom was out. I could only see him from the moonlight, streaming in through the windows.

"Uh, yeah, you are." Pete finished up and flushed. "You're really weird, you know that, Steph?"

Um. Duh. "Go back to bed, moron."

"Who's the moron?" Pete wanted to know.

But he went back to bed. And didn't notice the binoculars. Thank God.

I guess I should try to be a little more understanding of what his—Pete's—life must be like. Having the infamous Steph Landry for an older sister, I mean. Obviously, it must put him at a severe social disadvantage, at least in this town.

And yet he's borne it remarkably well . . . the teasing, the put-downs, the roughing up on the playground.

The way I see it, things could be worse. I mean, there was this girl in school last year, Justine Yeager, who was an actual genius—she had a perfect grade point average and got the highest score you can get on her SATs, even the essay part. But she had like zero social skills—she was BOOK smart, but not PEOPLE smart. I mean, worse than accidentally throwing a Big Red Super Big Gulp on the most popular girl in school. No one would sit next to Justine at lunch, not even the B-crowders, because all she ever talked about was how much smarter she was than everybody else.

So whenever things get really bad—like they are right now, when it's the last Saturday night of summer vacation and instead of being out on a date or at a party or the lake or whatever, I'm sitting in the bathroom spying on my best friend as he undresses and gets ready for bed—I think about how I could have been born Justine Yeager, instead of, you know . . . me. And it helps.

Sort of.

At least I'm not alone. In not being at a party or the lake, I mean. Jason's home, too.

And looking mighty, mighty fine.

Okay, this is sick. SICK. I am fully going to ask God for forgiveness about this during Communion in church tomorrow. Since I can't ask Father Chuck. Might as well go straight to the top. No more middlemen. That's what Grandpa always advises, anyway.

Although of course Grandpa doesn't know how much time I spend spying on the naked bod of my future step-whatever-Jason-is-going-to-be-to-me when his grandmother marries Grandpa.

But. Whatever.

What's the secret of popularity?
What makes some people so likable
and others not liked at all?

Popular people:
* Always have a ready smile for
  everyone.

* Show genuine interest in others and
  what they have to say.

* Remember that a person's name is
  the sweetest and most important
  sound to them! Popular people call
  others by their names, and do it
  often.

* Are good listeners who encourage
  others to talk about themselves.

* Make the person they are speaking
  to feel important—and do it sincerely.
  They always make the conversation
  about YOU, not about themselves!

 *Five*

I met up with Grandpa in the observatory while everybody else was having coffee and doughnuts in the church basement after Mass. I've had to give up crullers and elephant ears anyway, as they go straight to my butt. I have to ride my bike around town for like an hour to work off just one doughnut. It's totally not worth it. Unless it's a hot glazed Krispy Kreme, of course.

Grandpa says I inherited this tendency from his first wife, my grandma. I wouldn't know whether this is true or not, since Grandma died of lung cancer before I was born, even though she didn't smoke. Grandpa did, though, so Grandma blamed him for giving it to her. The cancer, I mean. I don't think that was very nice of her, even if it was true. You can tell Gramps felt plenty bad about it.

Although not bad enough to quit.

Until he started going out with Kitty, that is. All she had to say was, "Smoking is a filthy habit. I could never imagine myself with a man who smoked," and Grandpa quit. Just like that.

Which didn't endear Kitty much to my mom, but does go to show the power of The Book.

"Hey," I said after I'd let myself into the observatory, using the special code Grandpa had taught me on the electronic lock. The code is the date of Kitty's birthday, which I think is pretty romantic. Not as romantic as having the place built and naming it after her—the Katherine T. Hollenbach Observatory—and then donating it to the city, maybe. But up there.

My mom doesn't think it's so romantic, though. She calls Grandpa's spending since he got the I-69 money "conspicuous consumption," and says her father has made it so she's afraid to show her face at the Downtown Community sessions. Except that the Downtown Community is pretty stoked about the observatory, which is really state-of-the-art on the inside, though on the outside it was designed to blend in with the Square's 1930s WPA architecture.

But Mom says she's mainly referring to Grandpa's new condo on the lake and the butter-yellow Rolls-Royce he bought and is still waiting for to arrive, with specially ordered wheel-well covers.

"Hey," Grandpa said back to me from the rotunda, where he was tinkering around with stuff on the observatory deck. Since it was Sunday, none of the workmen were there. It was just Grandpa and me. The place is practically done, anyway. There's just a little more dry-wall that needs to be hung in the control room. "How goes it?"

"Good," I said, reaching into my skirt pocket as I climbed to the observation deck. "I've got eighty-seven dollars here for you."

"Why, thank you," Grandpa said. He took the money, shuffled it into a neater pile, folded it, and put it in his wallet. He didn't bother to count it. We both know I never make counting mistakes.

Then he took a notepad from his shirt pocket and carefully wrote out a receipt, which he handed to me. "Interest rate gap's narrowed."

"I saw that on the Web this morning," I said, slipping the receipt into my pocket.

Grandpa and I have always shared a mutual fondness for . . . well, money. In fact, I never really had a grasp for mathematics until Grandpa sat me down one day in the seventh grade and said, looking at the math problem that had me in tears, "Never mind how many apples Sue has. Let's say Sue's working a shift at the bookstore. But it's a Saturday night, and the only way you could get her to work was to promise her eight fifty an hour, as opposed to seven fifty, because she wanted to go out to Sizzler and a movie with her boyfriend. But you don't want to let your mother know you've been paying overtime when there hasn't, in fact, been any. How do you configure Sue's paycheck so she gets her money, without Mom knowing?"

My reply was instantaneous: Sue would get sixty-eight

dollars for working an eight-hour shift at eight fifty an hour. Sixty-eight divided by seven fifty rounds down to nine. So you put down that Sue worked nine hours instead of eight.

And then you'd go look for an employee who isn't as popular as Sue, so you can give them the Saturday night shift and not have to fudge the numbers anymore.

"Very good," Grandpa had said.

And that was the end of my problems with math. Thinking about numbers in terms of wages and hours finally cleared the mists from algebra for me, and actually made it comprehensible. Now I'm top of my class and have taken over payroll from Grandpa at the store, since Mom's falling out with Grandpa means he's not welcome there anymore.

"You get good deals, anyway?" Grandpa wanted to know, referring to what I'd bought with the money I'd borrowed from him.

I shot him an aggravated look.

"Gramps," I said. "Come on. It's *me* you're talking to."

"Just making sure," Grandpa said.

He had the air-conditioning in the observatory on full blast, which was good because it was about nine million degrees outside, with the humidity as high as it could get without actually raining. In other words, a typical Indiana August day.

"You transfer those funds from the savings account into checking like I told you to?" Grandpa wanted to know.

"Of course."

"Because bills are due out beginning of the month."

"Grandpa, I know. I've got it covered."

Grandpa shook his head. He is very dapper-looking for his age, although he's never gotten over the fact that he didn't grow to be taller than five seven. I tell him not to worry, since that's how tall Tom Cruise is and he did pretty well for himself—financially, anyway. Still, I suspect this is where I inherited my own lack of stature.

But at sixty-nine, Gramps can play eighteen holes of golf and still stay awake all the way through the eleven o'clock news. He's especially proud of his full head of (completely white) hair. He has a pretty decent mustache, too. It's white as well. The whole time I was growing up, his mustache was stained yellow from the cigarettes he smoked. Up until he started going out with Kitty, anyway. Now it's as white as snow.

"How's Darren working out?" Grandpa wanted to know. Darren's the Indiana University student we hired for the Sunday and evening shifts at the store. He likes working at Courthouse Square Books since there are hardly ever any customers, and he can get a lot of homework done during his shifts.

"Fine," I said. "He reorganized the layaway shelf the other night and found a Steiff bear no one's made payments on for an entire year. We put it back on the store shelves."

Grandpa clicked his tongue and went back to futzing with the sixty-inch telescope. Not that he knew what he was doing. Grandpa has NO interest in astronomy. He had to hire all these professors from Indiana University to help him design the observatory, and these grad students from there are getting college credit to run it. The only reason Grandpa decided to build an observatory in the first place is because he knows how much Jason loves looking at the stars, and he knows how much Kitty loves Jason. The whole thing is basically full-on sucking up to the woman he loves.

I would build an observatory for Mark Finley. If, you know, he liked stars, too.

"And how's your mother? She doing all right?"

"She's fine," I said. "Another month to go before she pops."

"How are you going to be able to run the store," Grandpa wanted to know, "and do this popularity thing at the same time, with your mom out of the picture for a while with this new little one?"

"Easy," I said. Grandpa is the only living soul on earth I've told about The Book. I even showed it to him. I had to, in order to get him to advance me the money. I didn't tell him where I'd gotten it, though. The Book, I mean. I didn't want him to think Kitty had used it to get him.

All he had to say about it was, "What do you care what Sharon Moffat's daughter thinks of you? That girl wouldn't know a T-bill if one came up and bit her on the derriere."

But I explained to him that this was something I simply had to do—the same way he'd had to build an observatory for the town, even though no one—with the possible exception of Jason, who has tried, unsuccessfully, to start an astronomy club every year in school since the third grade when he saw *Close Encounters of the Third Kind* on the Sunday Afternoon Movie and never quite got over it—actually wanted one.

But, as Grandpa put it, most people are too stupid to know what they really want, anyway.

"I still don't like it," Grandpa said. He was done doing what it was he'd felt was so vitally important to get done at the observatory that morning, and started heading toward the door I'd just come through, me following along behind him. "Kissing up to a little stinker who's done nothing but try to make your life miserable."

"I won't be kissing up to her, Gramps," I said. "Trust me. Besides, the whole thing was my fault in the first place."

"What?" Grandpa glanced at me as he threw open the door—letting the unbearable heat flood over us like spilled soup—looking annoyed. "You tripped! That's all! Somebody's got to go through the rest of her life being made fun of for tripping when they're twelve? It's ridiculous."

I smiled at him tolerantly. Grandpa has no idea what it's like to be a teenage girl. When his only child—Mom—was growing up, he'd hardly been around, since he'd been out running the farm. Watching me go through my own hideously painful adolescence has been his only experience in the Hidden Aggression of Teenage Girls and the Pain It Can Cause.

"There's your mother," Grandpa said, nodding toward the church doors, which you can see from the steps to the observatory. Even though a lot of people were streaming out of St. Charles at that moment, it wasn't hard to miss my family, primarily because of my mother's enormous stomach. But also because of the noise my brothers and sisters were making, which you could probably have heard from miles away.

Grandpa stopped going to church after Grandma died, according to my mother, which is yet another bone of contention between them. But Grandpa says he can worship God just as well on the ninth hole as he can in church—if not better, since he's closer to nature, and therefore God, on the golf course than he is in our pew at St. Charles. I fear for his immortal soul, and all, but I figure if God really is all-forgiving, like Father Chuck is always telling us, Gramps will be all right (and, considering what I was doing last night, so will I).

Fortunately for Grandpa, Kitty isn't exactly the most religious person, either. They're having a civil ceremony, performed by one of Greene County's judges, outside at the country club a week from today, instead of a church wedding.

"Right," I said. "I'd better go. You getting nervous yet?"

"Nervous?" Gramps threw me a reproachful look as he locked up. "What've I got to be nervous for? I'm marrying the prettiest gal in Greene County."

"I mean about having to stand up in front of all those

people next Sunday," I said dryly.

"Jealous," Grandpa said decidedly. "That's what they're all going to be of me. 'Cause she's marrying ME and not them."

The best part is, Gramps really believes this. He thinks the sun rises and sets on Katherine T. Hollenbach. Which I believe is due entirely to her having followed the instructions in The Book. The two of them—Grandpa and Kitty—have known each other since THEY went to Bloomville High School, back in the fifties. Only Grandpa says Kitty didn't even know he was alive back in those days, because she was so pretty and popular, and he was so little and shy. She didn't even acknowledge his existence until last year, when they met at the exclusive condo community they both moved to on the lake, Gramps after he got his I-69 money, Kitty after deciding she'd had enough of life in town.

"Any sign of weakening on *her* part?" Grandpa asked with a nod toward my mother. Mom's boycotting his wedding on principle, not because she doesn't like Kitty—although she's not exactly her favorite person in the world. Mom is not the only person to have pointed out to Grandpa that Kitty never glanced his way before he got his recent financial windfall. But Grandpa doesn't seem to care one bit about this—mostly because she's still so mad about the Super Sav-Mart thing.

She's letting the rest of us go, though . . . which is a good thing, since I'm Kitty's maid of honor, Pete's one of Gramps's best men (Jason's the other one), and Catie and

Robbie are the flower girl and ring bearer (Sara was judged too young to do anything).

I like Kitty a lot, and not just because everyone likes her (except my mom). But also because she's always kept my most shameful secret—which isn't that shameful now, because I realize it was just part of growing up.

But at the time, it was the worst thing that had ever happened to me. I had been invited by Jason to spend the night—way back in kindergarten, when it was still okay for girls and boys to have slumber parties together—while his parents were out of town and his grandmother was taking care of him.

One thing I had always admired about Jason's parents is that they knew enough to stop at just one kid—unlike my own parents, who just keep having more and more—so they can afford to do things like take romantic vacations to Paris together without Jason, and install a pool in their backyard (except, of course, whenever I complain about this to my mother, she's always like, "Well, which of you kids would you suggest I shouldn't have had?" which is a mean question, because of course I love my brothers and sisters).

(Though I don't think anyone would miss Pete much.)

Anyway, it had been my first overnight visit, and I guess I'd had a little too much excitement—or possibly Coke, which Kitty had given us, and of which I'd consumed far too much, having never been allowed to have Coke before, except on very special occasions like Thanksgiving and Easter—and I'd wet my underpants in what I'd assumed was the dead of night (although it had probably only been around midnight).

I remembered lying there in my wet panties, going, "What do I do now?" Jason was asleep, but even if he hadn't been, I wouldn't have told him what had happened. I was convinced I'd never have heard the end of it. "Wet the bed like a baby!" he'd cry. Well, knowing Jason, he probably wouldn't have said any such thing. But in my feverish four-year-old brain, I was convinced he wouldn't want to be my friend anymore if he knew I was a bed wetter. Also, of course, it would come up every time I beat him at anything: "Well, okay, maybe you're better at Candy Land, but at least I'm not a bed wetter."

Finally, as my undies grew colder and colder around me, I couldn't take it anymore, and I got up and padded to the master bedroom, where Jason's grandmother was sleeping.

She woke up right away, though she was a bit groggy.

"Oh, Stephanie," she said when she realized it was me. "Darling, it's not time to get up yet. See, in this house, we get up when the big hand is on the twelve, and the little hand is on the eight. Or nine."

But I explained to her I wasn't *up* up. I had had an accident.

Kitty was GREAT. She got me out of my wet undies and threw them into the washer, without waking up Jason.

And then when she'd tried to make me go back to bed, and I'd balked because I didn't have underwear on

(Yes. That's the kind of kid I was), she got out a pair of Jason's and told me boy underwear was just as good as girl underwear, and that I could wear it under my pajamas, and Jason would never know.

I was, of course, skeptical. I mean, boy underwear is nothing like girl underwear—it has a fly! Plus, Jason's underwear had Batman on them.

But it was better than nothing. So I went back to bed with Jason's Batman underwear on, with the promise that, in the morning, my own underwear would be returned to me, clean and dry.

I had lain there thinking, "I'm wearing Jason's Big Boy pants," because that's what he'd called them back when we were both transferring out of training pants— his were Big Boy pants and mine were Big Girl pants.

And the truth is, I'd felt kind of a thrill about wearing Jason's Big Boy pants. I was a sick kid, even way back then.

In the morning, while Jason was in the bathroom, Kitty smuggled my panties back to me, and I gave her Jason's Big Boy pants—which I was sort of sad to see go. And she never said a word—not to Jason, not to his parents or mine, nobody. To this day, I don't know if she remembers how she saved me . . . but I will never forget it.

And I'm glad she's going to be my grandma, because I think she's one of the finest grandmas a girl could have.

It's sad my mom doesn't agree. But maybe that's because Kitty never rescued HER from the mortal embarrassment of wet panties before.

"No," I said to Grandpa, in answer to his question

about Mom. "But don't worry. She'll come around."

I don't actually believe this. It's just something I tell Gramps when he looks sad, like he did just then. My mother is a very determined person. I once saw her physically throw a guy she suspected of being a shoplifter out of our store, just because he'd been hanging around the earring rack a little too long. He was way bigger than her, but it didn't matter. Mom's center of gravity is lower than most people's, I think on account of her having given birth so many times.

"I hope you're right, Stephanie," Grandpa said, his blue eyes narrowing as he stared at Mom over in the church parking lot. "I sure do miss her."

I patted him on the arm. "I'll keep you posted," I told him. "And expect another installment against my loan next week."

"I'll keep an eye on interest rates," Grandpa assured me.

Then I kissed him good-bye and ran through Bloomville Creek Park to join the rest of my family by the minivan. They, as usual, had no clue I'd even been gone.

Which is the only advantage of having soon-to-be five brothers and sisters.

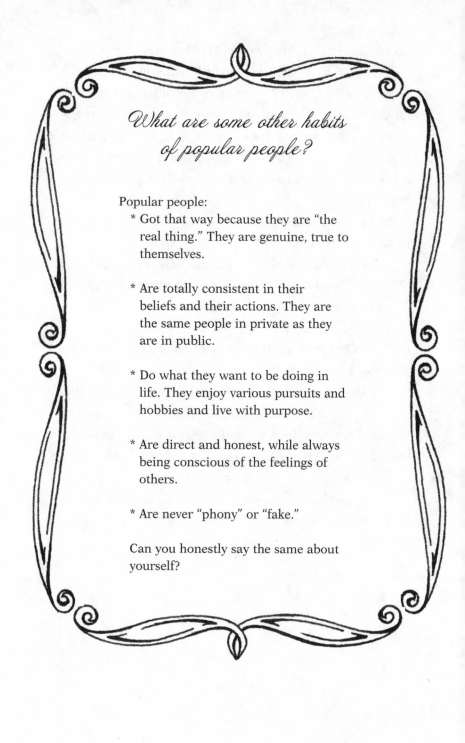

What are some other habits of popular people?

Popular people:

* Got that way because they are "the real thing." They are genuine, true to themselves.

* Are totally consistent in their beliefs and their actions. They are the same people in private as they are in public.

* Do what they want to be doing in life. They enjoy various pursuits and hobbies and live with purpose.

* Are direct and honest, while always being conscious of the feelings of others.

* Are never "phony" or "fake."

Can you honestly say the same about yourself?

 *Six*

STILL T-MINUS ONE DAY AND COUNTING
SUNDAY, AUGUST 27, 3 P.M.

Jason came over as I was laying out everything I was
going to need for the coming week. He went, "What are
you doing?"

"What does it look like?" I asked him.

"I don't know," Jason said. "Sorting through your
clothes?"

"See," I said. "They were right to let you go on to
eleventh grade this year, after all."

"Funny," Jason said. He was staring at all my clothes.
"Are those *new*?"

"They are."

"Where'd you get the money?"

I just looked at him. It is a well-known fact that Jason
cannot handle money. The only way he was able to save
enough for his car was by giving the money to me. He

got it back six months later with a healthy return.

I didn't think it was necessary to reveal that, in this particular case, I had borrowed from Grandpa. I had only needed to borrow from Gramps because all of my savings are currently invested in mutual funds.

"Well," Jason said, apparently realizing the stupidity of his question, "okay. But, like . . . since when do you care about clothes?"

"I've always cared about clothes," I said, genuinely startled by this question "I mean, I care how I look."

"Oh, really, Crazytop?"

"For your information," I said, "this haircut is all the rage on the runways in Paris." Well, the straightened version of it, anyway. But no way am I going to all the trouble to straighten my hair on a non–school day.

"Paris, Texas, maybe," Jason said, flopping down on my floor, the only place in my room not covered with the various ensembles I was putting together (because The Book very clearly states that you should pick out your clothes, including undergarments, well in advance of whatever event you are planning to wear them to, in order to avoid a last-minute fashion crisis).

"Whatever," I said. He'll so be singing a different tune when he sees the straightened version of my haircut. More importantly, so will Mark Finley. "Don't you have something you should be doing?"

"Yeah," Jason said. "I was thinking about taking The B to the lake." This is how Jason refers to his new car. As "The B." "Wanna come?"

As tempting as the idea of seeing Jason without his shirt on was—and without the benefit of Bazooka Joe binoculars—I was forced to decline, due to the busy afternoon I had ahead of me, cataloging my entire fall wardrobe.

"Aw, c'mon," Jason said. "When'd you get to be such a *girl*?"

I glared at him. "Thanks."

"You know what I mean," he said, rolling over and staring at the stick-on glow-in-the-dark constellations we'd pasted to my ceiling back when we were in the fourth grade. "I mean, you never used to care about clothes and your hair—and how big your butt's gotten."

"Well, not all of us can eat anything we want and not gain weight," I pointed out. "Not all of us NEED to gain weight. Like some people I could mention."

Jason propped himself up on one elbow. "Is this about Mark Finley?" he demanded.

I could feel myself flushing. Not because he'd mentioned Mark, but because when he leaned up on one elbow like that, I could see some of his underarm hair tufting out from beneath his shirt sleeve, and that reminded me of the hair I'd seen tufting out from other parts of his body. You know. Through the window. With my Bazooka Joe binoculars.

"No," I said, more loudly than I meant to. "Because if it were, I'd be crawling all over myself to go with you, wouldn't I? Since the lake's the most likely place Mark and all the other A-crowders will be today. Which begs the question, why do you even want to go there, considering how much you hate all those guys?"

Jason rolled over and scowled at my blue shag (Yes. I have blue shag. My parents are slowly renovating the house, but until my dad actually sells one of the mysteries he is constantly writing between mixing up batches of homemade granola, stuff like getting rid of my blue shag is so not on the horizon).

"I wanna take The B to the lake," he said. "She's never seen it. At least, not with me. Plus, you know, there are those curves over on the turnpike I want to try her out on."

"Oh my God," I said. "And you accuse me of being such a girl? You are such a *boy*."

With that, Jason got up and said, "Fine. I'll just go by myself."

"Why don't you ask Becca? She's probably just home scrapbooking, or something." Becca, now that she's moved away from the farm, isn't used to having free time, and so fills her days with craft projects, like making skirts out of pillowcases, and filling scrapbooks with pictures of adorable kittens she cuts from the Sunday *Parade* section. If she weren't my friend, I probably wouldn't even like her, based on that fact alone.

"She gets carsick on the way to the lake," Jason said. "Remember?"

"Not if you let her sit in front."

"Becca . . ." Jason hovered in the doorway to my room, looking . . . well, weird, is the only way I could think to put it. "Becca's been acting strange around me lately. Haven't you noticed?"

"No," I said. Because I haven't.

And also, if anyone should be acting strange around Jason, it's me. I mean, *I'm* the one who's seen him with his pants off, not Becca.

And may I just say what I saw was very impressive?

Not, actually, that I have anything much to measure by. Except my brothers.

"Well," Jason said, "she has. Pestering me to give her a criminal mastermind name. That whole thing last night about finding your soul mate. That kind of stuff."

"Come on, Jason," I said. "She just wants to fit in, be part of the gang. I mean, it's hard for her, living in town. She's used to hanging out with cows and stuff. Cut her some slack. Can't you just think of a criminal mastermind name for her?"

"No," Jason said bluntly. "Want to go to The Hill tonight?"

"No. Last time I had to dab myself with gasoline to get rid of all the chiggers that crawled into my underwear."

"We could go to the observatory, then."

"Why? The Perseids are over. And the Orionids don't start until October."

"There's other stuff to see in the sky besides meteor showers, you know, Steph," Jason said. "I mean, there's Antares. And Arcturus."

I swear, I wanted to be like, "See, Jason? This is why

you aren't popular. You could be popular—you have a decent-looking face and, as I know only too well, a killer bod. You have a good sense of humor and you're an only child, so your parents can afford to buy you the right clothes. You get good grades, which is a strike against you, popularity-wise, of course, but you play golf, a sport growing in popularity among teens. But then you have to go and ruin it all by talking about stargazing and BMW Courtesy. What is *wrong* with you?"

Only I couldn't. Because that would be too mean.

Instead, I just went, "It's a school night, Jason. I'm not going to the observatory."

"Who's not going to the observatory?" my dad asked, poking his head around Jason's shoulder.

"Oh, hi, Mr. Landry," Jason said, turning around. "Steph and I were just talking."

"I can see that," my dad said in his too-jovial I'm-talking-to-a-teenage-boy-standing-in-my-daughter's-bedroom voice. Except, of course, it was just Jason. "How's the new car?"

"Awesome," Jason said. "This morning I cleaned the bulbs on my dash gauges. Now they shine like new."

"Good for you," my dad said. And the two of them fell into a completely random conversation about wiring harnesses.

God. Boys are so lame sometimes.

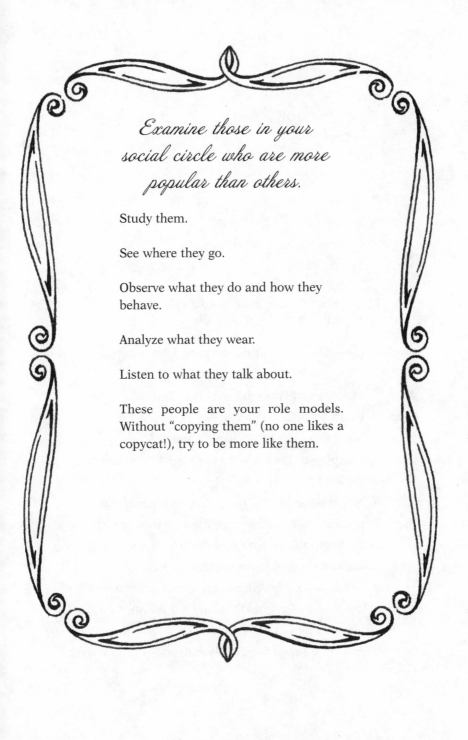

Examine those in your social circle who are more popular than others.

Study them.

See where they go.

Observe what they do and how they behave.

Analyze what they wear.

Listen to what they talk about.

These people are your role models. Without "copying them" (no one likes a copycat!), try to be more like them.

 *Seven*

Well. This is it. Everything is ready. I have my:

1. Dark denim stretch jeans (not too tight, but definitely not too loose).
2. Slim-fit cords in multiple shades.
3. Simple yet versatile two-piece sweater sets in various flattering tones.
4. Activewear (with hoodies)—no jogging pants, as drawstrings "draw" attention to your middle.
5. Jackets in corduroy and denim, nipped in at the waist to reveal my hourglass figure.
6. Skirts—knee-length pencil, again in corduroy and denim (one in khaki); mini (but no microminis . . . leave that to Darlene Staggs).
7. Multiple tops (none belly-baring—a girl should

save SOME secrets for the pool, or that special someone), including scoop neck and ruched tees; blouses with just a hint of ruffle at the cuff or neck, to maximize femininity.

8. Round-toe shoes such as Mary Janes; boots with flattering heel; slim yoga sneaker.
9. Close-fitting down-filled jacket for casual outings, and coat with flattering (imitation) fur collar for more formal events; matching cashmere scarf and gloves, for winter.
10. Dresses (not too revealing, full skirt) in black or pink for dances.

Of course, I had to fudge SOME of The Book's advice a little. I mean, The Book is pretty old. I didn't think a girdle or something called "pedal pushers" were going to fly in the halls of Bloomville High.

Not to mention the fact that if I walked around in white kid gloves for evening (even "unsoiled, unsplit" ones), I wasn't going to win any fashion points with Lauren and her friends.

So, obviously, I pretty much had to improvise with the clothes thing.

But with the help of a couple of teen fashion magazines and their back-to-school wardrobe tips, I think I did pretty well. Thank God for T.J.Maxx, is all I have to say. Oh, and the outlet stores outside the Dunes, where Becca's mom and dad took us that one weekend in July. How else would I have found

Benetton sweaters for fifteen dollars?

Anyway, I really do think I'm ready. Tomorrow morning—and every morning for the rest of my life, as per the instructions in The Book—I'll:

1. Shower—shampoo and condition hair, exfoliate, shave legs *and* underarms, then moisturize.
2. Use deodorant liberally (clear, quick-drying kind, so as not to leave unsightly deodorant stains on shirts).
3. Floss AND brush teeth (Crest Whitestrips to be applied for a half hour every morning and night).
4. Apply mousse, Frizz-Ease, blow-dry, and flat-iron hair.
5. Put on clean underwear, including bra that actually fits (thanks to saleslady at Maidenform outlet who actually measured me correctly, unlike Mom) and makes me look a size larger than the (wrong) bra size I used to wear.
6. Have shoes shined, cleaned, scuff-free.
7. Make sure nails are clean, filed, clear gloss applied, no chips, cuticles all pushed back (check into viability of weekly manicures in mall).
8. Wear perfect makeup—foundation, lightly applied in problem areas and well blended, with SPF of at least 15; cover-up for any acne flare-ups (to be controlled with Retin-A, prescribed by Jason's dad, as well as nightly routine of washing,

using astringent, and applying benzoyl peroxide before bed) and circles beneath eyes; long-lasting lipstick/gloss, subtle mauve only; eyeliner (lightly applied, soft shades, like gray and lavender); waterproof black mascara.

9. Make sure clothing is neat, no wrinkles, everything coordinated, nothing showing that shouldn't be showing. SET OUT CLOTHES THE NIGHT BEFORE!!!

10. Choose accessories—earrings (small studs or hoops ONLY) match; no more than one necklace, if any; watch on one wrist, bracelets (if any) on other; no piercings, anklets, belly chains, tattoos (as if); backpack (small to medium, new, no scuffs) in black or brown, or shoulder tote (ditto), small purse, designer ONLY.

Phew. That's a tall order for a non–morning person like myself.

But I figure if I start at quarter to seven, I'll have just enough time to grab a protein bar or whatever for breakfast and meet Jason and Becca at The B by eight to get to school by first bell at eight ten. I can grab a Diet Coke out of the machines by the gym for my caffeine jolt.

My mom just waddled into my room and sank down on the bed beside me.

"How are you doing, honey?" she asked. "All ready for school tomorrow? It's a big day . . . eleventh grade. I can't believe my baby's a junior already!"

"Yeah, Mom," I said. "Everything's great. Don't worry about me."

"You're the only one I don't worry about," my mom said, patting me on the leg. "I know what a good head you've got on your shoulders."

Then she noticed the outfit that was hanging on my closet door.

"Well," she said after a minute. "That's new."

She didn't exactly say it like she thought it was a good thing, either.

My mom is funny that way. I mean, I have tried explaining to her before that Wrangler jeans aren't the same as Calvin Kleins. I've tried telling her how "just ignoring Lauren" at school when she starts in with the Don't Pull a Steph stuff really doesn't work.

But my mom—and Dad, too—totally doesn't get it. I think because she never cared about being popular in school. All she ever did was read books. It was always her dream to open and run a bookstore, just like it was always my dad's dream to be a published mystery writer (a dream that still hasn't come true).

I've tried to explain to her that being popular isn't the point—getting people to give me a *chance* to be liked, a chance Lauren pretty much ruined for me that day in sixth grade—is all I ask for.

But she doesn't understand why I care about being liked by people like Lauren Moffat, whom she considers intellectually beneath me.

That's why I can't tell her about The Book. She'd just never understand.

"I suppose," Mom said still looking at the outfit, "that you borrowed the money for that from Grandpa."

"Um," I said, surprised. "Yeah."

My mom, seeing my questioning look, shrugged.

"Well, I know you'd never dip into your savings for new clothes," Mom explained. "That wouldn't be fiscally responsible."

I felt pretty bad then. I know how angry Mom is at her father.

"I hope you don't mind," I said. "I mean, that I still talk to Grandpa."

"Oh, honey," Mom said with a laugh, leaning over to brush my bangs away from the eye they fall over (in a look that Christoffe, Curl Up and Dye's leading hairstylist, assures me is THE hottest thing. "You are a gamine," Christoffe insisted, last time I saw him. "Insouciant! The rest of those girls at your school, with the part down the middle—phwah! You've got a look that says, 'I am sophisticated.'").

"You and your grandfather are so much alike," Mom went on. "It would be a crime to keep you two apart."

I liked hearing that. Even though Mom's mad at Grandpa, I'm glad she thinks that I'm like him. I want to be like Grandpa. Except for the mustache.

"I don't see why you two can't make up," I said. "I know you're still mad about the Super Sav-Mart. But it's not like Gramps is using the money all for himself. I mean, he built the observatory and gave it to the town."

"He didn't do it for the town," Mom said. "He did it for *her*."

Ouch. I guess my mom *really* doesn't like Kitty.

Or maybe she just doesn't like that Gramps gave up smoking for her, but wouldn't do it for his wife, even though she was dying of cancer.

Although Dad once confided in me behind Mom's back that Grandma was kind of a battle-ax, which was why Mom spent so much time reading as a kid. She needed to get away from her mother's constant harping and criticism.

Still, even if your mom was a total beeyotch, you wouldn't want to hear your dad going around calling some other woman the girl of his dreams, as Gramps often calls Kitty.

"What this town needs is a rec center for you kids," Mom went on, "so you don't have to spend your Saturday nights cruising up and down Main Street, or sitting on that wall, or lying on that hill with all the chiggers. If Gramps really wanted to be a philanthropist, that's what he'd have built, not a planetarium."

"Observatory," I corrected her. "And I get what you're saying. But are you and Dad *really* not coming to the wedding?"

Gramps's wedding to Kitty is going to be the event of the year . . . half the town has been invited, and Grandpa already confided it's costing him fifty thousand dollars. But he says it's totally worth it . . . since he's marrying the girl of his dreams.

Except of course, every time he says this, my mom's lips get all small. "Kitty Hollenbach never gave him the time of day before," I once overheard Mom complaining to my dad. "Now he's a millionaire, and suddenly she's all over him like sweat on a horse."

Which isn't a very nice description of Kitty, who is actually a very cool lady who always orders Manhattans when Grandpa takes her and me and Jason out for dinner at the country club. Grandma, from what I understand, thought it was a sin to drink alcohol of any kind and frequently told Grandpa, who is not what you'd call a teetotaler, so.

"We'll see," was what mom said in answer to my question about her going to the wedding.

I know what "we'll see" means, though. Around my family, it means "no way on God's green earth"—in this case, no way is Mom going to her dad's wedding.

I guess I can see why she's so mad. It really hurts small, locally owned businesses when places like Super Sav-Mart—which sell the same products for much less, and all conveniently located under one roof—move into town.

On the other hand, Super Sav-Mart's going to need someone to manage the book section of the new store, and who better than my mom?

Except that Mom says she'd rather eat her own young than don a red Super Sav-Mart apron.

"Well, good night, honey," Mom said, getting up from

my bed with effort and waddling to the door. "See you in the morning."

"See you," I said.

I didn't say what I wanted to, which was, "If you just asked Grandpa for the money to expand the store into the Hoosier Sweet Shoppe, which has closed down, so we can have a café, which is exactly what Courthouse Square Books needs to blow Super Sav-Mart out of the water, he'd give it to you. And then you wouldn't need to worry about having to wear that red apron."

Because I know if she took the money, she'd feel like she had to be nice to Kitty.

And that would just about kill her.

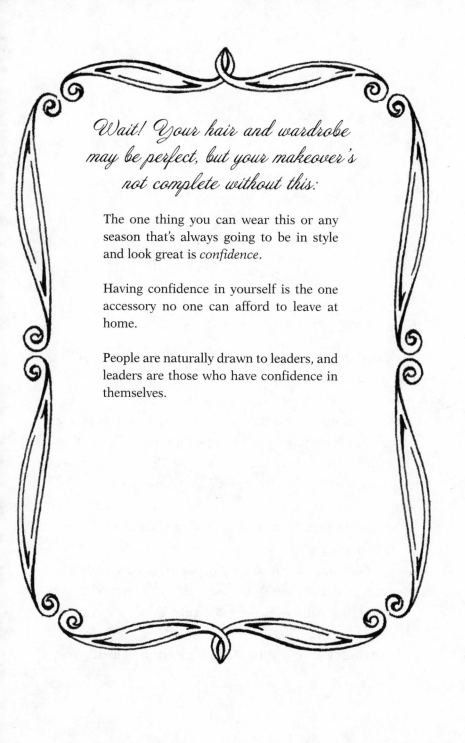

Wait! Your hair and wardrobe may be perfect, but your makeover's not complete without this:

The one thing you can wear this or any season that's always going to be in style and look great is *confidence*.

Having confidence in yourself is the one accessory no one can afford to leave at home.

People are naturally drawn to leaders, and leaders are those who have confidence in themselves.

 *Eight*

D-DAY
MONDAY, AUGUST 28, 9 A.M.

"Good morning, Crazyt—What happened to *you*?" is what Jason said when I climbed into the backseat of The B this morning.

"Nothing," I said innocently as I closed the door. We'd moved on from the 1977 compilation mix CD, I realized immediately when the sounds of the Rolling Stones assailed me. "Why? Is something wrong?"

"What happened to your hair?" Jason wanted to know. He actually turned around in his seat, as opposed to just looking at my reflection in the rearview mirror.

"Oh, this?" I pulled on my bangs to make sure they were hanging sexily in front of one eye, the way Christoffe had meant them to. They were. "I just used a flat iron, is all."

"I think it looks nice," Becca said indignantly from

the front passenger seat.

"Thank you, Becca," I said.

Jason was still twisted around staring at me, as Mick Jagger bemoaned the fact that he couldn't get any satisfaction.

"What kind of SOCKS are those?" Jason demanded.

"Thigh-highs," I explained patiently.

Although inside, I was wondering if I'd made a mistake. All the teen magazines had insisted sheer thigh-highs were THE must-have for fall.

But, judging from Jason's face, I might just as well have been wearing clown shoes.

"I think they look nice," Becca said.

"Is your skirt short enough?" Jason asked me, looking strangely red in the face. Especially since my skirt was strictly mini, not micromini. I wondered if maybe Jason's mom had made him eat hot oatmeal for breakfast. It always upsets him when she does this, something she tries every year on the first day of school. She puts raisins in it, too. Nothing disconcerts Jason more than raisins—he had an unpleasant experience involving one and his right nostril when he was three.

"That's the style," I said, shrugging.

"Since when do *you* care what's in style?" Jason practically shouted.

"Wow, thanks a lot," I said, pretending to be offended. "I didn't mean to try to look nice for the first day of school, or anything."

"I think she looks great," Becca said.

But Jason wasn't falling for it.

"What is this about, Crazytop?" he asked as he put the car in gear. "What's the plan?"

"There's no plan," I insisted. "And you can't call me Crazytop anymore, since my hair isn't curly right now."

"I'll call you Crazytop anytime I damn well want to," Jason said crankily. "Now what's the deal?"

No matter how much I assured him that there was no deal (even though, of course, there very much was one), Jason didn't believe me.

And when we pulled into the student parking lot at school right behind a certain red convertible, and watched as Lauren Moffat emerged from it, Jason seemed to reach a boiling point.

"She's wearing those same socks!" he cried—fortunately while we were still inside the car, so Lauren didn't hear him.

I looked and saw with some relief that the teen magazines had been right . . . sheer thigh-highs *were* in. At least they were if Lauren Moffat was wearing them.

Only Lauren's thigh-highs, unlike mine, which were navy blue, were white.

This was a blatant violation of one of The Book's strictest fashion mandates, which is that white stockings—even sheer ones—are fine only if you're a nurse, since pale colors have a tendency to make legs look larger than they actually are.

It was true, I saw, as Lauren, her cell phone glued to her ear, hurried across the parking lot. Her normally shapely legs looked as big as an elephant's. Well, more or less.

"What is the world coming to?" Jason wanted to know as we dragged ourselves to Bloomville High's back entrance (our first time using it, since in previous years we'd been dropped off in front of the building by our bus). "When Steph Landry and Lauren Moffat are dressing alike?"

"We're hardly dressed alike," I pointed out, pulling on the door handle. "I mean, she's wearing a micromini, and mine's just—"

But I didn't get a chance to finish, since my words were immediately swallowed up by the din that greeted us inside the school. Combination dials spun. Locker doors slammed. Girls who hadn't seen each other since school ended last summer let out piercing shrieks and hugged one another. Guys high-fived other guys. Teachers stood in the doorways to their classrooms, clutching steaming mugs of coffee and gossiping with other teachers. Vice principal Maura Wampler—or Swampy Wampler, as she was commonly referred to— was standing in front of the administrative offices, fruitlessly yelling, "Get to your homeroom! Get to your homeroom before the late bell! You don't want a detention your first day, do you, people?"

"Sit by you at the welcome back convocation?" Becca screamed at me above the chaos.

"See you then," I screamed back.

"I'm not through with you, Crazytop," Jason assured me as he reached his locker, and I had to keep going in order to get to mine. "Something's up with you, and I'm going to find out what it is!"

I couldn't help laughing at that one. "Good luck," I called to him, and hurried on without him.

As I got closer to my locker, things seemed to get quieter. Which is actually impossible, because my locker happens to be located at a point in the school where two main hallways intersect. There's a girls' bathroom AND a drinking fountain next to my locker, not to mention the doors leading downstairs to the cafeteria. Normally, this is the loudest corner of the school.

But today, for some reason, the hall seemed strangely hushed as I walked down it. And not, as I would have liked to think, because I looked so stunning in my new wardrobe and haircut, that everyone was shocked into silence, like when Drew Barrymore showed up at the ball in her angel outfit in the movie *Ever After*.

Actually, it was probably just as loud as usual. Things just SEEMED like they got quieter.

And that's because Mark Finley had entered my line of vision.

Mark's locker is across the hall from mine. He was standing there talking to some of the other guys from the football team as I walked by. In his purple-and-white jersey, he looked tanned and rested, his light brown hair bleached gold in a few places from all the time he'd spent out at the lake this past summer. Even his hazel eyes seemed brighter against the sun-darkened skin of his cheeks.

I, of course, couldn't take my eyes off him. Well, what girl could?

And with that kind of vision standing in front of me, was it really any wonder that I failed to notice that Lauren Moffat and her fellow Dark Ladies of the Sith, Alyssa Krueger and Bebe Johnson, were standing by the drinking fountain, staring at me?

"What," Lauren asked, her gaze going from the top of my insouciant, gaminesque head to the round toes of my platform Mary Janes, "are YOU supposed to be?"

Fortunately just last night I read the section of The Book revolving around jealousy, so I knew just what to do.

"Oh, hi, Lauren," I said, plastering a sunny smile on my face. "Did you have a nice summer?"

Lauren looked incredulously from Alyssa to Bebe, then back at me.

"Excuse me?" she said.

"Your summer." I hoped they couldn't see how badly my fingers were shaking as I twisted the combination to my locker. "How was it? Good, I hope. Did your mom like the books?"

Lauren's jaw dropped. I could tell I'd thrown her. See, most of our previous interactions—since the Super Big Gulp incident, anyway—had been like the one we'd had on Saturday night. Lauren says something mean to me, and I respond by saying . . . nothing.

The fact that this time I was responding—and in a manner that made it clear I refused to let her bait me— had her gears shifting into overdrive.

"I certainly hope so," I said.

Lauren's blue-glazed eyelids narrowed. "What?" she asked, sounding irritated.

"That your mom enjoyed the books she bought from our store," I said.

At that moment—thank GOD—the bell rang. I slammed my locker door shut, shouldered my new designer bag, and said, "Well, see you at the convo," and rushed down the hall . . .

. . . right past Mark Finley.

Who, I couldn't help noticing, had been looking in my direction, either because he'd noticed my interaction with his girlfriend, or—even though I knew this was too much to hope for . . . still, The Book said optimism is crucial for any successful social venture—he was taking in my sheer thigh-highs.

Either way, our gazes met as I hurried by.

I smiled and said, "Hi, Mark. Hope you had a good summer."

They were the first words I'd ever spoken to Mark Finley in my life.

And I think they had the desired effect. Because as I breezed past him, I heard him go, "Who was that?" and heard Lauren hiss, *"That was Steph Landry, you retard."*

Oh yeah. I'd pulled a Steph, all right.

And for the first time in my life, I felt GREAT about it.

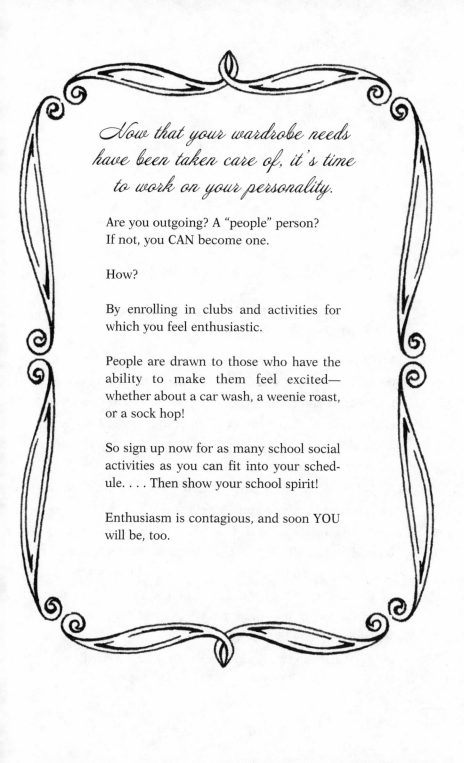

Now that your wardrobe needs have been taken care of, it's time to work on your personality.

Are you outgoing? A "people" person? If not, you CAN become one.

How?

By enrolling in clubs and activities for which you feel enthusiastic.

People are drawn to those who have the ability to make them feel excited— whether about a car wash, a weenie roast, or a sock hop!

So sign up now for as many school social activities as you can fit into your schedule. . . . Then show your school spirit!

Enthusiasm is contagious, and soon YOU will be, too.

 *Nine*

"This is so lame," Jason said as he started for our traditional places in the last row of the auditorium, where, last year, it had been my idea to roll soda cans down the entire length of the room during the student government's speeches. Since the floor is cement, they'd made an extremely satisfying racket.

No one had even suspected us, because we're such good students. Ms. Wampler yelled at some totally innocent guys in the row in front of us, just because they were horticulture (i.e., not college-bound) students. She'd have given them detention, too, if at the exact right moment I hadn't let loose one of my Diet Coke cans, causing Swampy's face to turn bright red as she shrieked, "WHO IS DOING THAT?"

I got a stitch in my side from laughing so hard.

"I've got an idea," I said before Jason could flop into a seat. "Let's sit closer."

Enthusiasm is contagious, all right. Becca was like, "Oh my gosh! Is this part of a criminal master plot?"

"Uh," I said. "Yeah."

"How'm I going to be able to roll my Coke can down the aisle if we're up front?" Jason wanted to know.

"You're not," I explained, selecting three empty seats just a few rows from the stage.

"Whatever your plan is," Jason said when he saw how close the seats were to where Ms. Wampler and the other school administrators were standing, "it better be worth it. We're going to have to, like, pay attention."

"Exactly," I said, and took the seat on the aisle.

"I don't get it," Jason said, shaking his head. "First the hair, then the socks, now this. Did you suffer a concussion this summer that I didn't know about?"

"Shhh," I said, because Ms. Wampler was starting the convocation. Which is what they call it at Bloomville High when we all gather in the auditorium to listen to ex–drug addicts and people who killed their friends in drunk driving accidents talk about their experiences.

While Swampy tried to get everyone to settle down (by saying, "Settle down, people. Now, people. Please settle down," over and over into the microphone at the podium), I watched as the A-crowd filed in and started filling up the first few rows in front of us. There was Alyssa Krueger, in Juicy Couture jeans and a glittery top, riding into the auditorium on Sean de Marco's broad shoulders, laughing hysterically.

There was Bebe Johnson, chattering away in her unnaturally high voice about nothing, as was her custom.

There was Darlene Staggs, surrounded by guys, as usual. One of them seemed to say something she found amusing, since she threw back her head and laughed, her honey-blond hair cascading like a waterfall down the back of her seat. All the other guys watched her truly magnificent chest as she jiggled. I mean, giggled.

And then, just before the bell rang, in came Lauren Moffat, hand in hand with Mark Finley. The two of them weren't looking at each other—no gazing deeply into each other's eyes, going, "I love you . . . no, I love YOU. No, I love YOU." Instead, they were gazing out across the sea of faces in the seats on either side of the aisle they were walking down, the way a bride and groom might smile and nod at people assembled for their wedding, or a king and queen might nod to their populace.

Which is, in a way, what Lauren and Mark are: the king and queen of our school. No matter how much Jason—who followed my gaze, saw who I was looking at, and made a very rude noise—might not like to admit it.

As soon as Lauren and Mark sat down—front row, since Mark, as senior class president, would be getting up to go to the podium to give us all a back-to-school pep talk, and also rally us to help the senior class raise enough money to send them all to Kings Island in the spring, a Bloomville High senior tradition—and

Principal Greer finally approached the microphone, the chattering hordes fell silent. They shut up because Principal Greer, who golfs, keeps a club in his office with which he often practices swings—without regard, rumor has it, to anyone who might happen to be sitting in his office at the time. There's a guy who works at the car wash who only has one working eye, and everyone says Dr. Greer is the one who put it out with his 5 iron the day the guy got sent to his office for mouthing off to Swampy Wampler.

Dr. Greer started his welcome speech—"Welcome, students, to another school year at Bloomville High"—and Jason, slumped in the seat next to me, slumped down even farther, putting his Converse high tops on the back of the seat in front of him and causing the person in that seat—Courtney Pierce, class suck-up—to turn around and give him an aggravated look, to which Jason responded with, "What? I'm not touching you," a line he actually learned from my little brother Pete.

Beside Jason, Becca, clearly bored, took out a purple sparkle pen she'd put on my employee account over at the bookstore ($1.12, seventy-three cents with my thirty-five percent off) and started making little stars on the white part of Jason's high tops.

And Jason, after throwing a startled look at me (as if to say, "Do you see what your insane friend is doing?"), just sat there and let her keep doing it. Like he was afraid if he moved, she might plunge the pen into his forearm, or something.

After Dr. Greer's mind-numbingly boring speech about how we should use the coming school year to Realize Our Full Potential came Swampy's reading of the highlights of the student code of conduct: no cheating, no violence, no harassment of any kind, or you will be expelled and have to go to Culver Military Academy or the alternative high school.

It was hard to see which would be worse. At Culver, you'd be forced to rise at dawn and perform drills. At the alternative high school, you'd be forced to put on performance pieces about your feelings concerning war. It was a lose/lose situation, either way. It was obviously better just to keep from violating the Bloomville High student code of conduct.

Finally, after she had the place alternately looking at the clock and longing for it to be lunchtime, and snoring, Swampy turned the mike over to Mark Finley, who sauntered up to the podium to thunderous applause that caused some people—like Jason, who'd nodded off—to start in their seats.

"Oh, man," Jason said looking down at his shoes. In addition to the stars, Becca had added tiny unicorns.

"Aren't they cute?" Becca asked, clearly thrilled by her own artistic prowess.

"Oh, man," Jason said again, not looking like he found them at all cute.

But I didn't have time to deal with Jason's shoe drama. Because Mark had started speaking.

"Hey," Mark said, his deep voice gruff—but totally

charming—in the microphone, which he'd had to adjust to his own height after the diminutive Ms. Wampler stepped away from it, to amused chuckles from the student body. "So, yeah. Uh. It's a new school year, and you know what that means . . . last year's juniors are seniors now, and—"

Here he was cut off by more applause and cheering as the seniors congratulated themselves for managing to make it through the summer without killing themselves in drunk driving accidents or by diving headfirst into the shallow end of the pool (not to mention not drinking any batches of lemon Joy lemonade).

"Um, yeah," Mark said when the seniors settled down again, grinning his sheepish little grin. "So, you know what that means. We gotta start saving up for our senior trip this spring. Which means we gotta make some money. Now, I know last year's senior class made like five thousand dollars doing weekend car washes. And I propose we do the same thing. The Red Lobster out by the mall said we could use their parking lot again, so . . . whadduya say? You folks up for a car wash?"

More applause, this time accompanied by whistling and shouts of "Go, Fish," which inevitably led to snickers about childhood card games.

I seriously don't know how our school got stuck with the Fighting Fish as its mascot. Because as mascots go, fish suck. Apparently it has something to do with the fish weather vane on top of the courthouse . . . which some people suspect is a crappie, the most commonly found fish in the lake. So I guess things could be worse. We could be the Fighting Crappies.

Mark looked around the room to see if anybody had anything but "Go, Fish!" to say. I looked around, too.

But the only person who raised his hand was Gordon Wu, the junior class president (elected solely due to having run unopposed, my class being—what's the nicest way to put this?—slightly apathetic), who stood up and asked, "Excuse me, er, Mark, but I was wondering if there weren't some other method by which we might raise funds, other than car washes? You see, some of us would prefer to have our Saturdays free for, um, lab work—"

This remark was followed by the hissing it deserved from the crowd and several shouts of "Don't be such a Steph, Wu!"

I couldn't believe my good fortune—I mean, that Gordon Wu, of all people, had actually cracked the door open for me to go barging through. Which I did without another second's hesitation, before Mark could say anything.

"Gordon brings up an interesting point," I said, standing up in my seat—so suddenly that Jason started and dropped both his feet from the back of the chair in front of him. He didn't seem aware of the loud thumping sound they made as they hit the cement auditorium floor, either. Instead, he craned his neck up at me and mouthed, "WHAT ARE YOU DOING? SIT DOWN!" while Becca, one finger in her mouth (she's a nail biter), stared up at me with a horrified expression on her face.

Silence roared through the auditorium as every face in the room turned toward me. I could feel heat rushing up to my cheeks, but I tried to ignore it. This, I knew, was it. My big chance to show my school spirit, after years of pretty much doing what Jason had been doing a second ago—dozing—through every school-related event I was forced to attend, and not showing up at all at the ones I wasn't.

Well, not anymore.

"We have a lot of very talented individuals in this room," I went on, glad that no one could see my knees from where I was standing (except Jason. But he wasn't looking at my knees) since they were shaking so badly. "It seems a shame to waste them. Which is why I was thinking a good way to raise money for the senior class trip this year would be to hold a student talent auction."

The crowd, which had been stunned into silence up until that point, began to buzz. I saw Lauren Moffat, her eyes alight with glee at what I was doing (making a public spectacle of myself . . . again), lean forward in her chair to hiss something in Alyssa Krueger's ear.

"Let me explain," I said hastily before the buzzing could drown me out. "Students like Gordon, for instance, who are very good with computers, could auction off a few hours of computer programming to a member of the community."

The murmuring became louder. I could feel the crowd growing restless. Soon, I knew, the "Don't be such a Steph"s would begin. I didn't have them yet. I needed to close the deal.

"Or, you, for instance, Mark," I said, looking up at the stage and meeting Mark's calm, hazel-eyed gaze. I wondered vaguely if he knew what an electrifying effect his gaze had on the female population of Bloomville High.

It's weird what you think about as your life is slipping away before your eyes.

"Being the school's quarterback, Mark," I went on, "you could auction off your time to film a local television ad for a community business. People would pay a lot for that kind of endorsement."

I noticed that, at the table behind the podium at which Mark stood, both Ms. Wampler and Dr. Greer were staring at me. Swampy even went so far as to lean over and say something to Dr. Greer, who, still looking at me, nodded. I wondered if she'd always suspected us for last year's Tin Can Rolling incident and had finally put two and two together. I tried to ignore them.

"It just seems like we have so many extraordinarily talented people in this school," I went on.

This was the tricky part. The Book was very explicit about not sounding like a suck-up. Although The Book doesn't call it sucking up. The Book calls it "currying favor." Under no circumstances were you to do it.

Still, it was hard, I was discovering, to suck up without *seeming* like you were sucking up.

"It would be a shame not to give them a chance to shine at what they're naturally good at," I said, "as opposed to forcing everyone to work . . . well, at a car wash."

Which was when a voice hissed, "What's YOUR talent, Steph?"

And another answered, "Oh, right. Super Big Gulp!"

I didn't need to look in their direction to know it was Alyssa and Lauren. I knew those voices plenty well.

"Which is not to say," I went on, conscious of the snickers from those who'd been seated near enough to hear Alyssa's question and Lauren's answer, "that we shouldn't have a car wash in addition to a talent auction, for the participation of those people whose talents are less marketable than others."

I wanted to add, "Or whose only talents are the kind you could go to jail for if you accept money for them," while looking directly at Lauren.

But The Book states very explicitly that if you want LASTING popularity, you aren't allowed to publicly slight your enemies.

Which makes me wonder if Lauren knows how limited her time at the top of the popularity totem pole might actually turn out to be.

"But," I went on, "I think we ought to consider a talent auction, as well."

And then I sat down.

Good thing, too, since my knees had finally given way. I couldn't have stood for a second longer. I sat there, my heart slamming against my rib cage, and looked at Jason and Becca. They were both staring back at me, their mouths slightly ajar.

"What," Jason asked softly, "was THAT about? Since when do you care—"

But I didn't get to hear what he said after that, since Mark, tapping on the microphone to get attention after everyone had started whispering among themselves, went, "Uh, okay. Thanks, uh, um—"

"*Steph Landry!*" Lauren screamed from her seat, where she'd dissolved in a puddle of white-thigh-high-wearing giggles.

"Thanks, Steph," Mark said. He looked back at Ms. Wampler and Dr. Greer. Both of them, I noticed, were nodding.

What did *that* mean? That they liked my idea?

Or that Mark should just ignore me and go on?

"Um, I think a, um, talent auction," Mark said, his hazel eyes looking right at me—no, *burning* right *through* me—where I had dissolved into my own seat . . . only not from a fit of the giggles, but from sheer mortification, "sounds like a great idea."

"*WHAT?*"

The word—which had come out of Lauren—cracked through the auditorium with the explosiveness of a starter's pistol down by the drag racetrack.

Everyone looked at Lauren, whose face was a comedic mask of outrage.

Or at least *I* thought it was comedic.

Mark looked from Lauren back to me, his bemused expression clearly indicating that he, Mark Finley, had no idea what his girlfriend's problem was.

"Great," Mark said to me. "So, is it okay if I put you in charge of signing people up for that, Steph? The, um, talent thingie?"

"Sure," I said.

"Great," Mark said again. "Then all we need next is a Bloomville Fighting Fish Slap. . . ."

And then Mark led us all in our school chant, a ridiculous thing you do with your arms, flapping one against the other to make a slapping sound like a fishtail on the water.

Then the bell rang.

Do not be surprised if a few acquaintances resent your newfound confidence and attempt to undermine your efforts at self-growth.

They are undoubtedly envious and perhaps concerned about their own social status in light of your meteoric rise to popularity. Do your best to soothe their fears and let old friends know they will always be important to you—as important to you as your new friends.

# Ten

STILL D-DAY
MONDAY, AUGUST 28, 1 P.M.

Everyone took off for lunch.

Everyone, that is, except for me.

And Jason and Becca, because they were pinned into my row by the fact that I wasn't moving.

But of course, I COULDN'T move. Because my knees were still wobbly. On account of what had just happened.

And things didn't get much better when everyone was filing past us, and people like Gordon Wu stopped by our row to say things like, "Great idea, Stephanie," or, "Do you think I can auction off drawing lessons for, like, little kids? Because I can draw. Does that count as a talent?"

Even Dr. Greer stopped by my seat on his way to his next round of golf and said, "Very nice suggestion, Tiffany. It's good to see you taking part in school activities for a change." He flicked a glance at Jason and Becca.

"Your friends here might want to follow your lead."

"It's Stephanie," Jason said as Dr. Greer went away. "Her name's Stephanie."

But Dr. Greer didn't appear to hear him.

Not that it mattered. Who cared whether or not the principal knew my name? Mark Finley knew it.

And that was all that mattered.

I knew Mark Finley knew my name because as he came down the aisle next to my seat, he grinned and nodded to me.

"Cool idea, Steph," he said. "See ya."

And, okay, his arm was around Lauren Moffat's neck as he said it.

But that's only because she picked it up and put it there. I SAW her do it. She was waiting as Mark came down off the stage and pretty much threw herself at him as soon as he set foot on solid ground.

And sure, she sneered at me as she went by, even as the guy she was attached to at the hip was smiling at me.

But who cares? MARK FINLEY SMILED AT ME.

Which is exactly what Becca said after everyone was gone.

"Mark Finley smiled at you." Her tone was reverential. "He SMILED. At YOU. In a NICE way."

"I know," I said. I could feel the strength slowly starting to return to my legs.

"Mark Finley," Becca murmured wonderingly. "I mean, he's like . . . he's the most popular guy in the whole school."

"I know," I said again. Empty, the auditorium is a very different place than it is when full. There is something almost restful about its echoey size.

"What the hell," Jason, who up until that point had been strangely silent, finally burst out, "is the matter with you, Steph? Did someone pour crack all over your cornflakes this morning, or something?"

"What?" I asked, trying to look—and sound—like I didn't know what he was talking about. And not about the crack, either.

"Don't give me that," Jason said. "You know exactly WHAT. What was all that back there? What's a talent auction? And what's with you volunteering to participate in one? What's with you showing SCHOOL SPIRIT?"

By that time my legs had stopped shaking, and I was able to climb to my feet.

"I just wanted to help out," I said. "I mean, someone'll do the same when it's our turn to go to Kings Island next year."

"You hate Kings Island," Jason said, climbing out of his seat. "You threw up on the log flume the last time we went there and refused to go on any more rides."

"So?" I said with a shrug. "Does that mean I'm not allowed to try to help other people enjoy something, just because I don't like heights?"

"Yes," Jason said, loping after me as I started up the aisle toward the exit to the rest of the building. "Because that is perilously close to school spirit. And you don't have school spirit."

"Actually," I said, "I've been thinking a lot about that, and—"

"Oh no," Jason said, reaching the doors before I did and barring the handles with his own body to keep me from slipping out before he'd had his say. "Don't even try to go there with me, Steph. How in hell can you want to help those people have a good time on their senior trip when all they've ever done is make your life miserable?"

"That wasn't them," I pointed out. "That was Lauren. She's not going to Kings Island."

"So what?" Jason demanded. "She's the enemy—and they're her friends. Ergo, they're your enemies."

I just stood there and looked at him. Well, not like I had much of a choice, since he was blocking the doorway.

"You're being really childish about this Jason," I said in my most reasonable voice. "There's nothing wrong with showing a little school spirit by trying to help out others who might be in need. We've only got two more years in this place. We should really try to enjoy the short time we have left."

At least, that's what it said in The Book. You know, about how you should try to enjoy your high school years while you can, because you will never get them back.

Jason, obviously, hadn't read The Book. But it was clear from his reaction to what I'd said that even if he had, it wouldn't have made much difference.

Because what he did next was reach out and plant a

hand on my forehead as if he were feeling for a fever.

"Does she seem hot to you, Becca?" he asked. "Because I think she might be coming down with something. Lassa fever, or maybe Marburg's. Either that or she's been body-snatched and replaced with a very clever clone. Clone!" He took his hand away from my forehead and peered down into my eyes. "Tell me what game Steph Landry and I used to play in the big dirt pile they made while they were digging my family's pool, back when we were both seven, or I'll know you're an alien replacement and you've got the real Steph up in your mother ship!"

I glared at him. "G.I. Joe meets Spelunker Barbie," I said. "And stop being so ridiculous. We have to go. We're going to end up at a bad table for lunch."

Finally Becca spoke up.

"I thought we were going out to lunch," she said. "You know. Since Jason's got a car now."

"We can't go OUT to lunch," I explained to them both. "Don't you get it? Lunch is the most important time of the day for social interaction in the school setting."

No sooner were the words out of my mouth than I realized how they sounded. They were, of course, a verbatim quotation from The Book.

But Jason and Becca didn't know anything about The Book. So naturally, they'd find the statement perplexing, as it did not actually sound the way I normally talk. I could tell they were confused before I even finished speaking.

"What I mean is, I can't just not show up down there,"
I explained in what I thought was a very reasonable tone
of voice. "I have to be available, in case anyone wants to
sign up. You know, for the auction. Do you see what I
mean?"

"Oh," Jason said, nodding. "We see what you mean,
all right. And if this isn't part of some greater diabolical
master plan—one that involves talking the school into
buying nonexistent swampland in Florida or something—then we're out. So. Is it?"

I shook my head. "Is it what?"

"Part of some diabolical master plan to take out Mark
Finley as senior class president and take over yourself, or
something?"

I didn't know what to say. It *was* part of a diabolical
master plan, of course. But not the kind he was hoping
for.

He seemed to realize this without my having to say
anything. Turning to Becca, he said, "Come on. Let's go."

Becca hurried to his side, eyeing me warily the whole
time as if I were a rabid dog, or a fried Twinkie, or something.

Still, I didn't get it. Not right away. Because the truth
was too horrible to believe, I guess.

I was like, "Good." I actually felt relieved. I actually
thought they understood. "Now, we'll just go down there
and hit the salad bar or whatever, and then sit by those
plants the horticulture club puts out, and if anybody
comes by, we'll—"

"WE won't do anything," Jason said, throwing open the doors and leading Becca out into the hallway.

"Well," I said, following them, still not getting it. "No, I mean, of course not, I realize this is my thing, and all. You guys don't have to help. But if—hey, where are you going?"

Because instead of making the turn for the cafeteria, they'd made the turn for the student parking lot.

"We're going to Pizza Hut," Jason said. "You're welcome to come with us, if you change your mind."

I just stood there, staring at them, not understanding what was happening. Jason and I ALWAYS ate lunch together. I mean, except for that fight in the fifth grade . . . ALWAYS.

And now he was ditching me? Just because I'd shown some school spirit?

"You guys," I said. I guess a part of me thought they might be joking, or something. "You can't be serious. I mean, come on. We can't be moody malcontents our whole lives. We've got to start participating in school activities, or people will never get to know us and realize how fantastic we are. They'll just be all, 'Don't be such a Steph' for the rest of our lives—you guys? You guys!"

But it was too late. Because I was speaking to an empty hallway, since they'd left.

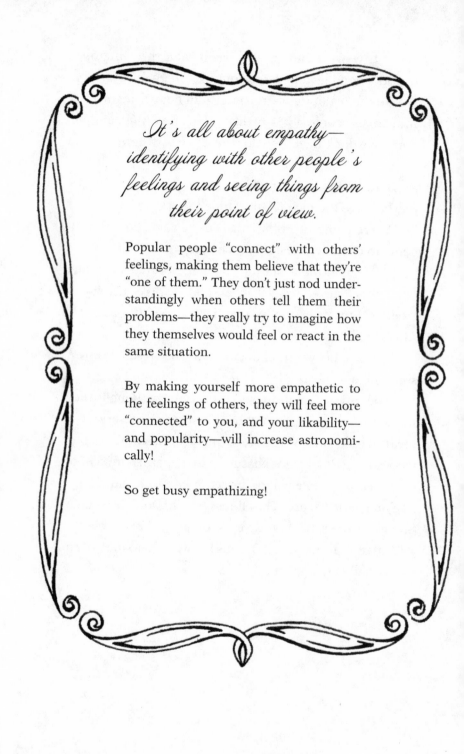

*It's all about empathy—
identifying with other people's
feelings and seeing things from
their point of view.*

Popular people "connect" with others' feelings, making them believe that they're "one of them." They don't just nod understandingly when others tell them their problems—they really try to imagine how they themselves would feel or react in the same situation.

By making yourself more empathetic to the feelings of others, they will feel more "connected" to you, and your likability—and popularity—will increase astronomically!

So get busy empathizing!

 *Eleven*

STILL D-DAY
MONDAY, AUGUST 28, 2 P.M.

The Bloomville High School cafeteria is a scary place, and not just because of the food. It's a lot like Main Street—the place to see or be seen—if you are a teenager in Bloomville, Indiana. The tables in there are round and only fit about ten people. This means that if you, like me, want to sit at a table filled with popular people, you have to find one with a space left for you to squeeze into.

More importantly, you have to find one the people sitting at will LET you squeeze into.

When I left the salad bar and stood there surveying the landscape before me, I saw that—just as I'd predicted back in the auditorium to Jason and Becca—almost all of the good seats were taken. There was a seat or two left at the "head" table . . . where Lauren and Mark and their entourage, including Alyssa Krueger and the rest of the football team, were sitting.

Meanwhile, there was PLENTY of room left at Gordon Wu's table. In fact, seeing me standing there, Gordon actually stood up and waved at me, and then moved his backpack off the chair next to him, as if he'd been saving me a place.

Which was very nice of him, and all.

But if I sat next to Gordon Wu, I'd still be no further away from jettisoning my Don't Pull a Steph reputation than I'd been this morning.

Which was when I noticed there was still a space at Darlene Staggs's table, right next to Mark and Lauren's table. Normally Darlene would have been at their table.

But since she grew what I have to say are probably the most impressive set of knockers in Greene County during winter break last year (some less generous people, like Jason, say Darlene's breasts are "store-boughts," but I refuse to believe that any parent—even mine—would be irresponsible enough to let their sixteen-year-old daughter get a boob job. You aren't even done growing at sixteen!), she's had to move to her own table in order to accommodate her ever-growing retinue of male admirers.

Darlene Staggs is possibly the dimmest person I have ever met who was not actually in Special Ed. Once in eighth grade biology, she finally figured out that honey comes from bees, and she was so grossed out that her favorite condiment came, as she put it, "out of a bug's butt" that she actually had to be sent to the nurse's office to have a cool compress applied to her forehead.

But while God was shortchanging Darlene in the brains department, He went overboard on the beauty. Though even before the miraculous Christmas visit by the boob fairy, you could tell Darlene was the kind of girl who, in a couple of years (after she'd become some banker's trophy wife and squeezed out a kid or two), was going to experience the same kind of battle with gravity that I am facing at the moment.

But for right now, she's the prettiest girl in our whole school and so is constantly surrounded by boys, who flock to her in hopes of someday being able to sink into her soft good-smellingness.

The other thing about Darlene is, when she, Lauren, Alyssa Krueger, and Bebe Johnson were in line to get meanness from God, Darlene must have seen a butterfly and gone running after it, or something, since she doesn't have a mean bone in her body. But Lauren still lets Darlene hang out with her and the other Dark Ladies of the Sith, because Darlene's too pretty not to keep her around, in case one of them needs to catch her dregs.

Which was why, with an apologetic smile to Gordon Wu, I made a beeline for the empty chair at Darlene's lunch table, which was just feet from where Lauren and Mark were sitting.

"Hi, Darlene," I said, putting my tray down across from hers. "Mind if I sit here?"

All eight of the guys at Darlene's table yanked their gazes off the front of her chest and looked at me. Or the area just above the sticky part of my thigh-highs, to be more exact.

"Oh, you're that girl from the convocation today," Darlene said amiably. Because that's how she does everything. "Sure, hi."

So I sat down and started in on my baked chicken, carefully peeling off the skin to avoid adding unnecessary saturated fats going to the Butt.

"Like your socks," Todd Rubin said to me with a grin I could only call lecherous.

Instead of being all, "Gross, get away from me, and by the way, in your dreams," as I might have done before reading The Book, I smiled at Todd and said, with a sly look, "Why, thank you, Todd. Say, Todd. Aren't you in my Advanced Trig class?"

Todd looked nervously in Darlene's direction, as if someone mentioning his math prowess might queer his chances of scoring with someone whose combined GPA was probably equal to the number of state capitals she could name off the top of her head.

Which, having been in World Civ with her last year, I happen to know is two.

"Yeah," Todd said cautiously.

"Maybe you could sign up for the talent auction, then," I said. "There are probably tons of cute freshmen girls who would bid to have you as their tutor for a day. Don't you think?"

Todd, with another glance at Darlene, who was staring at him vacantly as she nibbled a carrot stick, looked a little less alarmed, since what I'd just done was give him a compliment. In front of the woman of his dreams.

"Well," Todd said. "I mean, okay. I mean, whatever."

"Excellent," I said, and whipped out the clipboard I'd stolen from the main office on my way down to the lunchroom. "Sign yourself up, then. Wow, we'll probably make a fortune off this—enough for the senior class to go to France, at this rate. How about you guys? Anybody interested in having girls bid for you?"

Five minutes later, every guy at the table had signed up, listing, under the heading TALENT, skills as various as LAWN MOWING; THREE WHEEL ATV TRAIL GUIDE; TWO HOUR FISHING TRIP ON GREENE LAKE; WILL HOLD YOUR BAGS WHILE YOU SHOP AT BLOOMVILLE MALL; and ALMOST PROFESSIONAL CAR DETAILING. As other people noticed the guys at Darlene's table talking so animatedly, they stopped by to see what was going on, and then signed up themselves. By the time the next period bell rang, I had almost thirty volunteers—most of them A-crowd—including Darlene herself, who'd very charmingly asked, "But you guys, what about me? I have no talents."

"Of course you do, Darlene," I told her in the same animated voice I'd been using with all the guys. Because The Book says people are drawn to extroverts and other cheerful types. "Look how pretty you are. Why don't you volunteer to give someone a makeover?"

"Ooooh," Darlene said excitedly. "Like at the Lancôme counter in the mall?"

"Um," I said. "Yes." Then, seeing she clearly didn't

understand, I added, "Only you would be the one GIV-ING the makeover, not getting one. You'd probably have to use your own makeup on whoever wins it."

"Oh," Darlene said, looking disappointed. You could tell she'd totally thought she'd somehow be getting free makeup out of the whole thing. Which, given the fact that Darlene is probably given free stuff every minute of the day, is understandable. "But what if nobody buys me?"

"Don't worry, Dar," Mike Sanders hurried to say, since no human being could stand to see Darlene looking sad. "I'll get my mom to bid on you. She could totally use a makeover."

Darlene brightened. "Really, Mike?" she asked. "Would you really?"

"Of course, Dar," Mike assured her. And all the other guys at the table hurried to assure her their moms were dogs who needed makeovers, too.

It was as this was happening that the bell rang and everyone started getting up to go . . . including Mark Finley and Lauren Moffat, who ended up walking behind me as I was jotting down the names of some last minute sign-ups.

Even though Lauren had Mark's arm wrapped around her neck again, he didn't seem to be paying her much attention. He was looking at me, as a matter of fact.

"Hey," he said with a smile, nodding at my clipboard. "Gotta lotta names there, huh?"

I smiled at him sunnily, while at the same time avoided meeting Lauren's scowl.

"We do," I said chirpily. "People seem really into it. What I'm going to do next is take out an ad in the *Bloomville Gazette*, letting the people in town know about the auction, so they can come bid. What night do you think we should have it? The auction, I mean?"

"Thursday? Is that enough time to get the ad in?"

I said that'd be cutting it close, but that I'd take care of it.

"Hey, did you, uh, mean it?" Mark wanted to know, his hazel eyes looking almost green in the fluorescent lights. "That thing you said in the auditorium, about people maybe bidding on me to do advertising for their business?"

"Absolutely," I said. I darted a look at Lauren to see how she was bearing up, you know, under the circumstances. The circumstances of her boyfriend talking to me, I mean. She had her eyes half-lidded like a lizard's. It was clear she was wishing herself anywhere but there.

"Do you want to sign up?" I asked Mark, holding out the clipboard. "It would probably get a lot more people, you know, if they see your name on here."

"You think so?" Mark asked. But he was already reaching for the pen and scribbling his name. "What should I put for talent?" The smile he cocked at me was lopsided, a charming blend of uncertainty and self-effacement. "I don't know if 'spokesmodel' has the right tone."

"I'll put spokesperson," I said, smiling back at him. And, because I didn't want her to think I was trying to ignore her, or anything, I said to Lauren, "Would you like to sign up, Lauren? Maybe you could offer to chauffeur people in one of your dad's BMWs, you know, off his lot."

The look Lauren gave me was glacial. "Thanks," she said sarcastically. "But I'm not going to drive some schmo around all day in one of my dad's brand-new cars."

And, to emphasize just how bad of an idea she thought it was, Lauren flicked a glance at Alyssa, who nearly choked on her diet soda, she laughed so hard when Lauren added, "God, could she be more of a Steph?"

Mark, however, didn't seem to see anything funny about the situation.

"Jeez, Laur," he said, looking down at her pointed little rat face, framed by his (comparably massive) arm and shoulder. "It's for charity. Well, I mean, for the senior trip. What are you giving her such a hard time for?"

Now Alyssa actually *did* choke on her soda. She sprayed a mouthful of it across the (by now almost empty) cafeteria.

Lauren, for her part, looked up at Mark and, her rat face tightening, said, "Gawd. I was just kidding."

Then she snatched the clipboard away from me, scrawled her name on it, and wrote, WHATEVER, under TALENT.

Which is probably best, since I don't think there are

that many people who would bid to see Lauren KISS MARK FINLEY'S ASS, since we get to see that for free every day.

I made a mental note to remember to repeat that to Jason later, since I knew how much he would appreciate it, as witticisms go.

"Happy?" Lauren asked, shoving the clipboard back at me.

"Great, thanks so much," I said as if I were completely oblivious to her rudeness. "This is really going to make such a difference. You wait and see."

Then I gave her a final smile and a wave, and turned around to head to my next class.

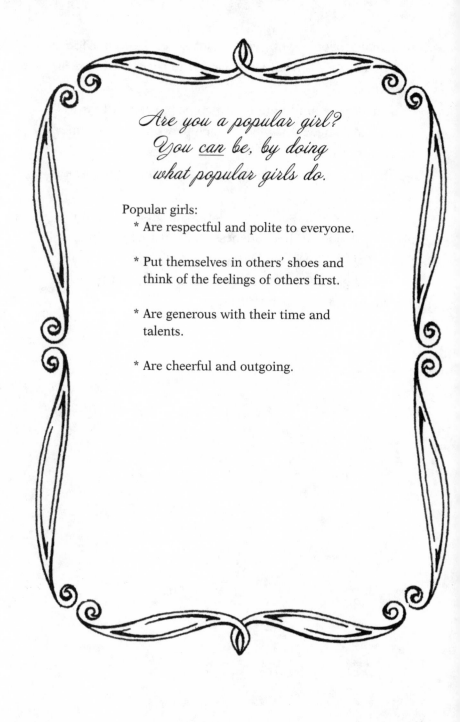

Are you a popular girl?
You <u>can</u> be, by doing
what popular girls do.

Popular girls:
  * Are respectful and polite to everyone.

  * Put themselves in others' shoes and
    think of the feelings of others first.

  * Are generous with their time and
    talents.

  * Are cheerful and outgoing.

 *Twelve*

STILL D-DAY
MONDAY, AUGUST 28, 4 P.M.

Jason and Becca were kind of quiet on the ride home from school.

I told myself it was because I was a little late meeting them by The B. That's because everywhere I went in the hallways, people were stopping me and asking if they could sign up for the talent auction. I had more than a hundred volunteers. That was way more than I'd anticipated. It was almost more than we could reasonably auction off in a night.

Jason and Becca didn't want to participate. Even though I pointed out they both had very marketable skills.

"Jason, you could give golf lessons. People would love it," I said to him in the car on the way home. "Or you could offer tours of the observatory. And, Becca, you could hold private scrapbooking seminars."

But Jason reiterated his refusal to take part in anything that might benefit Mark Finley. And Becca said only, "Oh, no way. I'm not good enough for that. Besides, I don't think my parents would let me, you know. Be auctioned."

"*You're* not being auctioned," I pointed out to her. "Your talent is."

But she just shook her head some more.

I could understand Becca, who, when not around us, is pretty shy and all, not wanting to be a part of it. But Jason is totally outgoing . . . if you can be outgoing and antisocial at the same time.

I didn't get a chance to really pester him in the car, but fortunately I got a call at home a little later from Kitty, letting me and Catie know that our dresses were ready—along with Pete's and Robbie's tuxedos—for our final fittings and asking if we wanted to come over.

"We'll be right there," I said, and went and got Catie—who was already doing homework, since fourth grade is the first year they give it in Greene County, and Catie was so excited about it, she couldn't wait (as this kind of nerdiness is typical of me and the rest of my family, I didn't become alarmed)—and Pete and Robbie, who were watching MTV2 in the family room, having figured out Mom's password for the parental V-Chip again.

Then, telling Dad where we were going and leaving Sara in front of *Dora the Explorer* (so he wouldn't figure out that we knew about the password), we all ran across the lawn to Jason's house, where the wedding finery was waiting.

I don't consider myself a super fashiony person. I mean, aside from the thigh-highs, which I changed out of as soon as I got home, I don't dress up much.

But the bridesmaid and flower girl gowns Kitty picked out for us are really something special. Sleeveless soft pink—but not in an annoying, girly way—satin shells with even paler pink chiffon floating over them, they are covered all over the hem with clear crystals of different sizes that catch the light and glitter . . . but not in a trashy, Princess Barbie way. I could totally remove the deep pink sash and wear the dress to the prom. You know, in the unlikely event anyone were ever to ask me.

And the best part of all is, Grandpa is paying for them. Because if it had been left up to Mom, we'd have had to wear matching dresses from the Sears sale rack instead of beautifully handmade gowns from Kitty's own personal seamstress and dress designer.

"Hello, kids," Kitty said when we came to the back kitchen door, which is the only one the Hollenbachs use. Their house, which Kitty grew up in, is one of the oldest on our block, a huge Victorian farmhouse (although the farm part got sold off long ago to build other houses on, like mine) with a fancy parquet entranceway the Hollenbachs never use. The house has a butler's pantry and maid's room (the attic room Jason had recently moved into), and a button under the dining room table you can press to ring for the maid in the kitchen, which

Jason and I used to press so many times when I'd go over there to play as a kid that his mom finally had it disconnected.

"Would you like some lemonade?" Kitty asked.

Which is one of the reasons I'd liked coming over to Jason's house so much when I was little. For one thing, it was the only house on the block with central air-conditioning, so it was always nice and cool.

But for another thing, his mother always had things like lemonade and fresh orange juice to serve. At my house, the only thing there is to drink, besides milk, is water. From the tap. My dad says we can't afford to have juice, even frozen concentrate, since it's so expensive (and besides, whenever by some accident it shows up in our fridge, it is immediately consumed by Pete), and he won't let any of us have soda or Kool-Aid, because all that sugar isn't good for you.

Jason can have as much sugar as he wants. And as a consequence, he never wants it.

We glugged down about two gallons of lemonade (Pete drank practically a gallon all on his own) before Kitty could finally persuade us to climb the stairs and try stuff on.

But when we did, it was totally worth it.

"Oh," Kitty said when Catie and I came out of Jason's old room, which had been converted into an impromptu sewing room. With race car wallpaper. "Look at you two! Like a couple of princesses!"

Catie looked down at herself in her flower girl dress,

which was exactly like mine, only in miniature, with just slightly less décolleté, and said, "D'you really think so?" looking extremely pleased with herself.

"I definitely think so," Jason's grandmother said. Mrs. Lee, Kitty's seamstress, studied us both, then came up to me and said, grasping the darts beneath my armpits, "It needs to be taken in a little here."

"Yes," Kitty said, nodding. "Just a little."

Pete, who was tugging uncomfortably on his bow tie—dyed the same pink as our dresses—let out a snort. I looked down and saw that Mrs. Lee was talking about my boob area, where the dress was sagging a little. That's because when she'd first fitted me, I hadn't had my new, correctly fitting bra, so I'd been all over the place. Now I was correctly proportioned—but the dress wasn't.

"Shut up, Pete," I said. "Will you be able to do it in time?" I asked Mrs. Lee, worriedly.

"Oh, of course," Mrs. Lee said. "I can do this in a jiffy." To Catie, she said, "Yours is perfect. You can take it off now." She looked at Pete and Robbie and said in a less friendly voice, "You, too."

The boys whooped and began stripping off their cummerbunds and jackets, almost before they even left the hallway for the bathroom, which was the boys' dressing room for the day.

But Catie looked about as ready to take off that dress as she was to eat a dirt sandwich.

"What's YOUR dress going to be like, Mrs. Hollenbach?" she asked Jason's grandmother.

"Call me Kitty, dear," Kitty said with a laugh. She'd asked all of us to call her by her first name, especially now that she was going to be our grandmother. But the littler kids kept forgetting.

"It's not as pretty as yours," Kitty assured us. "But I hope Emile will like it."

"He will," Catie assured her. "He's warm for your form."

"Catie!" I cried, shocked.

But Kitty and Mrs. Lee were laughing.

"Well," Catie said, looking up at me with a defensive expression on her face. "That's what Jason said. I HEARD him."

"Speaking of Jason," Kitty said, "where IS that boy? We have to make sure his tuxedo fits, too."

"Here I am, Grandma." Jason appeared in the doorway, spooning cereal into his mouth from a salad bowl. Not a bowl you'd put a single serving of salad in. But the actual wooden salad bowl itself, into which he'd poured an entire box of Honey Nut Cheerios and about a gallon of milk, his usual after-school snack.

"Oh, Jason," Kitty said with a sigh when she saw this. "What's your mother going to say when your supper's spoiled?"

"I'll be hungry again by dinnertime," Jason said with a shrug.

Kitty, who shared Jason's bright blue eyes and slender frame, but not his height or overlong dark hair—hers was cut into a pageboy, as pure white as Grandpa's hair, which is why they made such a cute couple, despite what Mom might think—shook her head.

"Must be nice, right, Stephanie?" she said with a wink at me. "To be able to eat like a horse and never gain an ounce?"

I didn't say what I wanted to, which was, "Yeah, but at least we don't look like one," meaning a horse, meaning Jason.

But I didn't think his grandmother would appreciate this little witticism. Though it would have served Jason right for being so mean to me in school all day.

Mrs. Lee made Jason go into the bathroom to change into his tuxedo. When he came out, followed by Pete and Robbie, who were back in their civilian clothes, he was still eating from the salad bowl.

Even so, seeing him in a tuxedo gave me something like an electric shock. Because he looked so handsome in it. Like James Bond, or somebody. If James Bond had ever eaten cereal out of a salad bowl.

"Dude," Pete was saying, gazing up at Jason, whom he worshiped for being over six feet tall and owning his own car, "the new 5 Series has got five-liter capacity, ten cylinders, 383 lb.-ft. maximum torque—it's the BOMB."

"I know," Jason said, chewing.

"What about your parents, Stephanie?" Kitty asked, a little too casually, as Mrs. Lee fussed around with Jason's cummerbund. "Any chance they'll be joining us Saturday after all?"

"I don't think so," I said, not meeting her gaze. I really

liked Jason's grandmother, and my parents' behavior—mostly on my mom's part, since my dad was just doing what she told him to do—embarrassed me. Grandpa's wedding was way more important than any stupid superstore opening in town. I don't know why my mom couldn't see that.

"Oh well," Kitty said with a sigh. Her smile, like her eyes, was still bright. "You never know. There's still time. I'm holding places for them at the reception, just in case. Jason, darling, are you going to get your hair cut before the wedding, or are you going to let it hang in your eyes like that?"

"I thought I might wear it like this," Jason said, and finger-combed his bangs over his eyes, so that he looked like the Snyders' sheepdog. Pete and Robbie giggled delightedly at this.

"Oh, Jason," Kitty said with a sigh. But you could tell she loved her grandson's teasing.

Which was when I noticed that Robbie had found Jason's cat, Mr. Softy, and was trying to pick him up, and that Catie was trying to take the cat away from him.

"Catie, leave Mr. Softy alone while you're in your flower girl dress," I said, and Mrs. Lee and Kitty immediately sprang into action, Mrs. Lee grabbing Catie by both hands and hauling her away from the all-black cat, who was known for his copious shedding, due to being a Persian, and Kitty distracting Robbie—and Pete—by asking if they wanted to come downstairs for homemade ice cream sandwiches.

They did, leaving Jason and me alone in the hallway,

eyeing each other in the awkward silence that followed. After he flicked his hair back, that is, so he could see again.

It was especially weird since Jason and I don't HAVE awkward silences. Ordinarily, we have so much to say to each other, it's like a race to see who can get it all out before the other one interrupts.

Now, however . . . silence.

I didn't think it was due to his hotness in a tux, either. I couldn't help but think our not having anything to say to each other was due to The Book.

I don't know why Jason couldn't just be happy for me. I mean, that I had finally got people to think about me some other way than as the girl who spilled the Big Red Super Big Gulp on Lauren Moffat's D&G skirt. It wasn't like I was going to forget about him and Becca once I got popular. I fully planned to bring the two of them along to all the parties I was bound to start getting invited to.

So what was he so mad about?

Jason was the one who broke the silence.

"Did you see what she did?" he demanded sort of angrily.

"Who?" I asked, thinking he meant his grandmother and wondering what she could have done.

"Your friend Becca," he said. And thrust out his foot to show me the soles of his high tops, the ones Becca had drawn on during the convocation.

"On the tops, man!" Jason cried indignantly. "She drew on the tops!"

"So?" I couldn't believe this is what had him so hot

under the collar. "Is your tongue broken? You could have asked her to stop."

"I didn't want to hurt her feelings," Jason said. "You know how she is. All sensitive."

"You are not," I said, holding up a hand, "laying the blame for this one on me."

"Why not?" Jason demanded. "She's your friend!"

"She's your friend, too," I reminded him. "Or wasn't she the one you took to Pizza Hut for lunch today?"

"Oh, like that wasn't a living nightmare. I'm telling you, there's something weird going on with that girl," he said. "Something even weirder than—"

He broke off. I stared at him.

"Go on."

"No," he said. "Nothing. Look, I gotta . . ."

"What?" I demanded. Suddenly, I felt hot in my bridesmaid's dress, despite the air-conditioning. "Just say it. Something even weirder than what's going on with me. That's what you were going to say. Right?"

"Well." Jason was spinning his cummerbund around, trying to unfasten it without putting down the salad bowl. "You said it. Not me. But, now that you mention it, yeah. What happened to you? What was all that today? I thought you hated that stuff."

"Here," I said, not being able to stand his fumbling around a second longer. "Let me do that." I went up to him and undid the cummerbund. "I don't see what's wrong with just giving the school spirit thing a try. I mean, not all of us are happy about being a social reject."

"I thought you loved being a social reject," Jason said, looking genuinely surprised. He held up his fingers like they were shaking a sugar packet. "'Merry Christmas, Mr. Potter!' Remember? We have fun being social rejects."

"I know," I said as gently as I could. I was using empathy, because I didn't want to hurt his feelings. "I just . . . I'm tired of being a Steph, you know?"

"But that's your NAME," Jason reminded me.

"I know. But I'm sick of that girl. I want to be someone different. And not," I added quickly, "Crazytop, criminal mastermind, either. I want to be Steph Landry . . . but a different Steph Landry. A Steph Landry who's . . . well"—I couldn't look him in the eye—"popular."

"Popular?" Jason repeated, like it was French or something. "POPULAR?"

But before he had a chance to say anything else, Mrs. Lee came out of the guest room, looking pained.

"Stephanie," she said. "Do you think you could come in here and convince your sister to take off her dress? She seems to want to keep it on until the wedding."

"Sure," I said. And I handed Jason his cummerbund. "Talk to you later, Jase."

"Yeah," he said, taking it from me. His expression, I saw, was a mixture of confusion and . . . well, there's no other word for it: hurt. "Whatever."

Except that what did *he* have to feel hurt about? *He* wasn't the one Lauren Moffat and her heinous cronies hadn't let pee for two days during Girl Scout camp. *He* wasn't the one all the girls ganged up on at once during dodgeball and pummeled with those stupid red balls. No one in our town ever said, "Don't pull a Jason," or, "You're such a Jason." Did they?

No. They did not. It was all well and good for Jason to say it like that—"POPULAR?"—but he didn't know, did he? He didn't know what it was like. He was a freak by CHOICE. He didn't HAVE to be a freak, with that body and those parents and this house. He could have been as popular as Mark Finley, if he'd wanted to.

He just didn't want to.

Something I would never, ever, in a million years, understand.

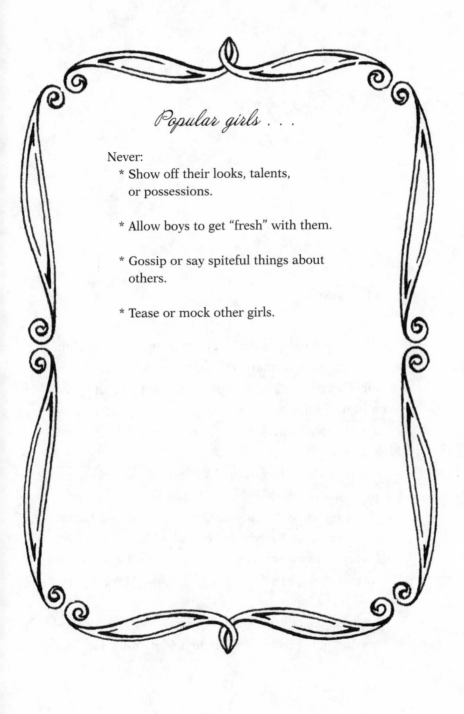

Popular girls . . .

Never:
* Show off their looks, talents, or possessions.

* Allow boys to get "fresh" with them.

* Gossip or say spiteful things about others.

* Tease or mock other girls.

 *Thirteen*

The talent auction was definitely on. And, so as to get the school year off to a financially advantageous start, it was on for Thursday night. I know because I got an e-mail from Mark Finley telling me so.

Yes. I, Stephanie Landry, got an e-mail from Mark Finley.

I have no idea how he got my e-mail address. But I guess if you're Mark Finley, Bloomville High quarterback, senior class president, and paramour of Lauren Moffat, you can get anybody's e-mail address you want.

I about died when I checked my e-mail account on the family computer, and there it was—Mark Finley's name—in my inbox.

It wasn't exactly a love letter, or anything. It was just a very factual, businesslike note to let me know he'd reserved the gymnasium—which seats more people than the auditorium—for the purpose of holding the talent auction, at seven P.M. Thursday night.

But it was still an e-mail from Mark Finley. My first e-mail from a popular person. Ever.

But apparently not destined to be my last, either. Because Mark's wasn't the only e-mail I got. Quite a few people wanted to volunteer their services for the talent auction. I had offers as varied as baby-sitting services to stump removal to an accordion concert in your home.

I had no idea the students of Bloomville High were so talented.

Then I noticed some e-mails that looked . . . well, not quite right. That's because their subject lines said Usuck and Ih8U. Plus, they all came from someone whose username was SteffMustDie.

Nice. They couldn't even spell my name right.

I knew what these were. I even had a pretty good idea who they were from.

But that didn't make it any easier. It didn't make me feel any less sick when I clicked on them. Because I *had* to click on them, of course, even if just to delete them.

WHY DON'T YOU GIVE UP AND STICK TO YOUR LOZER FRIENDS, FREAK, one not-so-friendly missive asked, not necessarily grammatically correctly.

STOP SUCKING UP, BROWN NOSE, she advised me, in the next.

And, yeah, okay. It hurt. They made my chest feel tight, those e-mails. Like I couldn't breathe. Who could hate me that much to want to make me feel that bad? Especially when I hadn't done anything to anybody—well, except spy on my next door neighbor and sprinkle sugar in Lauren Moffat's hair.

But she didn't know that was me. And she was the one who'd started it, with the Don't Pull a Steph stuff.

I've seen movies where girls got sent mean e-mails from their peers. In the movies, the girls always freaked out and started crying and printed out the messages and ran to tell their mothers, who then complained to the principal of their school, who then made it his mission in life to find out who was behind those messages.

In the movies, the principal always finds out and suspends the perpetrators, who, by the movie's end, apologize to the victim. And then they all become friends after they realize it was really just a big misunderstanding . . . usually after some pretty teacher the screenwriter based on herself intervenes and teaches them all to be More Empathetic.

Can I just say that in real life, this never happens? The people who send the mean e-mails always get away with it, and the victims just have to suck it up and go around wondering for the rest of their lives who could possibly hate them that much—always suspecting, but never knowing for sure. Always wondering if they had done or said something just a little differently, if the person would hate them less . . . but never knowing, since they have no idea what it was they did to make the person hate them in the first place.

Well, unless they're me. Then they have a pretty good idea what they did.

They just don't know why something that happened so long ago—and was a total accident, besides—has to haunt them for the rest of their lives.

I didn't start crying. And I didn't run for my mother, either. Instead, I just hit DELETE.

Because seriously. Who cares? I've had worse things said to my face. I wasn't exactly going to freak out because someone who didn't even have the guts to use her real screen name was upset with me.

Besides, The Book had fully warned that anytime you try to effect social change, there will be those who will feel threatened and/or insecure, and will attempt to stop you, either by intimidation or ostracism.

These people, The Book said, were to be ignored. There was simply no other way to deal with them, as their fear of change of the social order is completely irrational.

So what else could I do? Except delete. Delete. Delete.

Then I had an e-mail from Becca.

Scrpbooker90: Hey, it's me. So, that was weird today. I mean, cool. But weird. Can I ask you something, though? It has nothing to do with, you know. Your auction thingie.

My mom refuses to let us set up Instant Messaging accounts, as she considers them cerebral black holes that suck out your brain and leave you spending hours basically doing nothing (she feels the same way about MTV, which is why it's password protected).

So I had to e-mail Becca back and just hope she was online and would write back soon.

StephLandry (I know. That is the name of my e-mail account. My mom set it up): Sure, ask me whatever.

She was online. A minute later, I got the following:

Scrpbooker90: Oh, hi. Okay, I feel really stupid asking you this. But could you do me a huge favor and find out if Jason likes me?

I stared at the screen. I had to read her message like ten times, but still, I didn't understand it. Or, rather, I understood it . . . but I figured it couldn't mean what I thought it meant.

StephLandry: Of course he likes you. We're friends, right?

While I waited for Becca to write back, I listened to Robbie argue with my dad, who was making lasagna for dinner. Robbie hates lasagna—and all red food, actually—on principle and wanted chicken instead.

Scrpbooker90: Yeah, that's just it. I mean, find out if he likes me as more than just a friend. I THINK he does. Today, at Pizza Hut—well, you weren't there. But I was getting a vibe.

A VIBE? What was she TALKING about? What kind of vibe could JASON have been giving off? Except his usual, I'm-starving-and-I'm-going-to-eat-everything-in-sight vibe. Unless it was a why-is-Becca-acting-so-weird vibe that she was misconstruing as a Becca-is-hot vibe.

StephLandry: Um, Bex, you have to be mistaken. Jason likes Kirsten, remember?

In the kitchen, Robbie was losing the lasagna battle. He was going to have to fall back on his standard, "Fine, then I'll just have peanut butter and jelly" argument.

Scrpbooker90: He doesn't REALLY like Kirsten. Well, I mean, I know he does. But she's in COLLEGE. No way is she interested in HIM. Even now that he has a car. I seriously think he likes me. Like, LIKE likes me. Did you see how he let me draw all over his shoes today during the convocation?

Oh my God. What a mess.

Because of course there was NO WAY Jason LIKE liked Becca. Even if he hadn't just come out and complained about her to me barely two hours ago, there's the fact that . . . well, the entire time I'd known Jason—even as far back as nursery school—he had never liked anyone he had an actual chance of attaining. It had always been Xena Warrior Princess, or Lara Croft, or Stuckey's mom, or Fergie from the Black Eyed Peas. He had never liked a girl in any of our classes . . .

. . . as I knew only too well, given our fight in the fifth grade.

No, Jason wasn't likely to have fallen for Becca. But how to tell her that, without hurting her feelings?

I tried.

StephLandry: Becca, don't you remember what he said the other night, about how you don't want to "spit" where you eat and how dating in high school is stupid?

Becca wrote back almost right away.

Scrpbooker90: He said finding your soul mate in high school is stupid. He said he was all for dating—going to the movies and hanging out. That's all I want. For now. Until he, you know . . . realizes I'm The One.

The One? Oh, God, this was worse than I'd thought.

StephLandry: Becca, don't get me wrong, or anything, I love Jason and all—as a friend, of course—but as far as his being Your One . . . I really don't think so. I mean, Jason can't stand scrapbooking. He doesn't have an ounce of creativity in his body. Don't you think Your One would at least—I don't know—like art instead of golf?

But Becca had an answer for this one, too.

Scrpbooker90: He just hates art because he hasn't been exposed to it enough.

StephLandry: His grandmother took him to the Louvre last summer! And he said it would rock to install a nine-hole golf course in it!

Scrpbooker90: So what are you trying to say, Steph? That you don't think Jason likes me that way?

YES! I wanted to write. THAT'S EXACTLY WHAT I THINK.

But that would have been too mean. Even though it was true.

Instead, I wrote:

StephLandry: I just think you should keep yourself open to other guys, and not put all your eggs in one basket.

I knew Becca would appreciate this analogy, having grown up on a farm and all.

StephLandry: I will definitely ask Jason for you—you know, subtly. But I think you should prepare yourself emotionally for the cold hard fact that Jason's saving his heart for Kirsten. Or some girl he meets in college.

Becca, though, totally missed the warning part of my e-mail and honed right in on the part where I said I'd ask Jason if he liked her.

Scrpbooker90: THANKS, STEPH! You are such a good friend. Just for that, I have decided to take your advice and allow myself to be auctioned off. I suppose you're right, and there are a lot of people who'd like to learn to scrapbook. So I will auction off three hours of scrapbook mentoring. How about that?

I was guessing that no one was going to bid on Becca. Except maybe her mom. But I tried to be enthusiastic about it just the same, and thanked her.

It was as I was signing off that my mom came home from the store, aggravated, as usual, by how slow business had been.

"How much did we make on this day last year, Stephanie?" she asked me as she hung her purse and car keys on the hooks just inside the driveway door.

"Oh, Mom," I said with a groan, acting like I thought she was being a drag. But really, of course, I knew when I told her, she'd just get even more upset.

I was right. She made me look it up in my special Excel file for that purpose, and we were sixty dollars down from last year.

"But sixty dollars isn't that much," I tried to point out to her. "That might have nothing to do with Super Sav-Mart. It could just be, you know, we didn't sell a doll today, or whatever."

"God," my mother said, ignoring me. "I need a drink."

"Maybe you should think about installing that café like we talked about," I hinted. "Now that the Hoosier Sweet Shoppe closed down—"

"Closed down!" Mom interrupted, pulling down her not-so-secret stash of Tootsie Rolls from a top bookshelf (she doesn't care if I know about them, since I'd never gorge myself on them, being too fearful of going up another size, unlike my brothers and sisters) and helping herself to a handful. "They were driven out of business by Super Sav-Mart!"

Um, not exactly. The Hoosier Sweet Shoppe shut down last year after an ancient water pipe burst in the ceiling, destroying all of their stock. But you don't argue with a woman as hormonal as my mom.

"It wouldn't be hard to break through the wall to the Hoosier Sweet Shoppe," I said, "since it's right next door—"

"And where am I supposed to get the money for that, Stephanie?" Mom wanted to know. Then, before I could say anything, she said, "And DO NOT say from Grandpa. I will not kowtow to that man, trying to get his money. Unlike the rest of the people in this town, I have some dignity."

Talk about touchy.

I wanted to tell her not to worry—that everything was going to be fine. Because I had a plan that was going to bring tons of business to the store.

But I didn't want to jinx it. So I kept my mouth shut and went over to make Robbie a peanut butter and jelly sandwich, so he'd shut up already about not wanting to eat Dad's lasagna.

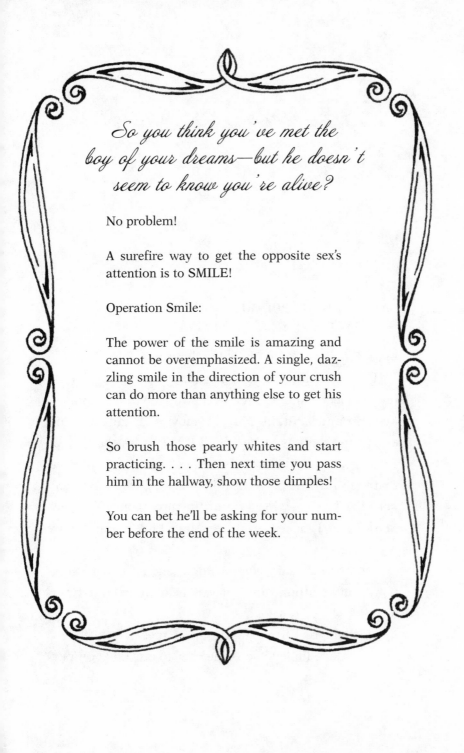

*So you think you've met the
boy of your dreams—but he doesn't
seem to know you're alive?*

No problem!

A surefire way to get the opposite sex's attention is to SMILE!

Operation Smile:

The power of the smile is amazing and cannot be overemphasized. A single, dazzling smile in the direction of your crush can do more than anything else to get his attention.

So brush those pearly whites and start practicing. . . . Then next time you pass him in the hallway, show those dimples!

You can bet he'll be asking for your number before the end of the week.

 *Fourteen*

Mark Finley spoke to me at lunch again today.

I was sitting there, trying to draw Darlene out on the few subjects she seems to know anything about—makeup and Brittany Murphy movies (I had just said everything there is to say about *8 Mile*, with the help of Darlene's assorted suitors, several of whom volunteered that their favorite part was in the factory, where Brittany licks her hand)—when one of the guys went, "Oh, hey, Mark," and I looked up to see Mark Finley standing by my chair.

"Hey," Mark said, and swung a chair from a neighboring table around until it was near mine, and straddled it.

"Listen, great flyer," Mark said to me.

Yes. Mark Finley had come over to our table on purpose to speak to me. ME. I can't get Jason and Becca to sit with me at lunch—Jason, still excited about the fact that, now that he has a car, he can leave campus for lunch every day, insists on doing so, and Becca, because of her conviction that Jason is The One, has to follow him . . . even though today Jason invited his friend Stuckey to come along with them, and Becca can't stand Stuckey, due to his custom of endlessly relating pivotal moments in Indiana college basketball games.

Clearly, they don't want to eat with me. Which is just as well, since the ride to school with them this morning was excruciating. As if it weren't bad enough that Jason felt compelled to comment on every article of clothing I had on—"What's wrong with that skirt? Why's it so tight? How are you supposed to run if Gordon Wu blows up the chem lab again and there's a fire and we all have to evacuate?"—there was the fact that Becca can apparently no longer speak in his (Jason's) company, on account of being too shy, since he's Her One, so I had to do all the talking.

I may just start taking the bus.

But Mark Finley doesn't seem to mind eating with me. At all.

"Oh," I said, immediately flustered. Because, you know, even though he had e-mailed me last night, and all, speaking to Mark Finley in person . . . well, that's totally different. Because of his eyes, which looked greener than usual for some reason.

"Yeah, it was nothing," I said.

It HADN'T been nothing. That flyer—advertising Thursday night's auction—had taken half the night to come up with. I'd had to blow off my homework, but it was worth it, since in the end, I'd come up with something semiprofessional-looking . . . which was good, since I had to buy ad space in the local paper to showcase the event, and needed something especially eye-catching.

I could, I suppose, have sought my mom's help on this, since ads and window displays are her best thing—her ONLY thing, really, that she's good at, insofar as running the store goes. She's great at figuring out what will sell like hotcakes in our town—biographies and Madame Alexander dolls—and what won't—tell-alls and Sanrio—as well as physically making sales.

But she sucks at the bookkeeping and bill paying . . . which makes it good that she has me around, now that she's given Grandpa the boot.

Still, I wasn't super enthused on letting my mom know what I was up to just yet . . . not that she isn't already suspicious, especially when this morning I came downstairs in one of my pencil skirts and she was like, "And you're going . . . where? To school? Dressed like *that*?"

I could see that I'd lived in jeans and sweatshirts for far too long.

"The ad should run tomorrow," I said to Mark. "I faxed it over first thing this morning. Hopefully we'll get a lot of bidders."

"Oh, we will," Mark said with that lopsided smile that made my heart skip a beat. I glanced over his shoulder and saw that Lauren was pretending to be deeply engaged in an animated discussion about her favorite soap opera, *Passions*, with Alyssa Krueger.

But her gaze kept darting nervously toward me. And Mark.

"It's gonna be awesome," Mark said. "People are *stoked*. The whole town's talking about it."

"Great," I said. And gave him my most dazzling smile.

Sadly, he didn't appear to notice—perhaps because at that same moment, Todd said, "Hey, Mark. You coming to the rager at the quarry on Friday, or what?"

"Of course I'm coming," Mark said with his trademark lopsided grin. "Never missed one of Todd Rubin's back-to-school ragers yet, have I?"

"Friday?" Darlene looked up from a detailed inspection of her cuticles. "It's supposed to rain on Friday."

We all looked at Darlene, because it was so unlike her to be at all familiar with current events.

The weather, however, appeared to be different than actual news, since Darlene explained, noticing our questioning stares, "I always check the five-day forecast before I plan my weekend tanning schedule at the lake."

Which of course explained everything.

"Can't have a rager in the rain, man," Jeremy Stuhl said with a frown.

Todd looked concerned. "I'll figure something out," he said, not very confidently.

Which was when Lauren suddenly appeared at Mark's side.

"Oh, Mark," she said. "Do you have your car keys with you? I think I left my Carrie Underwood CD in your car, and Alyssa wants to borrow it." Then, pretending to notice me for the first time, she said, "Oh, hi, Steph."

"Hi, Lauren," I said. And waited for the taunts to begin. What would it be this time? "Cute necklace. Not *real* gold, right? God, you're such a Steph." Or, "I see you're eating the chef's salad. What's the matter, afraid your butt's going to take over the cafeteria? Way to pull a Steph."

She didn't say any of those things. Instead, she said, wrapping both her hands around Mark's bicep, "My dad's real excited about the auction. Guess who he says he's going to buy?"

Mark looked delightfully bewildered. "Who?"

"*You*, silly," Lauren said, throwing her head back and laughing infectiously. Or at least, I suppose she thought it was infectious.

Mark frowned. "But I'd work for your dad for free, babe."

"Don't tell *him* that," Lauren said. "God, he'll have you out at the lot every single day. Do you have any idea how much business you'll bring in, hon? I mean, the QB? Especially if you guys get to State this year."

The chances of the Fighting Fish getting to State were extremely slim, and we all knew it—even, I suspect, Mark. But we all nodded and said, "Yeah, totally" like we actually believed it could happen.

"Gee, babe," Mark said. "That'd be cool if your dad bought me."

Lauren beamed.

I couldn't help feeling a little sorry for her. Because there was no way on God's green earth Lauren Moffat's dad was going to win Mark Finley on Thursday night. Not if I, and Emile Kazoulis's wallet, had anything to say about it.

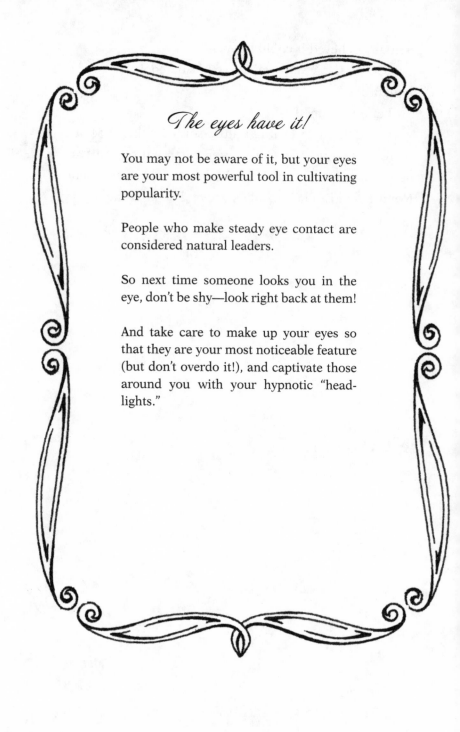

The eyes have it!

You may not be aware of it, but your eyes are your most powerful tool in cultivating popularity.

People who make steady eye contact are considered natural leaders.

So next time someone looks you in the eye, don't be shy—look right back at them!

And take care to make up your eyes so that they are your most noticeable feature (but don't overdo it!), and captivate those around you with your hypnotic "headlights."

 *Fifteen*

I think I died and went to heaven.

It didn't seem that way at first, of course. When I got to the student parking lot after school and looked around for Jason, I saw that his car wasn't there. Then I noticed Becca standing over by the bike racks, looking even more unhappy than she had when she found out Craig on *Degrassi* was bipolar.

"Where's Hawkface?" I asked her.

And the floodgates let loose.

"He said he had some important errands to run for his grandmother, for the wedding," she burst out, tears trembling on the ends of her eyelashes. "And that he was really sorry, but that he didn't have time to run us home first and that we were just going to have to take the bus! The BUS! How could he do this to us, Steph? I mean, the BUS!"

I thought she was being a little overdramatic, but I knew what she meant. Once you've ridden to and from school in a BMW, going back to riding the bus has got to be hard.

Even if you're getting a little tired of the Bee Gees.

"Don't worry about it," I said, patting her comfortingly on the back. "Things *are* a little nuts right now with the wedding, and all, and—"

"I think he was lying," Becca interrupted, wiping her tears with the back of one wrist. "I mean, he took Stuckey with him. STUCKEY! Do you know what Stuckey talked about all during lunch today? Indiana's 1987 NCAA Final Four victory. He wasn't even ALIVE in 1987. But he knew every stupid detail. And wouldn't stop talking about it. And Jason took HIM along to run errands, instead of us. I think he just doesn't want to hang out with us, because I'm so quiet around him, on account of my great love for him, and you're so—" She broke off and bit her lip.

"I'm so what?" I asked. Even though I already knew what she was going to say.

"You're just acting so weird!" Becca cried. Almost as if it were a relief finally to say it. "I mean, eating with Darlene Staggs? She's such a slut!"

"Hey, now," I said gently. "Darlene's not a slut. Just because she's got big boobs—"

"They're store-boughts!" Becca reminded me.

"They could be," I said. "But that's no reason to judge people. Darlene's really nice. You'd know that, if you'd come sit with me."

"Those people don't want to talk to me," Becca said, looking down at her shoes. "I mean, to them I'm still the dumb farm girl who used to sleep all through class."

"Well, maybe it's up to you to show them you're not that girl anymore," I suggested. "Now, come on, let's go around so we can get the bus before it—"

And then I let out an expletive that I was going to have to tell Father Chuck about at confession next week.

"What?" Becca asked. "What is it?"

I was looking at my watch. "We missed the bus," I said tightly.

Becca repeated my expletive. "Now what are we going to do?" she wailed.

"No problem," I said, rallying. It was hot out in the parking lot. I was beginning to sweat. Soon, I knew, my blow-out was going to start to frizz. "I'll just call my dad. He'll come get us."

"Oh, God," Becca moaned. Which I understood and wasn't insulted by. There's nothing worse than having to be picked up at school by your dad in his minivan.

It was right then that the miracle occurred.

"Oh, hey, Steph," a familiar—but still oddly thrilling voice—called from the doors to the school.

I knew who it was even before I spun around, because of the goose pimples of delight that had risen on my arms.

"Hi, Mark," I said as casually as I could, as I turned. . . .

And then I saw, with a pang of disappointment, that Lauren and Alyssa were with him.

Oh well. What did I expect? He's the most popular guy in school. Did I really think he goes *anywhere* alone?

It was right then, though, that things really started looking up. . . .

"What's the matter?" Mark asked, noticing Becca's tears (they were hard to miss, despite her attempt to mop them up). "Miss your ride?"

"Something like that," I said with a smile that only Mark returned. Lauren and Alyssa just stared at me stonily.

But that was okay. Thanks to The Book, I knew the most appropriate course of action to take under the circumstances was to smile sunnily back at them.

"Geez, that sucks," Mark said. I couldn't see his hazel eyes, because they were hidden beneath the lenses of his Ray-Bans. "I'd offer you a ride, but I gotta stay here for after-school practice. I was just walking Lauren to her car."

"Oh, don't worry about us," I said breezily. At least I hoped I sounded breezy. "We'll get a ride somehow."

"Oh, hey, I know," Mark said.

And I knew—I just knew, maybe because Mark is My One—what he was going to say.

"Why don't you give them a ride home, babe?" Mark asked Lauren.

Mark must be HER One, too, though, since she seemed to have known what he was going to say next and had an answer already prepared. Or at least it seemed that way, given how fast she came out with, "Oh, gee, hon, wish I could. But they live in town, and you know that's so far out of my way."

This was actually true. Lauren and her family lived in one of the newer McMansions out by the Y, three miles away from the turn-of-the-century (nineteenth, not twentieth) homes, just blocks from the courthouse, that Becca and I live in.

"Yeah, but weren't you gonna stop by Benetton downtown to pick up something to wear for the rager on Friday?" Mark asked. "I thought I heard you guys saying something like that."

Lauren was caught, and she knew it. Mark had made it clear how grateful he was to me for my brilliant talent auction idea. She didn't dare dis me right in front of him. There was nothing she could do but smile tightly and say, "Oh yeah. I forgot. You guys want a ride?"

Beside me, I heard Becca gulp. But I said, still sounding breezy (or so I hoped), "Oh, sure, Lauren. That would be great."

"Great," Mark said.

And then, super boyfriend that he is, he walked all four of us to Lauren's red convertible, which sat gleaming in the sun.

"Later, hon," Mark said, leaning down to kiss Lauren good-bye, after having held the front seat back for Becca and me to climb past (Becca was so stunned by this development, she didn't remember to voice her usual argument about how she had to sit in front due to a tendency toward carsickness), then helped Lauren behind the wheel, as tenderly as if she were made of china.

"Have a good practice," Lauren said, and twinkled her French manicure at him.

Then she pulled out of the lot.

And just like that, Becca and I? We were riding in the backseat of Lauren Moffat's BMW.

A part of me expected that as soon as we got to the corner, where Mark could no longer see us, Lauren was going to pull to the side of the road, with a squeal of brakes, and order us to GET OUT, in a voice like that poltergeist from *Amityville Horror*.

But she didn't. Instead, she started making small talk. LAUREN MOFFAT WAS MAKING SMALL TALK WITH ME.

"So," she said. "Don't you guys usually ride with that guy? That Jason guy? What happened to him?"

I loved how Lauren was referring to Jason as "that Jason guy." As if she hadn't sat next to him all through second grade, and acted as Snow White to his Prince Charming in the class play (I'd been cast as the Wicked Witch. And yes, tears were shed over getting this part and not Snow White, until Grandpa told me that without the Wicked Witch, there'd be no story, so it was really the most important part of all).

"He had to go run some errands," I said.

"For his grandma," Becca chimed in. "His grandma is marrying Steph's grandpa this weekend."

Whoa. Talk about TMI. I shot Becca a *Cool It* look. But she was too far gone. She was babbling like Bloomville Creek.

"Steph's the maid of honor," she went on. "And Jason is best man."

"Isn't that, like, incest?" Lauren asked, shooting Alyssa an amused glance. Alyssa, who was slurping on what had to have been her sixth Diet Coke of the day, stifled a laugh into the can.

"Why would it be incest?" Becca asked.

"Well, like, aren't Steph and that Jason guy going out?" Lauren wanted to know.

"WHAT?" Becca looked as if she'd been slapped. "No, they aren't *going out*."

"Really?" Lauren glanced at me in her rearview mirror. "I always thought you two were going out. I mean, you've been practically joined at the hip since, what? Kindergarten?"

I gazed steadily back at her reflection. "Jason and I are friends," I said.

"*Just* friends," Becca emphasized, leaning forward to grab the back of Alyssa's headrest. "They're *just* friends. Jason's single."

Seriously. I know she thinks he's The One and all. But could she calm down about it?

"Oh," Lauren said, cracking another smile in Alyssa's direction. "That's a relief."

"Really," Alyssa said, polishing off the remains of her soda. "I mean, that a catch like him is still available."

Then the two of them broke down in semi-hysterical giggles.

I glowered at the backs of their heads. Jason may be

a bit of a weirdo. But he's MY weirdo. How dare they make fun of him?

I wasn't too pleased with Becca, either. Why couldn't she learn to cool it once in a while?

Lauren pretended like she didn't remember where I lived, even after I pointed out that she'd been there. She acted like she had no recollection of the burnt oatmeal OR Navy Seal Barbie incidents.

There is nothing in The Book about needing selective amnesia in order to become popular, but obviously it is a crucial part of the process. You pretty much have to forget all the crappy things people did to you in the past in order to move on to a more successful future. Maybe when this is all over, and I am popular, I'll write my own book.

Oh, wait. I already AM popular: Lauren Moffat just gave me a ride home from school.

And she wasn't even that mean to me.

Jason freaking out and refusing to give me rides anymore might just be the best thing that ever happened.

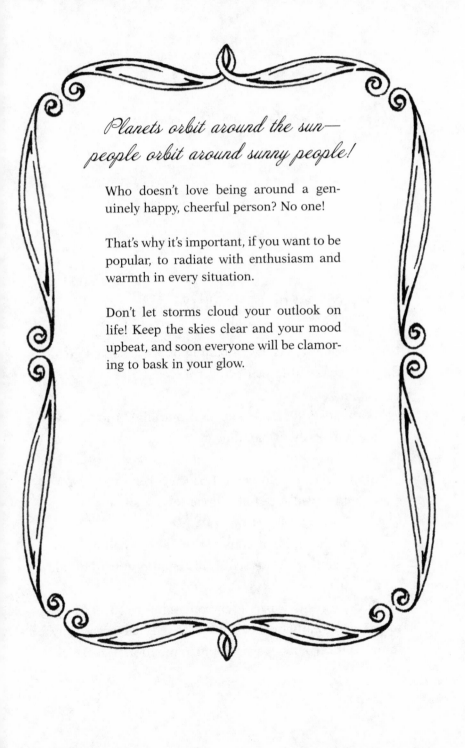

Planets orbit around the sun— people orbit around sunny people!

Who doesn't love being around a genuinely happy, cheerful person? No one!

That's why it's important, if you want to be popular, to radiate with enthusiasm and warmth in every situation.

Don't let storms cloud your outlook on life! Keep the skies clear and your mood upbeat, and soon everyone will be clamoring to bask in your glow.

 *Sixteen*

Not everyone thinks Jason bailing on us is such a good
thing. Becca is fit to be tied over it.

> Scrpbooker90: Have you spoken to him? Did he say
> anything? About me, I mean?

> StephLandry: How could I have spoken to him? You
> know I haven't seen him since school, same as you.

Except that this, of course, was a lie. I had actually
seen him getting undressed in his bedroom just half an
hour earlier.

But since this wasn't even something I was going to
mention to Father Chuck, to whom I tell everything
(almost), I certainly wasn't going to mention it to Becca.

Scrpbooker90: Well, what do you think is going to happen tomorrow? I mean, are we going to have to take the bus?

StephLandry: I think we're going to have to prepare ourselves for the possibility.

Scrpbooker90: I won't do it. I WON'T. I'm asking my dad to drive us. God, why is Jason DOING this to us? Do you think it might be because he's realized he has feelings for me, and so can't stand to be around me, since he thinks he can never have me, not knowing I feel the same way about him?

I could tell Becca had been reading some of Kitty's romance novels, which I'd lent her. I hoped she hadn't gotten to the Turkish-style part yet. Because I knew she'd ask her parents what it meant, and somehow, I'd be the one to get in trouble.

StephLandry: Um. Maybe.

Scrpbooker90: Well, will you please ASK him? Or— do you think he'd even TELL you? Maybe I should ask Stuckey to ask him. Do you think I should ask Stuckey?

StephLandry: Totally. You should totally ask Stuckey.

Anything to get her off MY back about it.

Scrpbooker90: I'm going to do it. I'm going to ask Stuckey. He's in my chem class. I'll ask him tomorrow. Oh, thanks, Steph! You're the best!

But Becca was actually one of the few people who was of that opinion—that I was the best, I mean. Because I was still getting e-mails from SteffMustDie.

Nice. Real nice.

I swear, if I didn't have Jason's window to look through every night, I think I'd have gone completely insane by now.

And I know it's wrong to spy on him like that. I KNOW.

But the sight of him—especially in his boxer shorts— just fills me with a deep inner calm unlike nothing I have ever known.

Actually, it's sort of like the deep inner calm I felt that night I had to wear his Batman underwear because I'd wet mine.

I wonder what that means, if anything?

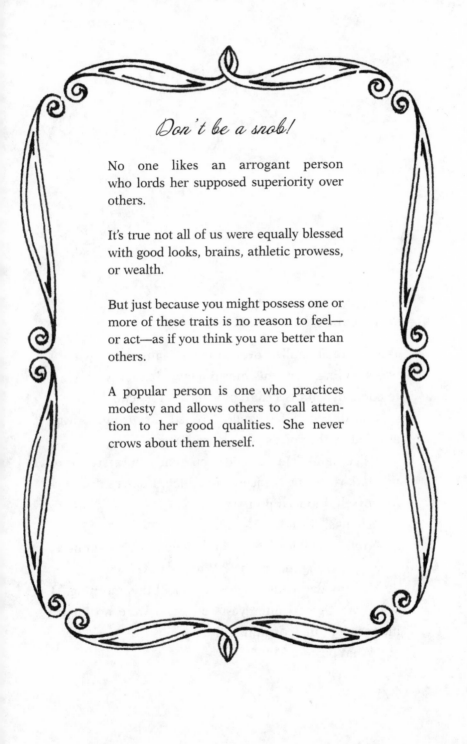

Don't be a snob!

No one likes an arrogant person who lords her supposed superiority over others.

It's true not all of us were equally blessed with good looks, brains, athletic prowess, or wealth.

But just because you might possess one or more of these traits is no reason to feel—or act—as if you think you are better than others.

A popular person is one who practices modesty and allows others to call attention to her good qualities. She never crows about them herself.

Seventeen

DAY THREE OF POPULARITY
WEDNESDAY, AUGUST 30, 9 A.M.

Jason actually pulled over in front of my house while I was standing there this morning, waiting for Mr. Taylor to come by with Becca to pick me up for school.

The driver's side window rolled down, and I was assailed by the vocals of Roberta Flack.

"Nice pants," Jason said, apparently in reference to my dark-rinse stretch jeans, in which, I don't mind saying myself, I looked pretty good.

"Thanks," I said.

"Well," he said sort of impatiently, after a minute, "are you getting in, or what? Where's Bex?"

"Becca's dad is driving us to school this morning," I said. "We figured after yesterday, you were no longer interested in the position."

"What position?"

"Of our chauffeur."

Jason brushed some hair from his face. Kitty is right. He DOES need to get his hair cut before the wedding.

"I told Becca," he said with what seemed like forced composure, "that I had some errands to run. That doesn't mean I never want to give you guys rides, ever. I just couldn't do it yesterday afternoon."

"Uh-huh," I said, unconvinced, and sounding it.

"I had to pick up the place cards from the calligrapher for Grandma," Jason went on. "For the tables at the reception."

"Sure you did," I said.

"And then I had to drop some stuff off at the printer. And I mean, it's not like you guys couldn't take the bus. It drops you off in front of your house, practically."

"Of course it does," I said. "I mean, if you'd told us enough in advance, then we could have gotten in front of the school to pick it up."

Jason stared at me. "You missed the bus?"

"Yes," I said. "But that's okay. We got a ride in Lauren Moffat's car."

Jason paled. "Not the 645Ci."

"That'd be the one."

Jason smacked the side of his fist against his steering wheel.

"What is going on?" he practically screamed. Which wasn't very cool, because we don't live on a very screamy street. I mean, there are a lot of rich elderly people on our street—even if my family isn't exactly what you'd call well off, let alone elderly. I could see a lace curtain move in Mrs. Hoadley's front room as she tried to figure out what was going on outside my house (it hasn't been easy for her, living across the street from a family of seven . . . soon-to-be eight. In fact, at Halloween, my mom makes us throw out anything she gives us, thinking it's probably poisoned. But since, for a rich person, Mrs. Hoadley is a total cheapskate and only gives out saltines, we've never minded).

But Jason seemed to neither notice nor care that his outburst was attracting the interest of our geriatric neighbors.

"What *happened* to you?" he yelled. "Why are you acting so *weird*?"

"I could ask you the very same question," I said calmly.

"I'm not the one acting weird," Jason yelled. "*You* are! And Becca—she won't quit following me around! It's like having a freakin' puppy on my heels all the damned time! And you—since when do you get rides home from LAUREN MOFFAT?"

At that moment I saw the Taylors' Cadillac pull up behind The B. Fortunately the windows were all rolled up, so it was doubtful Becca had overheard what Jason had shouted about her. Through the windshield, I saw Mr. Taylor, looking sleepy and confused, stare at Jason's car, stopped in the middle of the street, then tap gently on the horn.

"That's my ride," I said to Jason. "I gotta go."

And I left him to slip into the air-conditioned back-seat of the Taylors' car. No one inside of it was complaining about anyone killing them softly with his song, which was a relief. Mr. Taylor only listens to talk radio.

"What's Jason doing here?" Becca asked all excitedly. "Did he come to pick us up? Should we ride with him? Oh, gee, sorry, Dad, but—"

"Wait," I said as Becca reached for the door handle. "Don't. Just—"

"But if he wants to drive us, we might as well—"

Fortunately at that moment Jason put the pedal to the metal (in the vernacular of his favorite musical time period) and took off.

"Aw," Becca said, her hand still on the door handle. "He left!"

"Believe me," I said. "It's better this way."

"I do not understand what is going on with you girls," Mr. Taylor said in his slow, sleepy voice. "But can I take ya'll to school so I can get home and get back to bed?"

"Yes, sir," I said. "Sorry about that. Jason's just in a bad mood."

"Did he say anything about me?" Becca asked hopefully.

"Um," I said. "Not really."

Becca slumped in her seat, disappointed. "Dang."

But I knew the truth would have disappointed her even more.

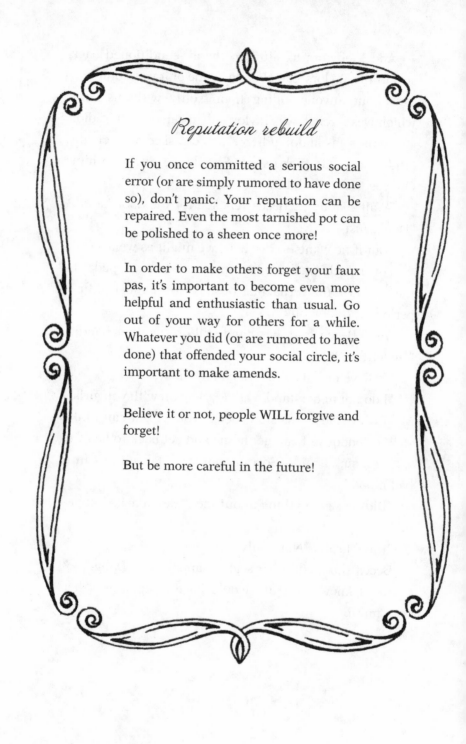

Reputation rebuild

If you once committed a serious social error (or are simply rumored to have done so), don't panic. Your reputation can be repaired. Even the most tarnished pot can be polished to a sheen once more!

In order to make others forget your faux pas, it's important to become even more helpful and enthusiastic than usual. Go out of your way for others for a while. Whatever you did (or are rumored to have done) that offended your social circle, it's important to make amends.

Believe it or not, people WILL forgive and forget!

But be more careful in the future!

 *Eighteen*

I was late getting to lunch because I'd been running around, enlisting the aid of teachers for tomorrow night's auction—Mr. Schneck, the drama director, has agreed to act as auctioneer, which should lend just the right note of campy fun to the proceedings . . . in my opinion, anyway, though probably not his—so I was kind of surprised when I got to my seat at Darlene's table and saw Becca sitting there, looking distinctly miserable.

She brightened up a little when she saw me, though.

"Oh, hi," she said. "Can I sit here? I mean, is it all right? I asked these guys"—she nodded toward Darlene, who was eating a banana, to the rapture of her entourage—"and they said it was, but—"

"Of course it's okay," I said, sitting down with my tray

of tuna salad. "But what happened to having lunch out with Jason?"

"Oh," Becca said, poking her burger (bunless . . . Becca has been on the South Beach Diet forever) with her fork and not looking me in the eye. "I talked to Stuckey."

I felt murderous rage sweep over me. If Stuckey had said anything to hurt her feelings—which I could totally see him doing, since he's so clueless about anything not having to do with basketball—he was a dead man.

"What did he say?" I asked, trying to sound calm.

"Just that if I wanted Jason to like me, I should make myself less available." Becca slurped sadly on her Diet Coke. "Stuckey says Jason's the kind of guy who likes a girl who plays hard to get."

Todd Rubin snorted, even though neither of us had been speaking to him. "Not me, man," he said. "I like a woman who knows her place." He indicated where that place was with a tilt of his pelvis, to the amusement of his buddies.

"Oh, really?" Darlene had finished her banana, and now she stretched, bringing every gaze at the table to her chest. "And what place would that be, Todd?"

"Um," Todd said, his mouth slightly ajar. "Any . . . place . . . you want. At all."

Darlene picked up her Diet Coke can and shook it, indicating it was empty. "Oh no. All gone! Can you be a sweetie and go get me another?"

Todd practically tripped over his own feet in his haste to get her another soda. Darlene glanced at Becca and me with a knowing smile. It was hard not to crack up.

And suddenly I realized Darlene isn't half as dumb as she pretends to be.

"I think Stuckey's probably right," I said, turning back to Becca.

"I know," Becca said with a sigh. "He really was very helpful. Stuckey, I mean. He said he doesn't think it's serious between Jason and Kirsten."

It was my own turn to snort. "Of course it's not serious," I said. "Because there's nothing actually going on between them. Except maybe in Jason's head. And even if there was, Kirsten's not right for him. Have you ever checked out her elbows?"

"Her elbows?" Becca echoed.

"Yeah. They're all gross and scaly."

"I hate that," Darlene said. "That's why I rub pure cocoa butter on mine every night." She pulled back her sleeve to show us. Darlene really did have the nicest elbows I'd ever seen, a sentiment with which every guy at the table, including Todd, who'd returned with Darlene's soda, agreed.

I'm going to have to remember that pure cocoa butter trick.

"Well, Stuckey said he doesn't think Jason even likes Kirsten—you know, in that way," Becca went on. "He says he thinks Jason just pretends to like Kirsten, so people won't figure out who he *really* likes."

This was intriguing. I had no idea Stuckey was such a keen observer of his fellow man.

"Well?" I said. "Who does Stuckey say Jason really likes?"

Becca shrugged. "That's just it. Stuckey doesn't know. He says Jason never talks about that kind of thing—girls—with him. But I couldn't help thinking . . . well, do you think the girl Jason really likes could be, possibly, well . . . me?"

"I don't know," I replied truthfully. Because I really didn't. I was careful not to add, "But I highly doubt it." Instead, I asked, "What else did Stuckey say?" Because the idea of Stuckey having a conversation with anyone that didn't involve Indiana college basketball was stunning to me.

"Oh, let's see." Becca thought for a minute, then brightened. "He said if I ever wanted to take a tour of the Indiana University campus to let him know, and he'd drive me over there and show me Assembly Hall, which is where the Hoosiers play basketball."

That sounded more like the Stuckey I knew.

Mark and Lauren chose *that* moment to make what seemed to be developing into a daily visitation to our table.

"Everything coming into place for tomorrow night, Steph?" Mark asked as Lauren twined an arm around his waist and sort of draped herself across him like a poncho. As usual, Alyssa Krueger lurked behind them . . . sort of Tinkerbell to Lauren's Paris.

"Looking good," I said, flipping open my official Bloomville High Talent Auction binder. "The ad should run in tonight's paper. We've got more than a hundred kids signed up. Depending on how many people show up, we stand to take in way more than any school-sponsored car wash has ever made."

"Hey," Mark said, his hazel eyes twinkling. "That's great! Good job."

"Thanks," I said. I was unable, of course, to repress a blush. Some things you just have no control over.

Like what happened next. Which was that as Mark, Lauren, and Alyssa passed by, a tightly folded note fell, seemingly from the air, and landed on my open binder.

No one but me noticed. Well, no one but me and Becca, who eyed me curiously as I picked the note up. It had the words TO STEFF written on it in block letters, indicating it was for me . . . or at least for someone named Steph, but who spelled it with two Fs instead of a P-H. I started to unfold it.

I only had to see the first few words—U STUPID HO, Y DON'T U GET A LIFE—before I figured out what it was.

And who it came from.

The blush that had crept over my cheeks at Mark's compliment turned into full-on flames. My face felt as if it were on fire.

But that didn't stop me from pushing my chair back and following after Mark and Lauren, the note in my hands.

"Um, guys," I said, catching the couple just as they—with Alyssa—were about to exit the caf, into the courtyard by the flagpole outside. "One of you dropped this. It says it's for someone named Steff, but that's not how you spell my name, so you must have meant it to go to some-one else."

And I handed the note to Mark.

Alyssa immediately started going, "What's that? I didn't drop that. I've never seen it before. Have you, Lauren?"

But Lauren just stood there, staring daggers at me.

And I stared them right back at her. *Don't even start with me, Lauren,* I tried to make my stare say. *Because I've got The Book now. And that means that you, Lauren Moffat, are GOING DOWN.*

Mark's face, as he read the note—who knew what it said after the first line? I had no idea, and I didn't actu-ally care, either—changed. I saw his jaw set, and his cheeks slowly turn the same color as mine. Only on him, it looked good.

He looked directly at Lauren. And she immediately turned to face Alyssa.

"God, Al," she said. "Could you *be* more immature?"

Alyssa's jaw fell. I could actually see a piece of chewed up Extra gum in her mouth.

"Lauren," she cried. "It was your—how could you—"

"How could *you*?" Lauren snatched the note from Mark's fingers and started tearing it up. "Why would you write something like this to poor Steph? She's only try-ing to help raise money for Mark's class. What's *wrong* with you?"

Mark, staring at Alyssa with narrowed eyes, slowly shook his head.

"That's low, Alyssa," he said in his deep voice. *"Real low."*

"But I didn't do it!" Alyssa insisted. "Well, I mean, I did, but it was—"

"I don't want to hear any more," Mark interrupted, in a tone that made it clear why he was voted last year's most valuable player and was chosen this year's quarterback. He would not tolerate any disrespect on his team. "I'd like for you to leave now."

Alyssa had started to cry.

"Leave . . . sch-school?" she hiccuped.

"No." Mark looked heavenward for patience. "Not school. My sight. Get out of here."

Alyssa, with a final, stricken glance in Lauren's direction, flung a hand over her face and hurried away, in the direction of the girls' room. Mark watched her go dispassionately, then looked down at Lauren.

"Why would she do something like that?" he asked her, seeming genuinely bewildered.

"I don't know," Lauren said, shrugging innocently. "Maybe she's jealous? You know, because I gave Steph that ride home last night? Maybe she's worried Steph and I are becoming friends and she's going to be left out, or something. You know how insecure she is."

My own jaw dropped at that one. I had never heard a bigger whopper in my life.

You had to hand it to Lauren: Whatever else you could say about her, she was a master manipulator.

"I better go make sure she's all right," Lauren said. "I

don't want her to do herself an injury, or anything."

Do herself an injury? Classic.

"Yeah, yeah," Mark said, nodding. "Go on." Then, when Lauren did—with a final *I'll Get You for This* glance in my direction—he put out a hand and very gently touched me.

On my bare arm. Mark Finley. Touched me.

"Hey," he asked softly. "You okay?"

I couldn't believe Mark Finley had touched me. And asked if I was okay.

"I'm fine," I said, nodding. Somehow, I managed to figure out how to make my mouth work again. "Don't worry about me."

"I can't believe she did that," Mark said. "I'm really sorry. I hope you won't take it personally, or anything."

Take it personally? I'd been hearing Alyssa Krueger— along with most of the rest of the under-eighteen popula- tion of Greene County—tell people not to be such a Steph Landry for the past five years. And here was the most popular guy in school—a guy who'd never been mocked or made fun of a day in his life—telling me not to take it personally. Yeah, no problem, Mark. Whatever you say.

"I won't," I said, giving him a tremulous smile . . . tremulous because I was really afraid, at that moment, that I might start to cry.

"Great," Mark said.

And laid a finger on my cheek. Just one finger.

But that was all it took. All it took for me to know with one hundred percent certainty that he was My One.

Even if he didn't know it yet.

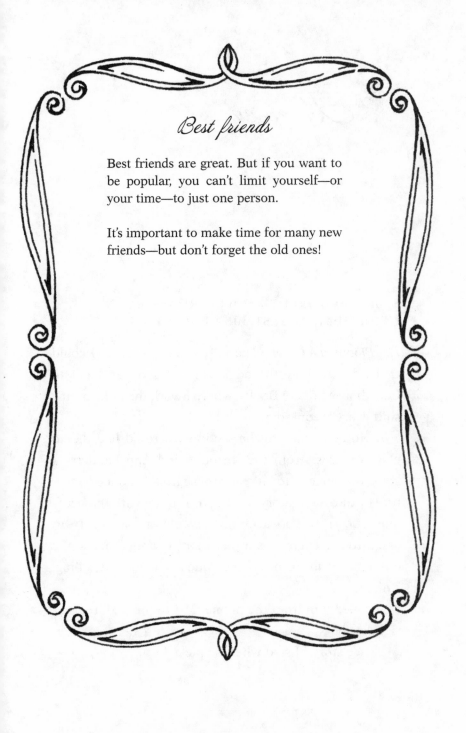

Best friends

Best friends are great. But if you want to be popular, you can't limit yourself—or your time—to just one person.

It's important to make time for many new friends—but don't forget the old ones!

 *Nineteen*

The Bloomville Gazette is an afternoon paper, so I could check to see how the ad looked as soon as I got to Courthouse Square Books, where I work the four-to-nine shift every Wednesday.

Before I turned to the section where I'd had the ad placed (across from the cartoons and Ann Landers—I know everyone in town reads those first), I noticed a picture of the observatory on the front page, with the headline, LOCAL MAN DONATES OBSERVATORY, DEDICATES IT TO BRIDE-TO-BE. There was a picture of Grandpa inside the observatory, his arms spread wide at the domed ceiling, smiling.

I called him from the phone next to the cash register right away.

"Nice story," I said when he picked up.

"Kitty," Grandpa said, sounding smug, "is pleased."

"She should be," I said. "Not many guys build something in your honor."

"Well," Grandpa said, "Kitty's worth it."

"Of course she is," I said. I truly believed that, too.

"Haven't heard from you in a few days," Grandpa said. "How's the popularity thing going?"

I thought about the way Mark's finger had felt against my cheek. He'd only rested it there for a moment. But it had felt like the longest moment of my entire life.

"Excellent," I said.

"Really?" Was it my imagination, or did Grandpa sound surprised? "Very good, then. Things are going well for both of us at the same time, for a change. And how's your mother?"

I had just seen Mom waddle out of the store, heading home to put her feet up. She was closing in on her ninth month, and her ankles looked like Lauren's legs in her white thigh-highs.

"She's good," I said. "But no movement, you know, on the wedding front."

Grandpa sighed. "Can't say I really expected much. She's a stubborn woman, your mother. Bit like you, in that way."

"Me?" I couldn't believe it. "I'm not stubborn."

Grandpa whistled, low and long.

"I'm *not*," I insisted.

Which was when the bell over the front door of the store tinkled, and Darren, my coworker for the evening, came back with Tasti D-Lites from Penguin for the two of us.

"Is it hot enough out there?" Darren wanted to know, handing over my fat-free, calorie-free, pretty much taste-free ice cream. "Can you say Indian summer or what?"

"Thanks," I said. "I just gotta finish up this phone call."

Darren waggled his fingers at me to show me he understood, and went over to the jewelry rack to organize the earrings, his favorite job-related activity.

"Um, Gramps," I said. "Oh, hey, listen . . . I might need to borrow a bit more money. As part of the plan. But it's to help the store this time. Not my social life." Well, not *totally*, anyway.

"I see," Grandpa said. "Well, I'll have to take a look at the interest rates. . . ."

"Understood," I said. I'm not insulted that my own grandfather charges me interest on loans. I would do the same thing if someone borrowed money from me. People on TV, like Judge Judy and my idol, Suze Orman, always say family should never lend other family members money. But it can actually work, if you're businesslike about it.

"Grandpa," I said. "Remember how you told me that you always liked Kitty, even back when you guys were in high school? But she always liked someone else?"

"Ronald Hollenbach," Grandpa said as if the name left a sour taste in his mouth.

"Right. Jason's grandpa. Well, I was just wondering . . . how did you finally get her away from him? Mr. Hollenbach, I mean?"

"That's easy," Grandpa said. "He croaked."

"Oh." This wasn't as helpful as I'd hoped it would be. I was looking for some advice on how to steal Mark Finley away from Lauren. Which I didn't actually consider an underhanded thing to do. Because Lauren is just plain mean, and Mark is the nicest guy in town. He deserves someone better than Lauren. Even if, you know, he may not know it.

"Getting all that dough from the good people at Super Sav-Mart didn't hurt much, either," Grandpa went on. "Kitty appreciates a nice steak dinner at the country club every now and then."

"Right," I said. Steak. Check. "But, like, I'm sure you had to charm her, right? How did you do that?"

"I can't tell you," Grandpa said. "Your mother'd kill me."

"Grandpa," I said. "She already wants to kill you. How much more trouble can you get in with her?"

"True," Grandpa said. "Well, the fact is, Steph, we Kazoulises, well, we're a passionate bunch, and we know how to please a woman."

I choked on a mouthful of Tasti D-Lite.

"Thanks, Grandpa," I said as soon as I could get the words out. "I think I get it."

"Kitty's a woman with needs, you know, Stephanie, and—"

"Oh, I know that, all right," I said quickly. I mean, I'd pretty much figured that out by how easily Kitty's copy of *Wicked Loving Lies* fell open to the Turkish-style scene.

She'd obviously read that part a *lot*. "Thanks, Grandpa. That's very helpful advice."

"I know you're half Landry," Grandpa said. "But you're a good fifty percent Kazoulis. So you shouldn't have any problems in the—"

"Whoa, look at that, a customer just walked in," I lied. "Gotta go, Gramps. Talk to you later. Buh-bye."

I stared at the phone after I'd put it down. It was clear that, while Grandpa was a pro at giving financial advice, when it came to matters of the heart . . . well, I was on my own. I was going to have to figure out how to win Mark away from Lauren without his help.

"Oh my God," Darren said, hurrying up to the counter with his ice cream. "D'you know what Shelley at the Penguin told me? The high school's holding a slave auction tomorrow night."

"It's not a slave auction," I said, showing him the ad in the paper. "It's a talent auction. People are volunteering their talents for the community to bid on. Not their— whatever you're thinking."

"Oh," Darren said, looking a little disappointed. "How do you know so much about it?"

"Because," I said. I tried not to sound proud, since pride is akin to arrogance, according to The Book, and arrogance is not a desirable trait in a popular girl. "I'm the one who came up with the idea. And I'm running it."

Darren looked shocked. "You? But you're—"

He stopped himself, though.

"It's okay," I said. "You can say it."

"Oh, thank God," Darren said. "It's just that—honey, you're such a Steph Landry!"

"But I won't be for much longer," I was able to inform him with total confidence.

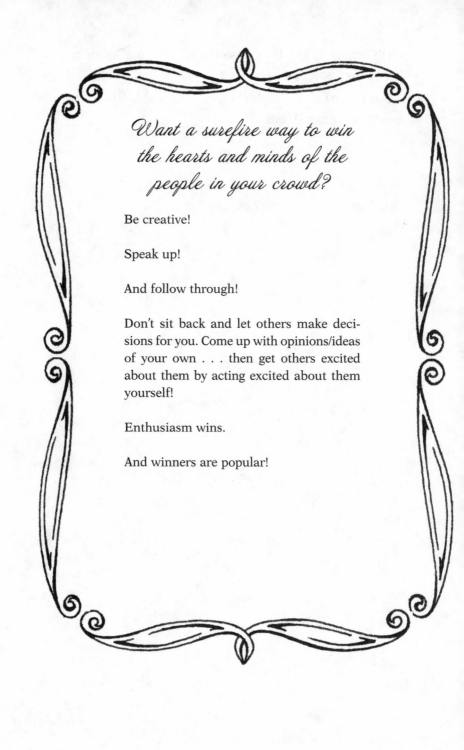

Want a surefire way to win the hearts and minds of the people in your crowd?

Be creative!

Speak up!

And follow through!

Don't sit back and let others make decisions for you. Come up with opinions/ideas of your own . . . then get others excited about them by acting excited about them yourself!

Enthusiasm wins.

And winners are popular!

 *Twenty*

DAY FOUR OF POPULARITY
THURSDAY, AUGUST 31, 6 P.M.

I was crazed all day getting ready for the auction: signing up last-minute people, then getting their names/tal-
ents to Mr. Schneck so that he could practice saying
them . . . getting the guys from the audio-visual club to
set up the sound system in the gym, so everyone could
hear the auctioneer . . . getting the bidding paddles
(hand-fans I got Day Mortuary to donate. But I'm sure
people won't mind. I mean, about being reminded of
dead people during the auction).

Things were so nuts, I didn't get lunch OR dinner. I
never even got to go home after school! Thank God
Becca stuck around to help . . . and, surprisingly,
Darlene. It turns out Darlene is a natural at getting people to do stuff. If I hadn't had her around all afternoon, I
don't know what I would have done. She just has to

lower her eyelashes and go, "You guys, will you move the podium over *there?*" and people—well, okay, guys—practically fall over themselves to do it for her.

And she really isn't as dumb as she looks. When the local cable television station showed up, because they want to record the auction and show it on public access this weekend, and they didn't have the right wires, Darlene turned to Todd and went, "Todd, run to the office and ask Swampy if you can borrow the coaxial cable from the teacher's lounge."

And the AV guys, their eyes all wide with worship, were like, "How did *you* know it's called a coaxial cable?"

And Darlene realized she'd accidentally let her smarts show, and was like, "Oh, did I say that? I don't know what I'm talking about."

But later, when the guys weren't around, and I asked her, "How *did* you know what kind of cable they needed?" Darlene was like, "Well, duh. Everyone knows that."

Which caused Becca to ask her, "Did you REALLY not know honey comes from bees that time in the eighth grade?"

And Darlene laughed and said, "Well, no. But that class was so boring. I just wanted to liven things up a little."

"But doesn't acting dumb make people look down on you?" Becca wanted to know.

"Oh no," Darlene said. "Because it gets people to do stuff for me, and then I have more time to watch TV."

Which actually makes sense. Sort of.

Darlene and Becca weren't the only ones helping out. Mark and a bunch of his team members came in after practice to help hang the FIRST ANNUAL BLOOMVILLE HIGH TALENT AUCTION banner that I spent my whole lunch period painting, with the help of some cool senior girls and—though she offered it begrudgingly, at best—Lauren.

Lauren came by after school, too, with Bebe Johnson. Her usual shadow, Alyssa Krueger, has been notably absent from Lauren's side since the TO STEFF incident. I caught a brief glimpse of her scuttling through the cafeteria when I stopped by to grab a soda before heading off to paint my banner, apparently hoping no one would see her buying a tuna sandwich and sneaking out to the flagpole to eat it by herself, since she's no longer welcome at Mark's table.

I probably should have felt triumphant, seeing one of Bloomville High's leading It Girls doing the Walk of Shame through the caf.

But the fact is, the sight just saddened me a little. I don't have anything against Alyssa Krueger. Much. I mean, she's a heinous troll, and all of that.

But it's Lauren I want to see go down.

And WILL see go down. Tonight. If there's any justice in the world.

While we were painting the banner, one of the senior girls accidentally dribbled paint on the free throw line of the gym floor, and Lauren started laughing.

"God, Cheryl," she said. "Way to pull a St—"

We all knew what she was going to say. But she stopped herself at the last minute.

I looked over at her and raised one eyebrow (a trick I'd spent hours in front of the mirror—much to the amusement of Jason—teaching myself in the fourth grade, after I became addicted to Nancy Drew, who was always going around, raising one eyebrow at people).

Cheryl, who didn't notice my eyebrow, went, "I know, I know. Way to pull a Steph Landry. Anybody got a paper towel?"

When nobody said anything, Cheryl looked up and saw everybody—including me—looking at her.

"What?" she said, genuinely not knowing.

"*I'm* Steph Landry," I said, trying not to let my anger show. Because anger isn't a desirable emotion to show if you want to be popular.

Cheryl, a pretty red-headed member of the school dance team, the Fishnets (after the Fighting Fish), went, "Right. Funny. Seriously, who has the roll of paper towels?"

"I *am* serious," I said.

Cheryl, realizing I was telling the truth, started to turn as red as the paint she'd spilled.

"But you're—I mean, you're—and Steph is . . . she's—" she sputtered. "I know *your* name is Steph, but I didn't think you were THAT Steph. I mean, that Steph . . . didn't she, like, shoot someone?"

"No," I said.

"No, but seriously. She put a car in Greene Lake or something. I *know* it."

"No," I said. "And I should know. Because I'm Steph Landry. And I didn't do any of those things. All I did was spill a Big Red Super Big Gulp on someone once."

And I shot Lauren what I hoped was a meaningful look.

"Is that all?" Cheryl wrinkled her little Fishnet nose. "God. I love Big Red Super Big Gulps. That's, like, the best flavor."

"Right," another senior girl said. "But it stains like crazy. I spilled one on my mom's white carpet, and I still hear about it sometimes when she's mad at me for something else."

"Totally," Cheryl said. "Come on, though, seriously, you guys. I have to clean this paint up before it dries. Does anyone have a tissue or anything?"

And that was it. Lauren, red-faced, went back to painting. And no one said another thing about it.

And after tonight? No one ever would again.

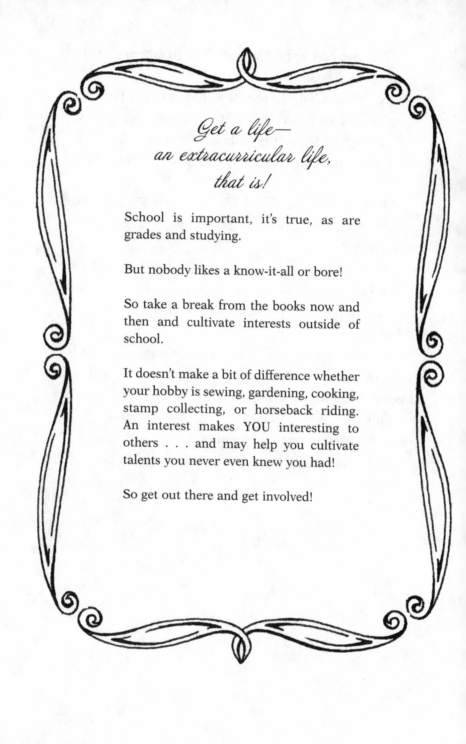

Get a life—
an extracurricular life,
that is!

School is important, it's true, as are grades and studying.

But nobody likes a know-it-all or bore!

So take a break from the books now and then and cultivate interests outside of school.

It doesn't make a bit of difference whether your hobby is sewing, gardening, cooking, stamp collecting, or horseback riding. An interest makes YOU interesting to others . . . and may help you cultivate talents you never even knew you had!

So get out there and get involved!

 *Twenty-one*

It's started.

And I don't think I'd be flattering myself to say that it's going GREAT.

And okay, we didn't get the seven thousand people who usually manage to drag themselves into the gym for basketball games.

But we've got a good three thousand, I bet. That's a heck of a lot more than we'd get for a car wash.

And people are spending money! Gordon Wu and his three hours of computer lessons went for thirty-five dollars. The guy with the stump grinder? Fifty-eight dollars. Some girl who claims she can teach anyone to make a perfect strawberry and rhubarb pie? Twenty-two bucks.

But by far the best-selling talent of the night so far has been Darlene's makeup lessons. Todd and those guys were all bidding against one another—ostensibly for their mothers. Todd won—for a whopping sixty-seven dollars.

I really hope his mom is worth it.

And so far, the one thing I was really worried about happening—someone standing down there on the little dais they've erected next to the podium and having NO ONE bid on them—hasn't happened. Even Courtney Pierce, our class suck-up, managed to get bids on her Spanish tutoring.

So I wasn't really worried when Mr. Schneck read off the name of the next person whose talent was to be auctioned off, and it was Becca Taylor. I mean, scrapbooking is a popular hobby in our town. There's a whole store devoted to it—Get Scrappin'—out by the mall. Becca's not popular, or anything—people still remember her sleeping-in-school days.

But *somebody* would bid on her.

"And here we have eleventh grader Becca Taylor," Mr. Schneck began in his auctioneer patter. He even had donned a bow tie and suspenders for the occasion. No one could ever accuse Mr. Schneck of not being devoted to his art. "Becca's offering up three hours of scrapbooking tips for any beginner scrapbookers out there. Any of you interested in scrapbooking, but need a little push to get started? Well, Miss Becca Taylor is your girl, then. She will come to your house, bringing with her her own scissors, adhesive, and journal pens, as well as layout ideas and plenty of refill pages to get you going on your album. Let's start the bidding for this very special service at ten dollars."

I looked around from my seat on the very bottom bleacher. The very bottom bleachers—the ones closest to the gym floor—are the ones the A-crowd always sit on, because they're the people who are usually being called over to the middle of the gym floor to receive awards or dance with the Fishnets or whatever.

And tonight, I was sitting with them. Not just with them . . . I was actually sitting *next to* Mark Finley.

And okay, Lauren Moffat was on his other side.

But he'd chosen to sit next to me—he'd walked into the gym, seen me on the first bleacher, where I'd been busy handing out Day Mortuary hand-fans, and he'd sat down beside me.

And the entire rest of the A-crowd—with the exception of Alyssa Krueger, who'd slunk up to the nosebleed seats where Jason and I usually sat, on the few occasions when we'd been forced to attend an event in the gym—had sat down with him.

And I was one of them. I was an A-crowder, one of the beautiful, popular people. I had made it.

And everyone knew it. I could feel their gazes on me—Courtney Pierce and Tiffany Cushing and all those other girls who, B-crowders at best, had still taken every opportunity to say, "Don't pull a Steph Landry" within my hearing. They were jealous. I *knew* they were jealous.

But they shouldn't have been. I'd worked to get to my position there on the bottom bleacher. I'd worked my butt off.

Almost literally.

The gym was crowded with familiar faces, not all of whom belonged to students at Bloomville High. I could see Becca's parents looking down on her fondly. They were excited their daughter was finally taking part in a school-related activity. They'd asked me at the door, when they'd come in, if my own parents were going to be here, thinking they could sit together. They looked kind of disappointed when I said my parents were too tired—Mom on account of the baby, and Dad on account of the younger kids—to come.

I didn't exactly mention that they didn't even know about it. Well, that they did—the whole town knew about it—but they didn't know I was the one running it.

And there was Dr. Greer, sitting with his wife and a guy who looked like the mayor—the MAYOR had shown up . . . alone, since he and his wife were in the middle of a nasty divorce we sometimes got to read about in the *Gazette*. Swampy Wampler was sitting with them, looking barely recognizable in jeans and a cotton sweater, as opposed to her usual gray or black suits. She kept looking over at Mayor Waicukowski and flipping her mouse-brown hair around. It was kind of obvious she was flirting with him.

And it was also kind of obvious he didn't mind.

At the last minute—just before Mr. Schneck had led us all in a ritual fish slap—I saw the last person I would have ever expected to see at a school-related event sneaking into the gym through a side door: Jason.

He had his friend Stuckey—a lumbering guy who traditionally wears nothing but excessively baggy Indiana University T-shirts and man-pris—with him. The two of them climbed the bleachers—not quite to the nosebleed seats, but close—and sat down, looking around. I saw Jason's gaze land on me. I lifted a hand to wave at him. After all, *he's* the one who apparently has a problem with me. I don't have a problem with *him*. Well, except for the whole calling me Crazytop thing.

Jason didn't wave back. And I *know* he saw me.

I hate to say it, but that sort of stung. I mean, that he'd ignore me like that. What did I ever do to him?

Except accept a ride in Lauren Moffat's 645Ci.

Which isn't exactly what I'd call very nice BMW Courtesy. His snubbing me like that, I mean, on account of being in someone else's 645Ci.

But fine. If he wants to be mad at me for that, he can be mad. What do I care?

It's just . . . well, it's going to be a little awkward when he has to escort me down the aisle at Grandpa's wedding on Saturday and we aren't speaking.

But whatever.

I looked at Becca, standing on the dais, looking pretty in khaki capris and a pink flowered shirt. She is on the big side . . . a lot like Stuckey, actually. Only she actually dresses in clothes that fit her. She was holding one of her scrapbooks and smiling at the crowd in the bleachers.

Except . . . except there was something sort of wrong with the way Becca was smiling. Her lips were curled up at the edges, and all. But the smile didn't seem to go all the way to her blue eyes. It sort of stopped at her gums.

That's when I noticed that the edges of her lips were trembling.

And that Mr. Schneck, the auctioneer, was saying, "Come on, folks. This is a service you can't get anywhere else. I know how popular scrapbooking is in this community, because there are nights when I can't get into the Sizzler because the Rather B Scrappin' Scrapbook Club is meeting there, and every table is filled up. So do I hear ten dollars for this little lady's valuable scrapbooking insights? Anyone?"

And suddenly it hit me, like a lightning bolt from the blue:

No one was bidding on Becca.

It was like a nightmare come true. Becca was standing there, trying to smile bravely and not burst into tears, while the knuckles on the hands that were clutching the scrapbook went whiter and whiter. . . .

"We have a bid of ten dollars," Mr. Schneck cried, to my intense relief. "Do I hear fifteen? Fifteen dollars anyone?"

I spun around in my seat to see who had raised their Day Mortuary hand-fan. . . .

And my heart sank. It was Mr. Taylor. Becca's DAD was bidding on her.

This was actually worse than if no one had bid on her at all.

"Something wrong, Steph?" a deep voice at my side asked.

I spun around the other way—

And practically bumped heads with Mark Finley, whose clear hazel eyes were gazing down at me with concern.

"You look upset," Mark said. "Is everything all right?"

Sputtering, I pointed at Becca.

"S-someone needs to bid on her," I said. "Someone who isn't her dad!"

And before I could say another word, up went Mark's Day Mortuary hand-fan.

"Fifteen dollars!" Mr. Schneck shouted, pointing at Mark. "We have fifteen dollars for the young lady's scrapbooking genius from the school quarterback. Do I hear twenty?"

The entire gym had fallen silent the moment Mark raised his paddle. It was as if no one could quite believe what they were seeing—the most popular boy in school bidding on the scrapbooking services of a girl who used to have to be shaken awake when it was time for recess. You could tell a lot of people thought he'd lost his mind—Lauren among them, since I heard her go, "Babe, are you *kidding* me?" under her breath.

But Mark didn't care. He held his Day Mortuary hand-fan high.

And the corners of Becca's mouth stopped shaking.

"Twenty dollars, folks," Mr. Schneck said. "Anyone care to bid twenty dollars? No? Becca Taylor's scrapbooking tutelage going for fifteen dollars, everyone. Fifteen dollars. Going once. Going twice. Sol—"

But before he could pronounce the *d* in *sold*, a voice rang out through the gym.

"A hundred and sixty-two dollars and fifty-eight cents!"

Every neck in the building cracked as people whipped their heads around to see who was willing to plunk down such an exorbitant sum on Becca.

I don't think I was the only one who was totally astonished to see Jason, standing with his paddle raised in one hand, and his wallet—whose contents he'd clearly just scanned—in the other.

"SOLD!" Mr. Schneck yelled. "To—to—that guy up there, for one hundred sixty-two dollars and fifty-eight cents!"

And his gavel came slamming down.

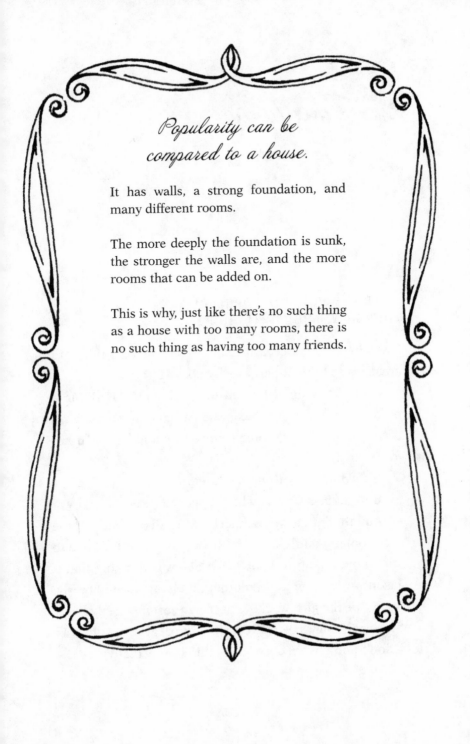

Popularity can be compared to a house.

It has walls, a strong foundation, and many different rooms.

The more deeply the foundation is sunk, the stronger the walls are, and the more rooms that can be added on.

This is why, just like there's no such thing as a house with too many rooms, there is no such thing as having too many friends.

 *Twenty-two*

I was happy for Becca. I really was. I mean, I think it's great Jason bought her. I really do.

I just don't think he had to make quite THAT big a production out of it. I mean, he basically wasted a hundred and forty-eight dollars, since he could have had her for twenty.

But whatever. I think it's sweet. I do.

But not as sweet as what happened next.

And that's that Mr. Schneck—after Becca had left the dais, looking all flushed and happy (and I didn't have to be a mind reader to know why: She was thinking that if Jason was willing to spend that much money on her, she MUST be the girl Stuckey suspected Jason secretly liked. She was going to be IMPOSSIBLE to deal with after this. I don't know what Jason was thinking. I really don't)—

cleared his throat into the microphone and said, "And now, all you Bloomville Fishes, the moment I know you've been waiting for—next up for auctioning off, the spokesperson talents of senior class president, team captain and quarterback, last year's Most Valuable Player, and all-around great guy, MARK FINLEY!"

The screams and applause followed by this statement nearly brought the steel roof beams crashing down. Mark stood up, grinning bashfully, and turned to wave to the crowd as he made his way to the dais. Perhaps the loudest shrieking of all was coming from his girlfriend, Lauren, who could barely seem to keep her butt on her seat, she was bouncing up and down so excitedly.

When Mark reached the dais, he waved to the other side of the gym as well. Then he turned to face Mr. Schneck, who was saying, "All right, folks, simmer down, simmer down. We know you all love Mark. Now it's time to see how much you REALLY love him. Mark has generously volunteered his time for use as an endorser of some lucky business . . . so let's find out who that lucky business owner is. We'll start the bidding at—"

Lauren's paddle flew up.

And hers was not the only one.

Mr. Schneck paused and said, "Um, folks, I haven't even—"

"A hundred dollars!" Lauren shrieked.

She was, I knew, just trying to imitate the sensation Jason had caused, offering such an outlandish sum he figured no one was going to outbid.

Too bad for her about ten other people had the same idea.

"A hundred and twenty!" a man I recognized as the owner of the Penguin cried.

"A hundred and forty!" shouted Stan, the manager of Courthouse Square Diner.

"One hundred and sixty," Lauren shot back.

"One eighty," Mayor Waicukowski, who owns an accounting firm in town—Waicukowksi and Associates: *We're more. More than just an accounting firm* (although no one seems to know what that means)—shouted, waving his Day Mortuary fan.

"Two hundred," Lauren shrieked.

Mark, on the dais, continued to look abashed—although he seemed to be enjoying himself, at the same time.

"Two twenty," Mayor Waicukowski called down from his seat by Dr. Greer.

Lauren, clearly tired of this, stood up, opened her purse, took out her checkbook, and read off the total amount in the account:

"Five hundred thirty-two dollars and seventeen cents."

Then she sat back down, looking satisfied by all the gasps the number had caused . . . and by the pleased grin on Mark's face.

I was sorry to have to ruin this touching moment for them. But, after all, I've got a business to run as well.

"A thousand dollars," I said, standing up.

The number of gasps for the number I'd just given,

versus the number of gasps for Lauren's number, rose exponentially.

"I beg your pardon, Stephanie?" Even Mr. Schneck looked shocked. "Did you just say a thousand dollars?"

"That's right," I said calmly. "Courthouse Square Books bids a thousand dollars on Mark Finley."

Now all eyes were on me, instead of on Mark . . . including Mark's. His expression was a combination of confusion and happiness mixed together—happiness over the fact that someone was paying so much for his services, I suppose, and confusion over the fact that it was me, and not his girlfriend, who was doing the buying.

"The little lady in the front bids a thousand dollars," Mr. Schneck said, picking up his gavel. "Do I hear a thousand twenty? Anyone? Going for a thousand, then."

Lauren was on her cell phone, desperately trying to reach her father. She was, I couldn't help noticing, given that I was standing right next to her, practically crying.

"But, Daddy," she said. "You don't understand—"

"Going once," Mr. Schneck said.

"—it's for a really good cause, and I'll—"

"Going twice," Mr. Schneck said.

"—never ask you for anything ever again, I swear, if you'll just—"

"SOLD to Stephanie Landry of Courthouse Square Books," Mr. Schneck cried.

And Lauren threw her cell phone across the gym so hard that when it hit the wall next to the exit, it exploded into a thousand little pieces.

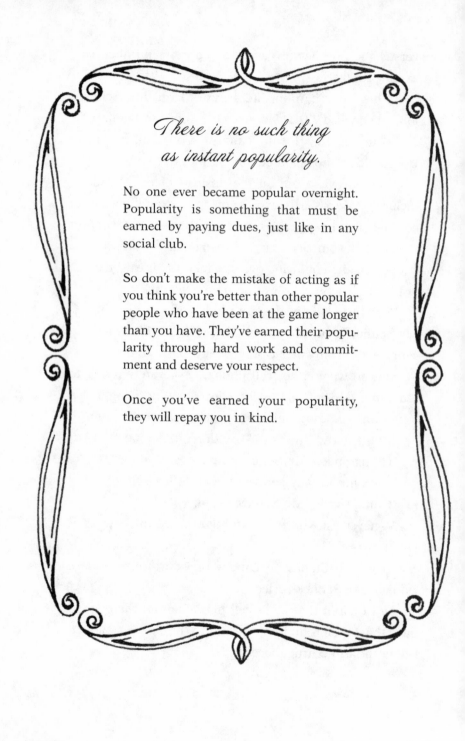

There is no such thing as instant popularity.

No one ever became popular overnight. Popularity is something that must be earned by paying dues, just like in any social club.

So don't make the mistake of acting as if you think you're better than other popular people who have been at the game longer than you have. They've earned their popularity through hard work and commitment and deserve your respect.

Once you've earned your popularity, they will repay you in kind.

 *Twenty-three*

I seriously don't get why everybody got so mad.

I bought Mark Finley—well, his services as a spokesperson for the store—fair and square, and that should be the end of it.

I don't know why Stan from Courthouse Square Diner had to call my mother and tell her about it, so the first thing that happened as I walked through the door after the Taylors dropped me off was my mother screaming at me that I was the town laughingstock.

First of all, *I* am the one who is going to be laughing when we start counting all the money from the new business Mark's image on our ads and flyers is going to bring in.

And second of all, Stan should mind his own business.

"He says you bought a boy in some auction," my mom kept repeating. "How could you buy a boy, Stephanie? How *could* you?"

This is what comes from too much *Law and Order* and ice cream. I'm dead serious. It warps your mind.

Not even Lauren was that mad. Once she got over her initial shock, and all. She and Mark both came over to say congratulations to me.

"Your endorsement is really going to help bring business to the downtown area," I said to Mark. You know, to make it clear I hadn't bought him for ME, but for the STORE. "The opening of the Super Sav-Mart has really hit us hard."

"Anything I can do to help," Mark said, looking like he meant it.

And Lauren was like, "Oh, Steph, I had no idea your parents' little store was in so much trouble. I'll tell all my friends to shop there from now on."

"Thanks," I said.

And I swear, for like a minute, I thought to myself that Lauren Moffat might not be all that bad.

But I didn't even really get to process that thought because Becca came up and was all over me wanting to analyze why Jason had bought her and what did I think it means and should she call him (since he left right after Mr. Schneck declared me the winner of Mark).

I told her of course she should call him, and that nothing was different—he'd been her friend before the auction, and he was still her friend.

"But he must like me as more than just a friend to spend that much money just to make me not feel bad about no one but my dad bidding on me," Becca said.

"Mark bid on you," I reminded her.

"He just did that because you made him," Becca said matter-of-factly. "No one made Jason do what he did. He must have done it because he thinks I'm The One. I'm going to call him as soon as I get home. Maybe I'll even stop by and see him."

I pointed out that it was after ten and that the Hollenbachs probably wouldn't appreciate her stopping by so late on a school night. I swear, sometimes I think Becca must have been raised by wolves.

Anyway, Mark is going to come by the store tomorrow after school to pose for some publicity photos and maybe hand out flyers on the square or something.

It will be a perfect opportunity for him to finally get to know me as a person, outside the confines of school.

And the confines of his girlfriend.

Because I really do think, if he'd just take the time to get to know me—REALLY know me—Mark would realize how much nicer I am than Lauren . . . despite what my mom seems to believe, which is that boys like Mark are only interested in one thing, and now that I've bought him, he's going to think I'm willing to give him that.

"You know that's why he's going out with that stuck-up Lauren Moffat," Mom said. "One reason and one reason only: because she puts out."

I almost started to cry, I thought this was so cute. Seriously, it reminded me of Kirsten's question, "But aren't the most popular people in your school the nicest ones?"

I don't think there've ever been two people more out of touch with reality than Kirsten and my mom.

Because if I were going out with Mark Finley, I would totally put out, too. Even Father Chuck would understand *that*.

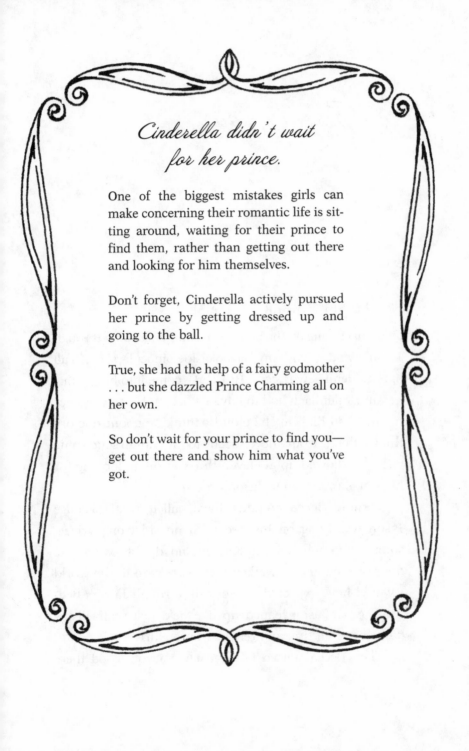

Cinderella didn't wait for her prince.

One of the biggest mistakes girls can make concerning their romantic life is sitting around, waiting for their prince to find them, rather than getting out there and looking for him themselves.

Don't forget, Cinderella actively pursued her prince by getting dressed up and going to the ball.

True, she had the help of a fairy godmother . . . but she dazzled Prince Charming all on her own.

So don't wait for your prince to find you—get out there and show him what you've got.

# Twenty-four

FRIDAY, SEPTEMBER 1, 12 A.M.

I was just sitting on the bathroom counter, looking through Jason's window with my Bazooka Joe binoculars, when all of a sudden I saw Becca—BECCA!—come into his room.

Dr. Hollenbach had to have let her in. He's always got his head so high in the clouds, thinking about doctory things, that it would never occur to him not to send some girl who showed up at eleven thirty at night, looking for his son, straight up to Jason's room.

I know Becca couldn't have called first, because Jason was lying on his bed with no shirt on, writing something—a haiku for Kirsten, no doubt—when the door opened and in walked the last person in the world I would have expected to see walk through Jason's bedroom door. Jason leaped up like he'd just realized his pants were on fire, and reached for a shirt (rats!).

Then Becca started talking, while Jason stood there

looking like he couldn't believe what was happening. After a while, he said something—I have no idea what . . . why didn't I take lipreading instead of Spanish??? WHY????—and Becca sank down onto his bed, looking all depressed.

That's when it happened. Jason sat down next to her and put his arm around her—

AND THEN THEY WERE KISSING!!!!

I have no idea who started it. I just saw their faces getting closer and closer, and then—

BAM!!!! They were smashing their lips up together.

And of course, as if that weren't weird enough, Pete had to choose that very moment to come barging into the bathroom.

"What are you doing sitting here in the dark again?" he wanted to know.

"Nothing! God! Don't you ever knock?" I whisper-screamed.

"Not when I don't see a light under the door," Pete said. Then, to my horror, he said, "Oh, wait, I know what you're doing in here. You're spying on Hawkface."

"I am not!" I practically shrieked. Only I had to keep my voice down, so as not to wake up Mom and Dad. "And don't call him that."

"Why not? You do. And you are so spying on him. You're holding binoculars. And you can see right into his bedroom from—Hey. Is that BECCA on his bed?"

"GET OUT!" I wanted to kill him.

"What's Becca doing making out with Hawkface?"

"Nothing. They aren't making out. See? They stopped."

Pete and I stood there and watched while Jason—the back of his head to the window—said something to Becca, who seemed to nod. It was kind of hard to tell what was going on.

But I saw Becca get up off the bed and leave.

"Whoa," Pete said. "Am I going to give HIM a hard time about this at the wedding."

I reached over and pinched him, hard enough to make him yelp.

"You aren't going to say ANYTHING to him about this," I hissed. "Because he can never know we were doing this. Spying on him like this."

"Why not?" Pete wanted to know. "You started it."

"I wasn't spying on him," I insisted. "I was . . . meditating."

"Sure," Pete said. And turned toward the toilet. "Whatever you say, Crazytop."

He screamed so loud when I pinched him for calling me Crazytop that he woke up Dad, who called sleepily from his bedroom, "What's going on up there?"

"Nothing," I called back sweetly. "Good night!"

I can't believe it. Becca and Jason? I mean, I knew she had a crush on him, and all. But I had no idea he felt the same way about HER.

Although I guess I should have known, seeing as how he bought her tonight.

Still. *Jason and Becca?*

The world has gone completely insane.

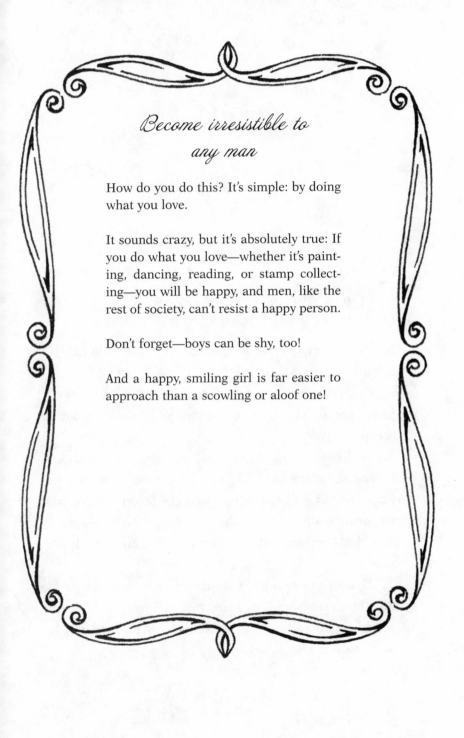

Become irresistible to any man

How do you do this? It's simple: by doing what you love.

It sounds crazy, but it's absolutely true: If you do what you love—whether it's painting, dancing, reading, or stamp collecting—you will be happy, and men, like the rest of society, can't resist a happy person.

Don't forget—boys can be shy, too!

And a happy, smiling girl is far easier to approach than a scowling or aloof one!

Twenty-five

She didn't say a word about it in the car on the way to school. Not a single word.

I can't believe she and Jason have a secret I don't know about. That I'm not supposed to know about, I mean.

That has to mean something? The fact that she didn't tell me about the kiss? I mean, the very fact that we were in her dad's Cadillac again, instead of Jason's BMW, had to mean something. If she and Jason were an item, wouldn't he have offered to drive her to school this morning?

That has to mean it was just a pity kiss. Becca probably confessed her true feelings for Jason, and he told her his heart still belongs to Kirsten. Or he gave her the soul mate speech again.

That has to be why she isn't saying anything.

Unless it means the OPPOSITE. What if it means that kiss was so special and sacred that Becca wants to keep it to herself—hug it to herself, like my secret about wearing Jason's Batman underwear that one time?

And the reason she had her dad drive us to school, instead of Jason, is that the two of them are waiting for the right time to break it to me—the truth about their love affair, I mean.

The real question is, why do I even care? I don't like Jason. In that way. Becca can have him. My God. I OWN MARK FINLEY FOR THE DAY.

I have got to chill.

Of course, the fact that Mark looked at me kind of funny when I was at my locker this morning hasn't helped matters anyway. He was like, "Hi, Steph—what happened to your hair?"

Which is when I realized I forgot to blow it out this morning.

But seriously, there is only so much drama a girl can handle. I was still all freaked out about Jason and Becca. Is it any wonder I'd forgotten to blow-dry my hair and that it was curling all over the place?

Except of course I couldn't say that to Mark. I couldn't be like, "Oh, yeah, I've got Crazytop this morning because last night while I was spying on my neighbor I saw my two best friends making out with each other."

So I just went, "Ha, yeah, trying out a new look."

"Well," Mark said. "It's . . . interesting. So is it okay if

I stop by the bookstore around six tonight? Because I've got practice after school."

"Totally," I said. "Perfect. See you then."

Mark raised his eyebrows. "Lunch. I'll see you at lunch."

"Right!" I said. "Sorry. Lunch."

"And, hey, listen . . . about last night."

Last night? How did HE know about last night? Had he seen Becca and Jason making out, too?

"The auction," Mark said, I guess because I'd looked a little confused.

"Oh, sure," I said with a laugh. "The auction. Right!"

"Yeah. I heard we raised seven thousand dollars."

"Seven thousand nine hundred and twenty-three," I corrected him. Because that is how I am.

"Right," Mark said with his trademark lopsided grin. "Seven thousand nine hundred and twenty-three dollars. I just wanted to say thanks. I mean, that's more money than last year's senior class managed to raise all year, and here it is still the first week of school."

God. Was it really only the first week of school? It seemed like it had been AGES since I'd first walked down this hallway in my navy blue thigh-highs and said hi to Mark as if I were a real person, not the social pariah I used to be.

"And I owe it all to you," Mark went on. "So . . . really. Thanks, Stephanie."

And then he leaned down and kissed me on the cheek.

Just as Alyssa Krueger went scuttling by on her way to the girls' room to repair the mascara rings under her eyes, since she'd apparently been crying . . . again.

It's funny, but there was a time when the thought of Mark Finley kissing me—even on the cheek—would just about have made my heart explode.

But today when it actually happened, I was just like—whatever.

What's happening to me?

I wonder if Jason and Becca used tongue.

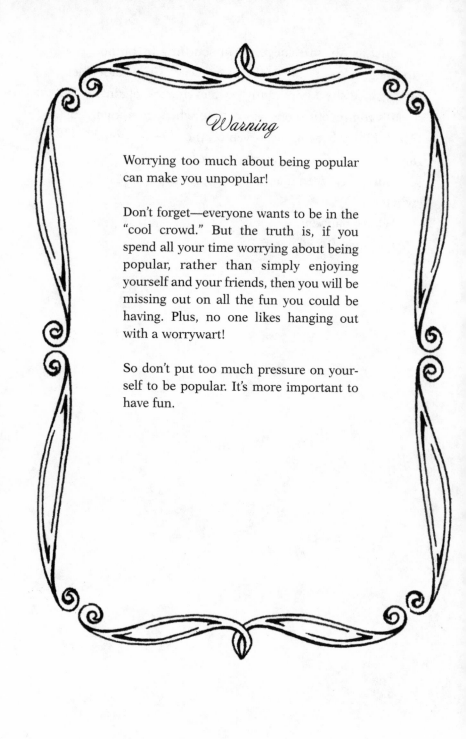

Warning

Worrying too much about being popular can make you unpopular!

Don't forget—everyone wants to be in the "cool crowd." But the truth is, if you spend all your time worrying about being popular, rather than simply enjoying yourself and your friends, then you will be missing out on all the fun you could be having. Plus, no one likes hanging out with a worrywart!

So don't put too much pressure on yourself to be popular. It's more important to have fun.

 *Twenty-six*

STILL DAY FIVE OF POPULARITY
FRIDAY, SEPTEMBER 1, 1 P.M.

Well. It happened. They warned me, but I didn't believe
them.

I couldn't face the lunchroom today. I don't know
why. I just . . . I couldn't do it. It was nothing against
Darlene. It was more . . . see, I was afraid that if I sat
there and Becca didn't show up, I'd know she was with
Jason and that it was true, about them being a couple
now.

And that just made me feel like I was going to throw
up for some reason.

So I grabbed a PowerBar and some diet soda from
the machines by the gym, and took off for the library,
since it was too rainy to eat outside. Besides, I figured no
one I knew was a big enough loser to be eating in the
library, so I'd be safe.

I was wrong.

Because sitting there, right where I'd been going to sit, in the study carrel in the biography section, where no one ever, ever went, was Alyssa Krueger.

I was going to sneak quietly away, but she saw me.

And lowered her own PowerBar and said, "Well, if it isn't Steph Landry," in a very unfriendly voice.

She didn't even bother whispering. That's because no one ever goes into the Bloomville High library, including the librarians, who are always in the back office, since they never actually have any customers, unless an English teacher makes her class go there to learn about the Dewey decimal system, or whatever.

"Look, Alyssa," I said, trying to remember The Book's advice on dealing with enemies. Empathy. It was all about empathy. "There's no sense blaming me for what happened between you and Lauren. You shouldn't have written that note to me."

"Lauren wrote it," Alyssa said bitterly.

"I know Lauren wrote it," I said. "You shouldn't have taken the blame for it. You should have told Mark the truth."

"Oh, right," Alyssa said, looking incredulous. "And then Lauren and I both could be eating in here, instead of the caf."

I pulled out a chair from a neighboring study carrel and sat down in it.

"If she were really your friend in the first place," I said, "she'd be in here with you now."

Alyssa's eyes filled up with tears. "I know," she said with a sob. "Do you think I don't know that? She's such a *bitch*." Alyssa threw down her PowerBar, unable to eat any more. "What am I telling *you* that for? You know. You've been a daily recipient of her bitchiness for the past—what is it now? Since you spilled that drink on her?"

"Almost five years," I said.

"Right. And now look at you."

I looked down at myself. I had on a pair of my slim-fit cords and a sweater set, because it was supposed to rain all day and cool things off a little . . . just in time for Grandpa and Kitty's wedding tomorrow. I'd checked the Weather Channel that morning and was relieved to find they were predicting clear skies for Saturday.

"Not what you have on," Alyssa said scornfully. "Your social standing. I mean, I saw Mark Finley *kiss* you this morning."

I took a bite of my own PowerBar. "Yeah," I said. "On the cheek. Big deal."

"He likes you, though," Alyssa said. "Seriously. He told Lauren. He thinks you're *nice*."

She said it like it was a dirty word.

"I *am* nice," I said. Then I remembered all the times I'd watched Jason get undressed through my Bazooka Joe binoculars. And the sugar I'd sprinkled in Lauren's hair. "Well, most of the time, anyway."

"I know," Alyssa said. "That's why Lauren's flipping out. Because you're making her look bad. In front of Mark."

"Lauren's making herself look bad in front of Mark," I corrected her.

"And then when you did that thing last night, where you outbid her for him—I mean, his sponsorship, for your bookstore, or whatever. I heard her later, in the girls' room. She was practically frothing at the mouth, she was so mad. She said she's going to get you, you know."

I took another bite of my PowerBar. "Oh, right," I said with my mouth full, even though The Book says bad table manners can keep you from becoming popular. "What can she possibly do to me that she hasn't already done?"

"I don't know," Alyssa said, her eyes red-rimmed and still teary. "But I'd watch out if I were you. Because I was her best friend, and look what she's done to me."

"Alyssa," I said. "You're only in this position because you LET her do this to you. If you'd just stand up and fight her—if everyone in this school would just stand up and fight her—"

"You're crazy," Alyssa said, wadding the remains of her lunch into a tight little ball, and standing up. "You know that, Steph? No one stands up to Lauren Moffat. Not even you."

"Excuse me," I said, swallowing. "What do you think I've been doing all week?"

"That's not standing up to her," Alyssa said. "That's playing her game her way. And you know what? You're going to lose. Because she's going to find a way—some vulnerable spot you don't even know you have—to get you, to make you look bad in front of all these new friends of yours. And then you're going to be right back where you started. You mark my words."

And with that, Alyssa left.

I thought about what she said the whole time I was finishing my PowerBar. But the truth was, I just couldn't see it happening. Lauren finding some way to pull the popularity rug out from under me, I mean. Because there was just no weapon she had that she could use against me. If anything, I had the upper hand. Because now I knew that Mark liked me.

And that Lauren was upset about it.

I was feeling pretty good about myself as I finished my lunch and got up to go . . .

Until I noticed who'd been sitting in a third study carrel, not ten feet away from me.

"What are *you* doing here?" I demanded.

"Trying to get some peace and quiet," Jason said. "And, man, did I come to the wrong place."

"Why didn't you just go sit in your car?" I asked.

Jason scowled. "Because everyone knows they can find me there."

I tried not to let myself think that by "everyone" he meant Becca, and that he was avoiding her. For one thing because I didn't care. And for another because it made absolutely no sense that I should be so happy that he was trying to avoid Becca.

"She's right, you know," Jason said, nodding in the direction Alyssa had stormed off. "About Lauren. She's going to figure out some way to get back at you for buying her boyfriend."

"Oh, please," I said. "Like I'm scared."

"You should be," Jason said. "She could make your life pretty unpleasant."

I just stared at him. "Jason, where have you been these past five years? What can she possibly do to me that she hasn't already done?"

"That's why I don't understand," Jason said, holding a bag of Funyuns toward me (and which I declined), "why you even want to be friends with her."

"I don't," I said.

Jason's scowl deepened. "Then what's this all about? This whole . . . *thing* this week?"

"I just want to be popular," I said.

"*Why?*"

The funny part was, he asked it like he genuinely didn't understand.

"Because, Jason," I said, not even quite believing I had to explain it, "my whole life—well, since sixth grade, anyway—I've been at the bottom. And now it's my turn to be on top."

"Yeah, but"—Jason chewed a Funyun—"what's so great about being there? You can't even be yourself."

"Yes, I can," I said.

"Oh, right. Because that's how your hair normally looks."

I raised an eyebrow at him, and he said, "Well, okay, today you've gone all Crazytop. But I mean the rest of this week—what does it take you, like half an hour to get it straight? Why do you want to be friends with a bunch of people who'll only give you the time of day if you have straight hair? What's so wrong with your old friends, who loved you the way you were?"

"Nothing," I said. I couldn't believe I was even having this conversation. "But what's so wrong with wanting to have other friends besides just you and Becca?"

"Nothing," he admitted. Grudgingly. "But *Lauren Moffat*? Or is it just her boyfriend you're trying to steal?"

"I'm not trying to steal him," I said, feeling myself flush.

"Oh, you're not? You just spent a thousand bucks of your hard-earned cash on him for no reason?"

"No," I said, forgetting about limiting my saturated fat intake and reaching into the bag on his desk for a Funyun. "You know why I did that. To bring business to the store."

"Oh, sure. And you don't have a crush on him."

"Right. Just like you don't have a crush on Becca."

Even as the words were coming out of my mouth, I was longing to stuff them back in. But it was too late. They were already out.

"Becca?" Jason made a pretty funny face as he said the name, for someone who, only twelve hours ago, had been kissing her. "Since when do I have a crush on Becca?"

"Well, you bought her," I pointed out. Since I couldn't very well mention that I'd seen the kiss.

"Of course I bought her," Jason said. "What else was I supposed to do? Let her stand up there and be humiliated because only her dad was bidding on her? I couldn't very well let *Mark Finley* buy her."

"What's wrong with Mark Finley?" I demanded. "He's a really nice guy."

"Sure," Jason said with a sneer. "If you like mindless clones who just do whatever their girlfriend—or you— tells them to."

"Mark's not like that. He—"

"Whatever, Steph," Jason said, standing up. "You know, Alyssa's a troll, but she's right about one thing. The only thing you're going to get out of hanging around the likes of Lauren Moffat and her golden boy is burned. And I just hope when it happens, I'm there to see it."

The weirdest part of it all is, when it happened?

He *was* there.

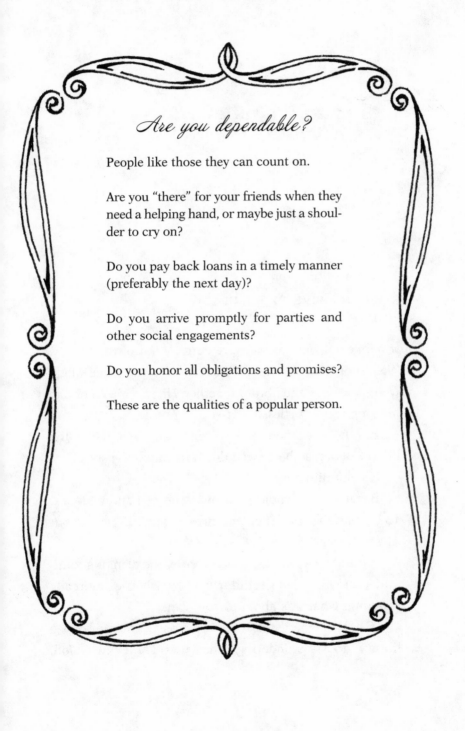

Are you dependable?

People like those they can count on.

Are you "there" for your friends when they need a helping hand, or maybe just a shoulder to cry on?

Do you pay back loans in a timely manner (preferably the next day)?

Do you arrive promptly for parties and other social engagements?

Do you honor all obligations and promises?

These are the qualities of a popular person.

 *Twenty-seven*

It happened right as we were coming out of the library. Well, not "we" exactly, since Jason and I definitely weren't leaving the library together. He was ahead of me, his long legs effortlessly out-striding mine.

But he saw who was waiting for me outside the library doors, so he slowed down to watch the show.

Nice of him, wasn't it?

Because the whole gang was there. Lauren. Mark. Todd. Darlene. Darlene's entourage. Bebe. Everyone but Alyssa Krueger.

But not to worry. I saw her over by the drinking fountain, pretending to be refilling her water bottle, but really watching what was about to go down.

"Oh, there she is," Lauren cried as I came out of the library doors, wondering what was going on. "God,

Steph, we've been looking for you all over!"

"Yeah, how come you didn't come down to the caf for lunch?" Darlene wanted to know. She, at least, looked as if she'd genuinely missed me.

"I, uh, had some studying to do," I said lamely. "I've got a chem quiz later."

"Bummer," Darlene said sympathetically.

Lauren was the one who got down to business first.

"This guy right here," Lauren said, holding up the front page from Wednesday's *Bloomville Gazette*. "Isn't he your grandfather?"

I looked at the picture of Gramps holding his arms outstretched in the rotunda of the observatory. I could not imagine where Lauren was heading with this.

"Um," I said. "Yeah."

"So he owns this?" Lauren said, tapping another photo that accompanied the article, of the outside of the observatory. "Right?"

"Well," I said. "Yeah. I mean, he had it built. He's donating it to the city—"

"But he hasn't yet," Lauren said. "It's not open to the public yet, right?"

"Right," I said. "Not till next week—"

"So it's empty?" Lauren asked.

I seriously did not see where this was all going. Maybe I'm a moron. But I just didn't get it.

"Yeah," I said. "Well, I mean, there're workmen there—"

"During the day."

"Right. . . ."

"But it's empty at night."

"Yeah," I said. "Why—?"

"See?" Lauren threw a triumphant look up at Mark. "I told you. It's perfect."

"Perfect for what?" I asked, just as the bell signaling the end of the lunch period rang.

"For Todd's rager tonight," Lauren said. "Normally he has it out at the quarry, but it's going to rain all day and into the night, too. He was going to cancel it, but then I remembered your grandfather was the guy who was building the new observatory, and that it wasn't open yet, and that you could probably get us in there."

"You can let us in, right?" Todd asked eagerly. "I mean, I know it's probably locked. But you have the key or the code or whatever, right?"

"Well," I said. "I mean, yeah, I do, but—"

"See?" Lauren grinned up at Mark. "I told you! Steph, you're the best!"

"But," I said. This wasn't happening. No way could this be happening. "How many people are we talking about here?"

"Just a hundred," Todd said. "Tops. Well, maybe a couple dozen more. But seriously, Steph, my ragers are exclusive—invitation only. We'll post someone at the door, keep an eye out for the cops, the works. It's supposed to rain all night, so it's not like there'll be people out on Main or The Wall, or anything. I swear, no one will even know we were there. All we need for you to do is open the doors for us around ten o'clock. That's it."

I thought of the observatory's clean white walls and spotless floors. I thought of the massive central telescope pier, and the twisting halls around it, and the wide observatory deck.

Then I thought of all the images of teen parties I had seen on TV and at the movies (since I'd never actually been to one).

And I said, "I really don't think this—"

"Aw, come on, Steph," Mark said, looking down at me with those hazel eyes of his. "We'll be careful. You won't get busted. And if you do, well, I'll take the rap for you. I swear."

I stared up at him, hypnotized as always by those golden-green irises.

"All right," I heard myself murmur.

"Yeah!" Todd said, and he and Mark high-fived each other. Lauren looked pleased, and Darlene said, "Wait, so . . . that means the party's on after all?"

"Party is *on*, baby," Todd said, and tried to put his arm around Darlene's waist, but she stepped quickly away, saying, "Oh, good, I can wear my new suede pants."

"You're the best," Lauren said to me. "I just knew we could count on you, Steph."

Then the second bell rang, and everyone took off.

Everyone except Jason, that is.

Who looked at me and said, *"I just knew we could*

225

count on you, Steph."

But in a completely different tone of voice than Lauren had said it.

And then walked away.

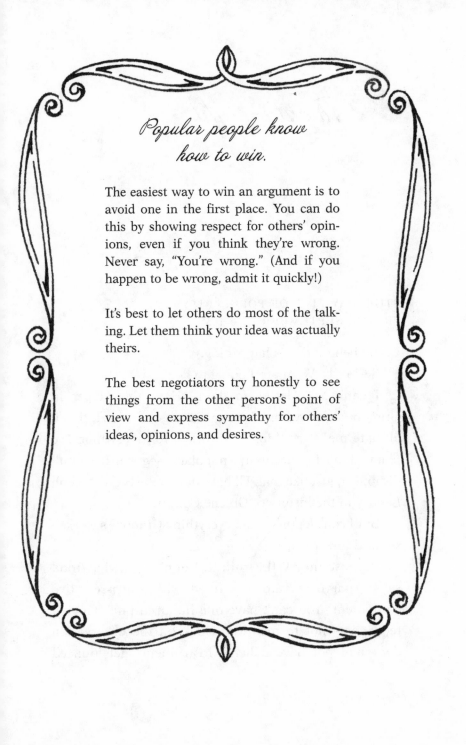

Popular people know how to win.

The easiest way to win an argument is to avoid one in the first place. You can do this by showing respect for others' opinions, even if you think they're wrong. Never say, "You're wrong." (And if you happen to be wrong, admit it quickly!)

It's best to let others do most of the talking. Let them think your idea was actually theirs.

The best negotiators try honestly to see things from the other person's point of view and express sympathy for others' ideas, opinions, and desires.

Twenty-eight

STILL DAY FIVE OF POPULARITY
FRIDAY, SEPTEMBER 1, 4 P.M.

I can't believe this is happening.

Seriously. What am I going to do?

I can't NOT let them do it. Have their rager in Grandpa's observatory, I mean. Because if I don't, they'll all hate me. Everything I've worked for, everything I've planned, all my newfound popularity—gone. It will all disappear, just like that. I'll have pulled the biggest Steph Landry in the history of Greene County.

But I can't let them ruin everything Grandpa's worked so hard for, either.

Because they WILL ruin it. I don't care what Todd says. That observatory is filled with super-sensitive equipment. You can't have one hundred plus dancing teenagers—not to mention a DJ—on the observation deck and not have delicate instruments get jounced around or even destroyed.

I can't let them do it. I can't let them mess up Grandpa's wedding gift for Kitty.

But I can't pull a Steph Landry, either.

WHAT AM I GOING TO DO?

Mom just asked, "What's the matter with you? You've been jumpy ever since you got here." Here being the store. Since I'm meeting Mark here to take the photos for the ads he's agreed to be in for the store.

"Nothing's the matter," I said. "Everything's fine."

What if Jason tells on me?

I asked him if he was going to. I waited for him after school, out by the student parking lot. He came running by so fast, he was practically a blur. I don't know who he was hiding from, but I don't think it was me, because when I called his name and he turned around and saw it was me, he looked relieved.

Although the whole time we were talking, his gaze was darting around, like he was looking for someone.

"What?" he said in a totally non-friendly manner.

"I just need to know," I said. "Are you going to tell?"

"Tell who about what?" Jason asked.

"You know what. About the rager tonight. Are you going to tell your parents? Or Kitty?"

"It's none of my business," Jason said. "I wasn't invited, remember?"

"I know," I said. I didn't bother telling him he was invited. He wouldn't come, anyway. "But are you going to try to stop it?"

"You know what, Steph?" Jason said. "You've made it very clear this past week that you make your own decisions, and don't need anybody's help—or opinions. You've been doing fine without me so far. So why should I interfere now?"

I felt my shoulder slump a little in relief.

"So . . . you're not going to tell?"

"I'm not going to tell," Jason said. "I'm going to trust you to make the right decision. Since you're so convinced you always do, anyway."

I stared at him. "If I don't let them in to have this party," I said, "they'll all hate me."

"Yeah," Jason said. "They will."

"But if I do let them in to have this party," I said. "You'll hate me. Assuming you don't already."

"Assuming that," Jason said. "Also assuming you care how I feel about you."

"I care," I said, stung by his implication that I didn't.

But I don't think Jason heard me, since at that moment something he saw over the top of my head caused him to go pale, and he said, "See you."

Then he took off for The B.

But when I turned around, all I saw was Becca and Jason's friend Stuckey coming out of the school.

"Wasn't that Jason you were just talking to?" Becca wanted to know when she reached me.

"Yeah," I said. Clearly, whatever had gone on between them last night, all was not wine and roses today. It was obvious Jason was doing everything he could to avoid Becca.

Only why? I mean, why, if he'd bought her—*and* kissed her?

But I didn't want to hurt her feelings. So I said, "He had some errands to run. For the wedding."

"Oh," Becca said. "Stuckey's giving me a lift home. Want to ride with us?"

I said sure. I wasn't super enthused about having to listen to the trials and triumphs of the Indiana Hoosiers basketball team. But it seemed better than the bus.

And surprisingly, Stuckey was actually able to converse about one or two topics that weren't basketball related, including scrapbooking (clearly he's been spending too much time with Becca) and tonight's rager at Grandpa's observatory.

"D'you know they're planning on having it there, Steph?" Stuckey wanted to know. "'Cause I couldn't imagine you'd know and not, you know, be trying to stop them. I've heard about Todd Rubin's ragers. He had one at this kid's house last year, on account of the kid's parents being in Aruba, and they caused ten thousand dollars' worth of damage. Someone lit the living room carpet on fire. With lighter fluid. They wrote their name in flames."

"Oh, Steph would never let them do something like that to her grandpa's observatory," Becca said knowingly. "You must have heard wrong, John."

It's funny, but I never even knew Stuckey HAD a first name, let alone that it was John.

Whatever.

Anyway, there's only one thing I can do. It took me a

while to figure it out. But there IS a way to get out of having this party AND retain my popularity.

Unfortunately, it isn't going to be easy.

But I think I've learned enough from The Book by now to pull it off.

Of course, a lot of it depends on Mark . . . .

But that's all right. Because Jason's totally wrong about him.

And Mark's going to make everything all right. I just know it.

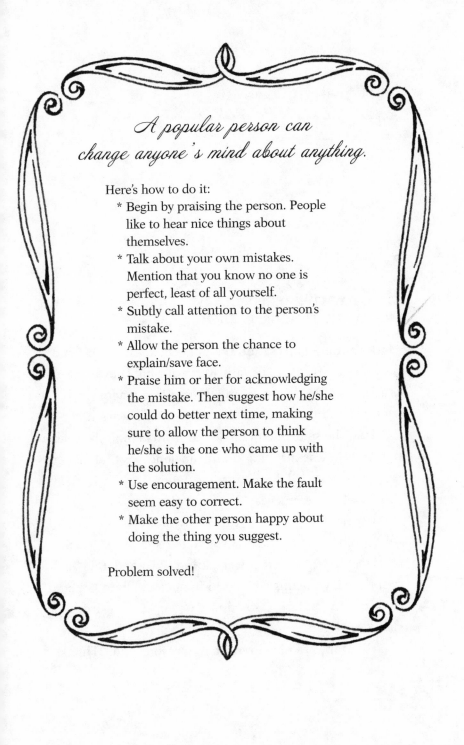

A popular person can change anyone's mind about anything.

Here's how to do it:
   * Begin by praising the person. People like to hear nice things about themselves.
   * Talk about your own mistakes. Mention that you know no one is perfect, least of all yourself.
   * Subtly call attention to the person's mistake.
   * Allow the person the chance to explain/save face.
   * Praise him or her for acknowledging the mistake. Then suggest how he/she could do better next time, making sure to allow the person to think he/she is the one who came up with the solution.
   * Use encouragement. Make the fault seem easy to correct.
   * Make the other person happy about doing the thing you suggest.

Problem solved!

 *Twenty-nine*

Mark showed up at six on the dot, exactly when he said he would. His hair was still wet from his shower after practice—and possibly from all the rain outside.

But it didn't matter. He looked hot, as always.

"Hey," he said when I came out from behind the cash register. He was dripping on the ancient A-B-C alphabet carpet. But it was hard to mind when I got a look at those golden-green eyes. "How's it going?"

"Great," I said. "Mark, this is my mom."

My mom, who'd waited around to meet Mark, despite the fact that her ankles were killing her and Dad had spent all day making his world-famous (well, in Greene County, anyway) chili for dinner, stepped forward and shook his hand.

"Hi, Mark, it's nice to meet you," Mom said. "Thanks

234

so much for agreeing to do this. You don't know how much it means to Steph. I mean, to me. I mean, to the store!"

Mark laughed along with my mom. It was kind of gratifying to know he could disconcert a late-thirty-something female—even one who was eight months pregnant with her sixth child—the same way he did her sixteen-year-old daughter.

"It's my pleasure," Mark said. "Great to meet you, too."

Leaving me to do my own thing—for once—Mom gathered up her umbrella and said good-bye.

"The weather being like it is," she said, indicating the rain streaking the display windows, "you shouldn't be bothered with too many customers. And Darren's in the back having a quick bite. Just holler if you need anything."

"Will do," I assured her. And didn't miss her mouthing, *You're right. He's cute!* on her way out.

Thank God Mark was looking at a copy of *Sports Illustrated* on the magazine rack at the time, and didn't notice.

I had the family digital camera ready to go, so I wouldn't waste any of his time. "I was going to have you pose outside, but with the rain and all, would you mind just sitting in one of the chairs over in the Popular Fiction section?" I asked.

Mark said, "No problem," and followed me.

I had him sit in the beat-up old leather armchair and

propped a copy of the latest John Grisham hardback in his hands.

"This'll be good," I said. "It'll be like, 'When he's not leading the Bloomville Fish to the State Finals, you can find Mark Finley relaxing at Courthouse Square Books.'"

Mark smiled modestly. "Well, if I actually manage to lead us to the State Finals, you mean."

"Oh, you will," I said as I started snapping away. "Lift your chin up just a little. Great. You can do anything you set your mind to. You're just that kind of person."

"Well," Mark said, smiling a little more broadly, "I don't know about that."

"It's true," I said. "You're really amazing. Not just on the field, but off it, too."

"Come on," Mark said, rolling his eyes. But he was still smiling.

"Come on, yourself," I said. "You know it's true. I wish I could be more like you."

"Oh, now," Mark said. "You're pretty great yourself. I mean, nobody else in the history of the school has ever figured out a way to raise as much money as you did in just one night."

"Oh, I'm good at money stuff," I said, snapping away with the camera. "But I'm not so hot with people. Your girlfriend, for instance. Hey, could you swing one leg over the chair arm? Yeah, like that, nice and casual-looking."

"Lauren?" Mark had stopped smiling.

"Yeah, Lauren. I mean, you probably don't know this,

but she's hated me for years."

"No way," Mark said. He was smiling again. "Lauren thinks you're great! She even told me about how you two used to play Barbies together, when you were little."

"She told you that?" I forgot about taking pictures for a second. "Did she tell you about the Super Big Gulp?"

"I might have heard something about that once or twice," Mark said. Now he looked a little uncomfortable. "But that was a long time ago, right? I know Lauren— and everybody else—is super stoked about you agreeing to let us have our party in your granddad's building."

"Yeah," I said. "Listen, why don't we take some at the counter, like you're buying something. Okay?"

"Cool," Mark said, and got up, giving me a picture-perfect view of his backside in his snug, faded jeans.

"It's just," I said, swallowing hard. "About that. The party, I mean."

"It's so great of you to agree to let us have it at the observatory," Mark said, posing at the counter with one hand on his chin. It was kind of obvious from his ease in front of the camera that he'd done this kind of thing before. The hand on his chin looked kind of Sears catalog-y. But I didn't want to say anything. "You've really saved our butts. Again."

"Right," I said. "I know. But this thing with Lauren—"

"What thing with Lauren?"

"This thing between Lauren and me—"

"That's what I keep trying to tell you," Mark said with a laugh. "There's no *thing*. I mean, not on Lauren's side.

She totally likes you, Steph. You saw how she cut Alyssa Krueger off for sending you that nasty note. If she didn't like you, why would she drop her best friend?"

To hang on to you, was what I wanted to say. But instead, I said, "I think it's a little more complicated than that. And I'm worried that—"

"Wait." Mark froze, one elbow on the counter, one hand on his hip. "I know what this is about."

I stared at him in astonishment. "You . . . do?"

"Yeah."

And that's when he did it. He reached out and took my hand—the one not holding the camera—and drew me to him.

I didn't really understand what was happening until I was standing about two inches away from him, and he had reached down and stuck a finger under my chin to tilt my face up so I was looking him in the eye.

"You're worried," Mark said, grinning down at me—that lopsided grin that made my heart hurt every time I looked at it, "about people trashing your grandfather's place tonight."

"Well," I said. Thank God. He'd finally figured it out. Without me having to tell him. "Yeah. Actually. And I was hoping maybe you could talk to Lauren and everybody and help them understand that I really can't—"

"God. You are so *nice.*"

"Um," I said. If only he knew the truth. "Not really. So do you think you could maybe—"

But before I could say another word, Mark had

leaned down and put his mouth over mine.

That's right. Mark Finley was kissing me.

On the lips, this time.

I have no idea whether or not I kissed him back. I was so surprised, I didn't know what to do. It's not like I have a lot of experience with kisses, never having been kissed before. I think I just stood there, letting him kiss me, aware of the sound of the traffic in the rain outside, and the taste of his lips—like ChapStick—and the warmth from his body.

Mark Finley is kissing me. That's what kept going through my head the whole time. *Mark Finley is kissing me.*

I know when you get kissed, fireworks are supposed to go off, or something, inside your head. You're supposed to hear an angelic choir singing in your ears, and little birds singing, like in cartoons when someone gets hit in the head with a frying pan.

So I kept my eyes closed and tried really hard to see the fireworks and hear the choir and the birds.

Mark Finley is kissing me. MARK FINLEY IS KISSING ME.

And I saw them. And heard them. Did I ever.

Finally Mark lifted his head. Looking down at me with his eyes half-hidden by his thick brown eyelashes, he said in his deep voice, "God, you're cute. Has anybody ever told you how cute you are?"

I shook my head. I don't think I could have spoken if I tried. All I could think was, *Mark Finley kissed me. Mark*

Finley thinks I'm cute.

MARK FINLEY THINKS I'M CUTE.

"I didn't think so," he said, gently stroking my tingling lips with his thumb. "Sorry about that." He meant, I knew, the kiss. "You're so cute, I guess I just couldn't resist. Forgive me?"

Forgive him? For kissing me? It was all I could do to keep from dropping to my knees and thanking him. *Mark Finley had kissed me. MARK FINLEY HAD KISSED ME.*

"I won't let anything happen to your granddad's building, Steph," he said in the same deep voice, gazing deeply into my eyes. "Don't worry."

I shook my head. Of course I wasn't going to worry. Because he's . . . well, he's Mark Finley. MARK FINLEY. And he kissed me. And he thinks I'm nice. And cute.

"You got enough pictures for now?" Mark asked me softly, still holding on to my face.

"Yes," I heard myself say. I couldn't believe my lips were even capable of forming words, they were still so tingly from his kiss.

"So is it okay if I go now? I have to pick up the keg for tonight."

"Yes," I heard myself say again. I couldn't figure out what was wrong with me. It was like I was on the outside of my body, watching this girl named Steph in a love scene with a guy named Mark. A guy named Mark who'd kissed her.

"Cool," Mark said.

And then he kissed me again, this time lightly, and just once, on the forehead.

"See you at ten," he said.

And left.

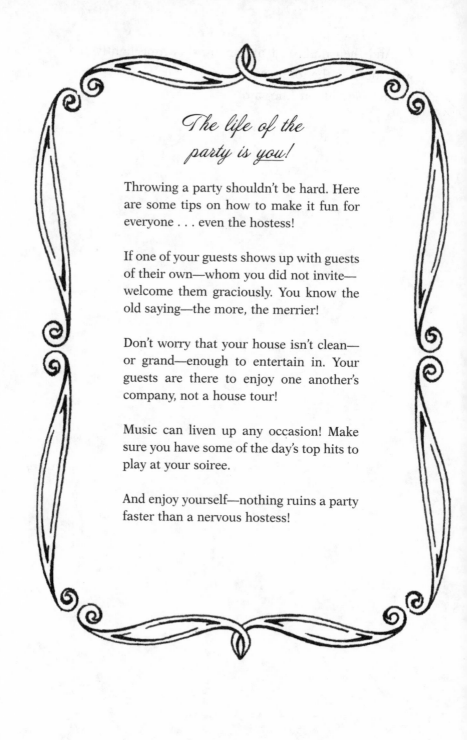

The life of the party is _you_!

Throwing a party shouldn't be hard. Here are some tips on how to make it fun for everyone . . . even the hostess!

If one of your guests shows up with guests of their own—whom you did not invite—welcome them graciously. You know the old saying—the more, the merrier!

Don't worry that your house isn't clean—or grand—enough to entertain in. Your guests are there to enjoy one another's company, not a house tour!

Music can liven up any occasion! Make sure you have some of the day's top hits to play at your soiree.

And enjoy yourself—nothing ruins a party faster than a nervous hostess!

 *Thirty*

Darren came out of the back room just as Mark was leaving. He walked up to the register and went, "Who was THAT?"

"That," I said, watching Mark head out to his four-by-four parked right in front of the store, "was Mark Finley."

"*The* Mark Finley?" Darren whistled. "And were mine eyes deceiving me, or was he just KISSING you?"

"Yeah," I said. "Yeah, he was."

"Congrats, girlfriend," Darren said. "See? You didn't believe me. I knew you'd get a date to the prom."

And with that, I was jolted forcibly back to reality.

"No," I said faintly. "He already has a girlfriend."

Darren looked shocked. "Well, that's no way for a taken man to behave. What's he thinking?"

The birds that had been twittering around inside my

head fell silent. The tingling sensation in my lips vanished.

That's right. Mark had a girlfriend. What WAS he thinking, kissing me, anyway?

He'd said I was cute, and that he couldn't resist.

But . . . he'd never seemed to have any trouble resisting me before now.

Was I really supposed to believe that he just couldn't resist me, on account of my being so cute and—what was that other thing he said? Oh yeah—"nice"?

Although, I guess, after Lauren, "nice" would probably seem like kind of a change of pace.

But I didn't imagine Lauren acted mean around Mark. I *knew* she didn't.

She blamed her meanness on other people. People like Alyssa Krueger.

Who was right. Lauren *had* figured out a way to get me back.

It was because of Lauren I was sitting here right now, listening to the rain patter against the rotunda in the big, dark, empty observatory, waiting to let everybody in.

So they could destroy it. Everything my grandfather'd worked so hard for this past year.

Because no matter what Mark promised, that's what was going to happen. Now that the tingling from his kiss had faded—and I'd been brought back to reality—I knew it. They were going to wreck the place. They were going to rip it apart.

But what about everything *I'd* worked so hard for? What about *me*? I mean, I finally got people to stop talking about me in a mean way—Don't pull a Steph Landry!—and start talking about me in a nice way . . . even kissing me, if they happened to be Mark Finley . . . and now I was just going to ditch it all because I was such a prude—such a freak—I couldn't stand the idea of a bunch of my peers having what, according to all the books and movies I'd read and seen, is a normal teen experience?

Was I *really* that nice?

I wasn't. I knew I wasn't. I mean, I rolled empty soda cans down the school auditorium floor. I sprinkled sugar on Lauren Moffat's head. I spied on my future step-grandbrother while he was naked. I was not nice. I was *not*.

So why couldn't I do this?

I *had* to do this. When they knocked on that door, I would open it. I *had* to. I was not letting them down. I was not letting things go back to the way they were. I was not pulling another Steph Landry.

Grandpa would understand. I had enough money saved up, I could probably pay for most of the damage myself. So long as it wasn't more than a few thousand dollars, since I'm a little short on account of buying Mark for the store.

But Kitty. What about Kitty? She'd be hurt.

Still. I bet she did things like this when she was my age. Grandpa never did—he was too busy working like a zillion jobs to help support his immigrant family.

But Kitty would get it. After all, she'd read The Book. She KNEW. She KNEW how hard it was.

Jason, though.

Oh, now why did I have to think about him? I wouldn't think about him. I *wouldn't*.

I just knew we could count on you, Steph.

That's what Lauren said.

And what Jason said, too. Only he meant something completely different than Lauren.

Well, what did I care what Jason thought? I mean, he was the one going around kissing Becca in his bedroom. Not like I care that he's been kissing other girls. I didn't even like him in that way.

Besides, I've been kissing other boys. Well, one other boy.

Still. Why *Becca*? Why did he have to kiss *her*? Why did he have to *buy* her?

Oh my God. There I go again.

WHY DID I EVEN CARE???? WHY DID IT BOTHER ME SO MUCH??? I mean, I should be happy for them. If, in fact, they WERE a couple.

If they were a couple, I'd throw up, just like that time at Kings Island after I got off the log flume.

No, I wouldn't. I'd be happy for them. They were my best friends. They deserved to find romantic joy.

But why did Jason have to find it with BECCA?

What was WRONG with me? Why couldn't I stop thinking about Jason? I just got kissed by MARK FINLEY. On the lips. I saw fireworks! I heard an angelic choir!

It was just . . . .

What if it wasn't just hormones? How I felt when

Jason and I leg-wrestle, I mean. Or why I couldn't stop spying on him. What if it was something more than just normal teen curiosity about the opposite sex?

It couldn't be. It COULDN'T be. I LOVED MARK FINLEY. I LOVED HIM. I—

I didn't love him. Oh, God. I didn't think I even *liked* him anymore. Because what kind of guy even *did* that? Kissed one girl while dating another? That wasn't right. That wasn't nice. That was kind of gross, actually. It was completely phony. It was the total OPPOSITE of the way The Book said popular boys should act. Popular boys weren't supposed to have a roving eye. They were supposed to be true to their steady girlfriends.

They weren't supposed to kiss girls in public.

They weren't supposed to kiss girls just to get them to do what they wanted them to do.

They were supposed to be nice. They were supposed to be funny. They were supposed to be true friends.

Like Jason.

Oh, God. What was happening to me?

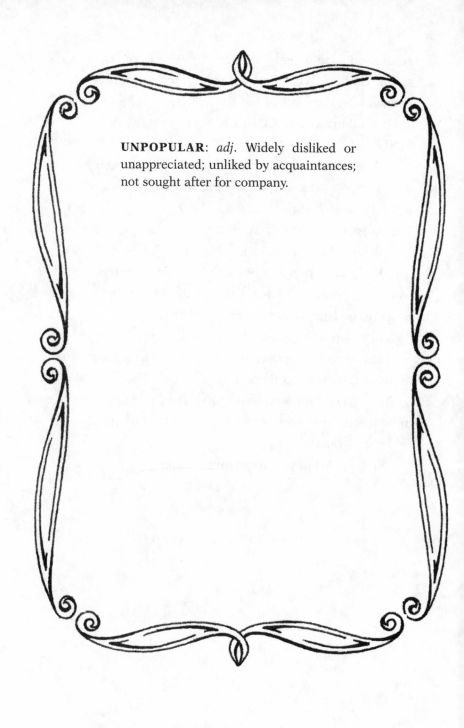

UNPOPULAR: *adj*. Widely disliked or unappreciated; unliked by acquaintances; not sought after for company.

 *Thirty-one*

I couldn't do it.

I couldn't open the door.

I wanted to. I really did. Or at least, a part of me did.

Especially when I heard Mark say, "Steph? Hey, Steph, are you in there? It's me, Mark. Open up, okay? It's raining pretty hard out here."

But then I heard Lauren say, "Oh my God, my hair. Steph! Steph, hurry up! We're getting soaked!"

And then I heard Todd say, "Man, this keg weighs a ton."

I stayed where I was by the door. I didn't get up to open it. I didn't move.

I just called, "Um, you guys?"

"Steph?" Mark thumped on the door with a fist. "Is that you? Open up, will you?"

"Yeah, about that." I took a deep breath. "I can't."

"Can't what?" Mark called. "Figure out how to open the door?"

"No," I said. "I know how to do that. I can't let you in. I'm sorry. I changed my mind. You can't have the party here."

This was met with silence. For a moment.

Then Todd yelled, "Very funny, Landry! Open the freaking door. We're getting poured on out here!"

"I don't think you understand," I called. "I'm not letting you in. You're going to have to take your party elsewhere."

More stunned silence.

Then everyone started banging on the door at once.

They tried the latch. They started kicking it (that was Lauren, I'm sure). They pounded on it.

But I didn't budge.

Not even when I heard Mark yell, in an unfriendly voice that I'd never heard him use before, "Steph! Steph, come on! Joke's over! Open up!"

Not even when I heard Lauren shout, "Steph Landry! Open the freaking door *right now!*"

I closed my eyes. *Grandpa*, I thought. *Here's my wedding present to you. I'm not going to let my so-called friends trash your observatory. Congratulations!*

As gifts went, I realized it was kind of lame. But it was the best I could do, under the circumstances.

And the truth was, I *was* making an incredible sacrifice on Grandpa's and Kitty's behalf. Even if they didn't know it.

After a while, when I didn't unlock the door, the banging stopped. And I heard Todd go, "She's blowing us off. I can't believe it. The bitch is blowing us off."

"Maybe something happened to her." That had to have been Darlene. "Steph? Are you okay?"

"I'll tell you what," Lauren said, sounding furious. "Something's *going* to happen to her on Monday. I'm going to make her wish she was never born. That's what."

So, you know. I have that to look forward to.

And Mark didn't say a word to defend me. Not a single word.

Not that I ever really thought he liked me in the first place. That's not what that kiss had been about. That kiss—I know now—wasn't because he thought I was so cute and nice that he couldn't resist me. That kiss was supposed to make me do what he wanted me to do.

Which, in this case, was open the door.

Too bad for him it didn't work. That's the problem with fireworks. They fade away pretty quickly.

They finally went away after that, Lauren complaining about what the rain was doing to her hair and Todd saying something about some freshman kid who'd said his parents were going to be in French Lick for the weekend, so maybe they could all go there. . . .

I wonder what Lauren's going to do to me on Monday.

Oh well. It doesn't really matter. It can't be any worse than what I've already been through.

That's when a voice from the darkness—from INSIDE the observatory—said my name.

And I screamed.

"Whoa," Jason said, stepping out of the shadow of the telescope pier. "It's just me."

"What are YOU doing here?" I screamed.

"Making sure you made the right decision," Jason said.

"You mean—" I couldn't believe it. My heart was pounding so hard, I thought it was going to slam right out from behind my ribs. I don't know what had surprised me more—his stepping out of the dark like that, or the fact that he was there at all. "You were here the whole time?"

Jason shrugged. "I let myself in before you got off work."

"And you just sat here," I said, feeling what I could only describe as a murderous rage toward him, "in the dark with me the whole time, and didn't say anything?"

"This was something you had to work through on your own," Jason said. "Besides. I knew you'd do the right thing."

"Oh, right," I said. I wanted to throw something at him. I really did. "And if I hadn't?"

Now Jason brandished something that he'd been holding behind his back. It was a golf club.

"I figured Big Bertha here would drive them away," he said.

For some reason, this statement drove every last ounce of rage from me. I just couldn't be mad at him anymore after seeing that stupid golf club.

It also seemed to drive away the last of the strength from my knees. I slumped against the wall, then slid all the way down until I was sitting on the brand-new industrial carpeting—the industrial carpeting I had protected from being doused with lighter fluid—with my face in my hands.

I heard, rather than saw, Jason slide down onto the floor beside me.

"Cheer up, Crazytop," he said after a few minutes. "You had a good run."

"All that work," I said to my knees. I wasn't crying. I *wasn't*. Okay. I was. "So much work. And all for nothing."

I felt Jason's hand on my back, patting me comfortingly . . . not unlike the way he'd comforted me when I'd been barfing my guts up into that trash can after we got off the log flume.

"Not for nothing," Jason said. "You were the most popular girl in school—well, practically—for a week. Not many people can say that."

"It was a total waste of time and energy," I said, still not looking up. My jeans were doing an adequate job of absorbing my tears.

"No, it wasn't," Jason said. "Because it showed you that what you thought you were missing out on wasn't actually all that great. I mean. Was it?"

"I don't know. I was working so hard to get popular—and then stay that way—I didn't actually ever have a chance to enjoy it." I lifted my head and looked at him, not even really caring anymore if he saw that I was crying. "I don't even know. I don't even know if I'd have liked it or not."

"Hey," Jason said gently, looking somewhat alarmed by my tears. "Hey. It's not worth crying over. *They're* not, anyway."

"I know," I said, dragging the back of my wrist across my eyes. They had stopped streaming, for the most part. Which was a relief. I leaned my head back and rested it against the wall behind us. "God. I can't believe they actually expected me to let them have one of their stupid ragers in here."

"Well, you had me fooled. I really thought you were going to let them in."

"I couldn't do that to Grandpa," I said. "Or Kitty."

"It wouldn't have been a very nice wedding gift," Jason agreed.

Which was funny. Since that's exactly what I'd been thinking.

"I can't believe I blew my hair straight for them," I said. "For a *week*."

"You look better with it curly, anyway," Jason said.

He was just being nice. On account of my having been crying, and all. I knew that. I *knew* he was just being nice. He didn't say it because he liked me, or anything. As anything more than a friend, anyway.

But still. Something—I have no idea what—made me ask, completely out of nowhere, "Jason, are you in love with Becca?"

Jason's back straightened away from the wall as if

he'd been electrocuted.

"*What?*" He blinked at me in the semidarkness. "What gave you *that* idea?"

"Well," I said, realizing, belatedly, the grave I'd dug for myself. What was I doing? *What was I doing?* And why on God's green earth was I doing it? "You did buy her—"

"I *told* you why I did that," Jason said. "Because I didn't want her to feel bad."

"Right." It was like my mouth was disconnected from the rest of my body, or something, and just going off on its own crazy mission all by itself. "Because you love her."

"Do I have to remind you what she did to my shoes?" He held up one massive foot for me to see that the soles of his high tops were still covered with purple stars and unicorns.

I stared at them. Jason put his foot down.

"Geesh," he said.

But it didn't do any good. My mouth just kept going, despite my brain—and heart—going, *Shut up. Shut up. Shut up.*

"If you don't love her, then why"—*Shut up. Shut up. Shut up*—"did you kiss her in your room last night?"

SHUT UP. Oh my God. I am the stupidest human being on the face of the planet.

Jason's mouth fell open. "How did you—"

"I can see into your room from our bathroom," I said fast. Suddenly, my brain decided to pitch in and help my mouth out. Better late than never, I guess. "Not that I ever look. Really. Much. It's just that last night, I was in there, and I happened to sort of look out, and I saw her—you—both of you. And you were kissing."

Jason shut his mouth. He wasn't smiling.

"Becca didn't tell you?" he asked finally.

"She didn't say a word," I said. "And I didn't want to bring it up. Because—"

"Because you didn't want her to accuse you of being a peeping Tom."

Oh, God. But he was right. He was right. I was going to confession on Monday. I was going to tell Father Chuck everything.

And it wouldn't matter if he told my mom, because Jason already knows, now.

"I wasn't peeping," I said. "Exactly. I mean, Pete saw you, too—"

"Oh, great! Your brother knows?"

I was beginning to feel uncomfortably warm. I had no idea why. The observatory has really great air-conditioning.

"Yes, Pete knows," I said. "I mean, the two of you were going at it right there in the window." *Going at it* was a strong term to use. I have no idea where it came from. "If you had bothered to lower the blinds—"

"I don't have blinds in there yet," Jason said. "But you can bet I'll be getting them now. What else have you seen me doing in there?"

Naked push-ups, I wanted to say. This time, however,

my mouth actually did what my brain told it to, and so instead I said, "Nothing. I swear." Forgive me, Father, for I have sinned. It's been—how long since my last confession? Well, it doesn't matter, because there's this one thing I didn't tell you, and it's been going on for a few months now, and—

Oh, whatever. God will understand.

"So come on," I said to Jason. Because my chest was feeling tight. I had to know. I just had to. "What's going on with you and Becca?"

"Aw, geez." Jason slumped back against the wall, his eyes closed. "Nothing, all right? She got the wrong idea—exactly like you did—about my buying her stupid scrapbook mentor thing. She came over—just showed up—and my dad let her in, because, well, he's my dad. I was just lying there, reading, when she came walking in, and she was all . . . you know."

I stared at his profile. His nose looked bigger and more crooked than ever. And for some reason, I wanted to lean over and kiss it.

I had gone mental. Lauren Moffat and those guys had finally driven me completely insane. Since when did I go around, wanting to kiss Jason Hollenbach's nose?

"No," I said. "I don't know. Becca was all . . . what?"

"All lovey-dovey," Jason said, finally turning his head to look at me. "She thinks—Jesus. She thinks I'm The One. *Her* One. Her soul mate. And for the record, *she* kissed *me*. Not the other way around. I had to tell her—well, I had to tell her she was barking up the wrong tree.

I'm not the guy for her. No matter what she might think."

I felt a wave of relief wash over me that was so intense, I actually felt physically weak from it.

Why? *Why* did I feel relieved at hearing Jason say he wasn't the guy for Becca?

Why did hearing that *she* had kissed *him*, and not the other way around, make that angelic choir—the one I'd willed myself to hear when Mark Finley kissed me, and that I knew now hadn't been the real thing . . . not at all— suddenly spring to life inside my head?

"Oh," I said. It was hard to hear myself talk above all the singing.

"Why do you think I was hiding out in the library today?" Jason asked. "I was trying to avoid her."

"Oh," I said again. Little birds were tweeting in my ears, and no one was even kissing me. It was crazy. But it was true.

"It's all Stuckey's fault," Jason grumbled.

"Stuckey?"

"Yeah. He was the one who kept telling me to buy her."

"Stuckey?" I was sure I hadn't heard him right, what with all the birds and singing.

"Yeah. He'd have bought her himself. Only he didn't have any money."

"Stuckey likes Becca?" I asked. The choir burst into the "Hallelujah" chorus. Especially when I thought about how Stuckey had been talking about scrapbooking the whole way home from school in his car today. And that tour of Assembly Hall he'd offered to give Becca.

"I guess," Jason said. "How should I know?"

"Well, wouldn't he have told you?"

Jason shot me a very sarcastic look. Ordinarily, when Jason does this, I shoot him a sarcastic look right back. This time, all I could think about was how I wanted to kiss his nose.

"Guys don't talk about that kind of thing with each other," he informed me.

"Oh," I said.

"Besides," Jason said, "you bought Mark Finley. Does that mean you're in love with him?"

"Obviously not," I said. I didn't think it was necessary to mention that Mark and I had kissed, just as Jason and Becca had. Also that I would much rather have been kissing Jason. "I mean, you saw me not letting him in just now, right?"

"Well," Jason said, "you could have fooled me."

"What's that supposed to mean?" The chorus and birds shut up abruptly.

"Just that for someone who claims not to have been in love with a guy, you gave an awfully good imitation of it."

I thought about that. It was a fair statement, actually, under the circumstances. Mark's gold-green eyes . . . his deep voice . . . the way his butt looked in his jeans. These were all very compelling images.

But that, I realized, suddenly, is all they were. Images. What did I know about Mark the person? Nothing.

Nothing except what Jason had said . . . that he was a mindless clone who just did whatever his girlfriend—or anyone, it seemed—told him to. He was so dumb, he didn't even know Lauren was the one who'd written me that note. He actually believed her when she told him she liked me. He couldn't see that his own girlfriend was the hugest phony in the whole world.

And the truth was, he was a bit of a phony himself. I mean, kissing me, then telling me he'd done it because he couldn't resist my cute niceness? When really he'd done it to get me to open the door.

So why had I ever thought I liked him?

I knew why. I knew perfectly well why, and it wasn't a pleasant thought.

Because he was popular.

But that was before, I told myself. Before I knew what being popular really meant. At least at Bloomville High School.

And that was not being yourself.

"Haven't you ever thought you might be in love with someone," I asked Jason, "then figured out you were wrong?"

"No," Jason said shortly.

"Ever? What about Kirsten?"

"I don't love Kirsten," Jason said, looking down at his shoes and not at me.

"Come on. Not even a little? Are you saying all those haikus in her honor were just for fun?"

"Exactly," Jason said, leaning forward to scrub ineffectively at one of the unicorns with his thumb. "Look, we'd better go. The wedding's tomorrow, remember. We gotta get up early to get ready for it."

But I put out a hand to stop him before he could get all the way up.

"Seriously," I said, craning my neck to look up at him. "Are you saying you've *never* been in love? With anybody?"

Jason sank back against the wall with a sigh.

Then, still not looking at me, he said, "Remember in the fifth grade when I kept pinching you, and stuff, and you said your grandpa said I was doing it because I was a little bit in love with you?"

"Do I," I said with a laugh. "You didn't talk to me for like a year after that. Until after the Super Big Gulp thing."

"That's because your grandpa was wrong."

"Um, that was fairly obvious, given the whole silent treatment."

"I wasn't a *little bit* in love with you," Jason said, finally looking at me. And his eyes, I noticed, for the first time that night, were the same color blue as Sirius, the dog star. "I was a *lot* in love with you. And I didn't know how to handle it. I still don't."

I could barely hear him on account of the choir and the birds starting up again inside my head. It was like Handel's *Messiah* and a trip to Six Flags Wild Safari all rolled into one.

"Wait," I heard myself—barely—say. "Did you just say—"

And a million crazy thoughts flooded my head. I remembered that day in fifth grade, when I'd said the thing about him being a little bit in love with me, and how red his face had gotten—on account of rage, I'd thought then. I remembered his ignoring me, and how lonely and miserable I'd been during that time—right up until the day I spilled that stupid drink on Lauren, and Lauren and all of her friends invented the Don't Pull a Steph thing and wouldn't sit by me in the cafeteria, and made fun of anyone who did. So no one did.

No one except Jason, who put his tray down next to mine and started telling me about an episode of *The Simpsons* he'd seen the night before, as if there'd never been a rift between us in the first place, and as if people in the hallways didn't accuse him of Pulling a Steph.

But he didn't care.

I remembered all those nights on The Wall, making each other laugh until I thought I'd wet my pants (again), mocking the popular crowd, and eating Blizzerds. And those nights on The Hill, lying in the cool green grass, gazing up at the massive night sky, Jason pointing out constellations and musing about the possibility of life on other planets, and wondering what we'd do if one of those meteors turned out to be an alien spacecraft and landed right next to us.

And I thought about how many nights I'd said good night to him, after spending the entire day together at the lake or the movies, and then gone inside my house, only to sit in the dark and watch him in his room, as if I just couldn't get enough. Of Jason.

Jason. *Jason.*

God. I must be the stupidest girl on the entire *planet.*

"Did you really just say you're in love with me?" I asked him, just to be sure. Because I was afraid it had all been a dream and that I was going to wake up all alone in my room.

Jason closed his mouth. Then he opened it again and said, "Well. I guess I did."

And that's when I kissed him.

"Avoid popularity if
you would have peace."
—Abraham Lincoln

 *Thirty-two*

SATURDAY, SEPTEMBER 2

He loves me.

He loves me.

He loves me.

He says he always has. He says all that stuff he said before, about not believing in soul mates and how people shouldn't fall in love in high school, was just to try to talk himself into not loving me so much, since he didn't think I felt the same way about him. He had no idea that, just like he's always loved me, I've always loved him.

Even if I didn't exactly realize it until a little while ago.

Oh well. No one's perfect.

But it's okay. I've totally made up for lost time. We've been kissing so much, in fact, my lips feel a little chapped. But in a good way.

I've told him everything—and I do mean *everything*:

about my thinking he got hot while he was in Europe (he claims he's thought I was hot since the second grade); about my spying on him (He didn't get mad. In fact, I think he was kind of flattered. Although he says he's getting blinds tomorrow); about how jealous I was when I thought he loved Becca ("Becca?" he choked. "Oh, God!"); about how jealous I was when I thought he had a crush on Kirsten, to the point where the sight of her elbows actually sickened me ("Her *elbows*?" he echoed incredulously); I even told him about the time I wore his Batman underwear. And how I kind of liked it.

I saved The Book for last. We had a good laugh over that one.

"Wait," Jason said. "Let me get this straight. You found some old book of my grandma's, and you thought it was your ticket to popularity?"

"Well," I said. We were still sitting in the same spot where we'd first kissed. Only now my head was resting on his chest. It felt really good there, as if Jason's chest had been made to fit the exact shape of my head. "It worked, didn't it?"

When I paraphrased some of the choice chapters, he laughed so hard my head started jiggling up and down, so I had to sit up.

"You laugh," I said. "But that book taught me a lot."

"Oh, right," Jason said. "How to act like a big phony and drive all your friends insane."

"No," I said. "How to be the best you that you can be."

"You already were the best you that you could be,"

Jason said, pulling me back down against him. "You didn't need any book to help you with that."

"I did," I said to his shirt. "Because if it weren't for the book, I'd never have tried to be popular, and if I'd never tried to be popular, I'd never have realized how I really feel about you." And I'd never have discovered that *I'm* the girl Stuckey was saying Jason has always secretly been in love with.

"Well," Jason said, wrapping his arms around me more tightly than ever, "then we better take that book and get it bronzed."

He was joking, but I actually think he's right. I owe everything to that book. Even if, ultimately, I didn't actually get to be popular.

I got something much, much better, instead.

"Whatever is popular is wrong."
—Oscar Wilde

Thirty-three

SATURDAY, SEPTEMBER 2, 9 A.M.

I woke up to the sound of someone yelling my name.

When I lifted my head, I had no idea where I was. Also why my neck was so stiff.

Then I rolled over and saw Jason, sleeping next to me.

Then I sat up so fast, I actually caused my neck—stiff from sleeping on the industrial carpeting—to make a cracking sound.

"Jason," I said, poking him. "Jason, wake up. I think we're in big trouble."

Because of course we'd stayed up so late talking—and kissing—we'd fallen asleep. In the observatory. On the floor of the observation deck, under the rotunda.

I was so, so dead. Even though of course we hadn't actually *done* anything. Besides kiss.

But who was going to believe that?

My grandpa, it turns out. When he came in a second

later, took one look at us, and called back over his shoulder, "It's all right, Margaret. They're in here."

The next thing Jason and I knew, my mom and Grandpa were standing over us, all yelling at the same time.

"How *could* you?" my mom was shrieking at me. "Do you have any idea how worried we've been? Why didn't you call? And Jason—your father's been checking hospital emergency rooms all over Indiana all night long. He thought you'd been in an accident!"

"You really ought to have telephoned," Grandpa said. "What in the Sam Hill are you two doing here?"

"I think it's pretty obvious what they were doing here, Dad," Mom said bitterly. Which was totally unfair, considering we both still had all our clothes on.

"We just fell asleep," Jason said. "Honest. We were talking, and—"

"But why didn't you call?" Mom wanted to know. "Do you have any idea how out of our minds with worry we've been?"

"We just forgot," I said. I did feel horrendously guilty. I couldn't believe I hadn't thought to call.

But I couldn't very well sit there and go, *We were just way too busy making out to think about calling home, Mom.*

"Well, you, young lady, are grounded," my mom announced, pulling me to my feet with surprising strength for a woman so far advanced in her pregnancy. "Maybe that will teach you not to *forget* to call."

"Your parents are going to be very disappointed in you, son," was all Grandpa had to say to Jason, who never gets punished for anything. His parents just get disappointed in him. "Your poor grandmother's been up all night, and today is her wedding day!"

Grandpa and Kitty's wedding! I'd totally forgotten!

"Oh, Gramps," I said. "I'm so sorry. We just didn't check the time."

"But what were you *doing* here?" my mom wanted to know.

I sucked in my breath, prepared to confess all. Well, not the making out all night with Jason part. But the part about Mark Finley and the rager. Because, as long as I'd come clean with Jason, I figured I'd better come clean with everybody else, too.

But before I got the chance to, Jason stepped forward and said, "We were just looking at the stars. And I guess we fell asleep."

"The stars?" My mom looked totally confused. Then she seemed to remember we were standing in an observatory. "Oh. Well."

"See, Margaret?" Grandpa said. "I told you. They're fine. They were just looking at the stars. And they fell asleep. No harm done." Then, to my surprise, Grandpa put an arm around Mom's shoulders.

What was even more surprising was that she actually *let* him.

"I told you this observatory was a good idea," Grandpa said. "Give the kids in this town something to do at night, instead of getting into trouble."

Jason and I exchanged glances. Grandpa had no idea how close his observatory had come to getting a LOT of kids in this town into trouble.

My mom shook her head, then lifted trembling fingers to her temples. "God, I wish I could have a drink," she said to her belly.

"Well, maybe at the wedding reception, someone'll slip you a glass of champagne," Gramps said, giving her a squeeze.

This was even more shocking than the fact that she was letting him hug her. Mom was coming to his wedding after all? They were on speaking terms again? When had *this* happened?

"Oh, Dad," Mom said. She threw him an aggravated look.

But underneath the aggravation, I saw a hint—just a hint—of affection.

Then the next second, the look was gone, and she was glaring. At *me*.

"Well, come on, young lady," she said. "Get in the car. I'm taking you home."

"Okay," I said, throwing Grandpa a perplexed look. What was going on? How had he gotten back on Mom's good side?

Grandpa saw my look. I know he did.

But he just winked, then put his arm around Jason.

"Hey, kid," I heard him say as he and Jason followed us out of the building. "Ever ride in a Rolls before?"

"Avoid popularity;
it has many snares,
and no real benefit."
—William Penn

# Thirty-four

The wedding was beautiful. The rain cooled things off, so it was actually pleasant to be outdoors for a change. The sun shined in a cloudless blue sky—the same color as Jason's (and Kitty's) eyes—making it one of those glorious late summer, early autumn days that's just perfect for apple-picking or boating on the lake.

Or getting married next to one.

The bride certainly didn't look like a woman who'd been up all night, worrying over the whereabouts of her grandson. She glowed in a beaded ivory evening dress, looking elegant and yet relaxed at the same time. Grandpa, seeing her in her wedding finery, actually got a little misty-eyed.

He told me later it was because he'd got something in his eye. But I know the truth.

Just like he knows the truth about what Jason and I

were really doing in the observatory. Well, not the part about the rager. But the part about not looking at the stars.

But that's okay. Everything else went great. Mom and Dad—to everyone's surprise but Grandpa's—did show up, with Sara in tow. Kitty was so happy to see them, she started to cry. Then my mom, seeing that Kitty was crying, started crying, too. Then the two of them hugged, crying, which caused Sara to cry, because no one was paying any attention to her.

Meanwhile, Robbie didn't lose the rings, and Jason looked so incredibly handsome in his tux, I thought *I* was going to cry. Although that might have been due to lack of sleep.

I even avoided a falling-out with Becca over the guy she had a crush on turning out to be MY One instead of hers. That's because Becca had her new One at her side to keep her occupied. The Stuckeys and the Taylors weren't even assigned to the same tables, but Becca had obviously done a little bit of pre-reception switching of the place cards, since when I walked into the dining room, there she and John were, smooching over the salad course.

I walked right up to them and went, "Excuse me. Becca, can I have a word?"

She followed me, blushing, over to the champagne fountain.

"It's not what you think," she said to me right away.

"How do you even know what I'm thinking?" I asked.

Because the truth was, that what I was thinking was "How am I going to explain to her about Jason and me?"

"I'm not on the rebound," Becca said. "I feel totally different about John than I did about Jason. And not just because John actually likes me back. This is it, Steph. This is the real thing."

"I wasn't going to accuse you of being on the rebound," I said. "I was just going to say I'm happy for you."

"Oh." Then Becca beamed at me. "Well, thanks. I just wish you could meet Your One, too. Hey . . . I know you're going to think this sounds crazy, but have you ever thought of asking Jason out?"

I just stared at her.

"I'm serious," Becca said. "Because I think he likes you. The other night—well, I didn't tell you this, because it's sort of embarrassing. But after he bid on me—you know, at the auction—I went over to his place and I sort of . . . well, I told him I liked him. Don't laugh."

"I'm not laughing," I said.

"Thanks. Anyway, that was before I figured out that I really love Stuckey. But, anyway, Jason said he was sorry, but that he didn't feel the same way about me. And I asked him if it was because of the whole not-believing-in-soul-mates thing, and he said he'd actually lied when he'd said that. He told me he thought he'd found his soul mate already, but that he didn't think she liked him back, because she's in love with a popular boy . . . and, well, call me crazy, but I couldn't help wondering if maybe

Jason was thinking about you."

"Wow," I said. And even though I already knew Becca was right, and that it HAD been me Jason was talking about, I felt a little thrill of pleasure, just hearing it all over again. That's how far gone I was. "Thanks for telling me. I will definitely think about asking him out."

"You should," Becca said. "Because, you know, I asked John, and he said it's possible—just possible—that the person Jason is secretly in love with is you. And if it is, then we could double date! Me and John, and you and Jason! Wouldn't that be fun?"

I said I couldn't think of anything more fun.

After all the toasts, the bride and groom danced their first dance—to "I've Got a Crush on You," Grandpa's favorite Frank Sinatra tune—then danced with their children, and finally their grandchildren. That was when I finally got the chance to ask Grandpa how he'd gotten Mom to forgive him for the Super Sav-Mart and come to his wedding.

"Well," he said as he moved me around the dance floor in time to "Embraceable You," "I'm sorry to say I took advantage of the fact that she was a woman in a vulnerable state—eight months pregnant, deathly worried over the whereabouts of her eldest child, and convinced she's in severe financial trouble—and put my foot down. I told her I've bought the Hoosier Sweet Shoppe, and am putting a café in there, and knocking the wall between her place and mine down, and she can either let go and like it, or learn to live with it. Your dad did a pretty good job of convincing her to let go and like it."

"Grandpa!" I beamed up at him. "That's so great!"

"We've still got a ways to go toward patching things up," Grandpa said, nodding in the direction of Mom and Kitty, who were still chatting away. "But it's a good start."

"Between the new café," I said, "and the ads we're going to run, featuring Mark Finley, I bet the bookstore will be outselling Super Sav-Mart in no time."

"That's the plan," Grandpa said. "Now why don't you tell me what you and Jason were *really* doing at the observatory last night. And don't say stargazing, young lady, since—though your mother doesn't seem to remember, I do—it was pouring rain all night. You couldn't have seen a thing through that telescope."

Oops.

So I told Grandpa. Not about the rager. But about me and Jason. I figured everybody was going to figure it out sooner or later anyway. Especially since Jason had already asked me for the next dance, and neither of us was a very good dancer, so it was going to be sort of obvious we were just standing there next to each other in order to be standing there next to each other.

Grandpa heard it all with raised eyebrows. He likes Jason, so it wasn't like I was worried he was going to disapprove. But I did want him to be happy for me—as happy for me as I was for him.

"Well, well, well," was all he said, when I was through. "And what's he planning on studying in college?"

"I don't know, Gramps," I said with a laugh. "We have a ways to go before college."

"Just make sure it's astronomy," Grandpa said. "I don't want to have spent all that money on that building for nothing."

I assured Grandpa I'd do what I could.

Then later, when I went to the ladies' room, I ran into Kitty, who was reapplying her eyeliner, which was smudged on account of all the crying she'd done with my mother. I knew she knew—about me and Jason—the minute she saw my reflection in the mirror and spun around to take my hand.

"Stephanie," she said excitedly, "I'm so happy for you both. I always wondered . . . but I thought you'd been friends for too long for it to ever work."

"Oh, it's working," I assured her. And then, because she was my new grandma—well, step-grandma—I felt like I could add, "And, you know, a lot of it's really because of your book."

"My book?" Kitty looked blank.

"You know, that book you let me have," I reminded her. "The one in that box I found in your attic, when we were cleaning up for Jason to move his stuff up there? That book on how to be popular? I, um. I sort of took its advice. I figured if it worked for you, it could work for me. Things didn't turn out quite the way I'd planned— but now I'm glad. And it's all because of you. Well, your book."

"A book on how to be popular?" Kitty looked perplexed

for a moment. Then her face brightened. "Oh my goodness. That old thing? Someone gave that to me as a joke.
I never actually *read* it."

I didn't know quite what to say to that. So I said the
only thing I could think of. Which was, "Oh."

"Well." Kitty adjusted her short, chic veil. "How do I
look?"

"Beautiful," I said truthfully.

"Thank you, my dear," Kitty said. "I was just thinking
the same thing about you. Well, I have to get back out
there. Your mother and I are finally getting properly
acquainted, and I don't want to keep her waiting." She
patted me on the cheek before she left, beaming.

Jason was waiting for me when I got back to the
dance floor.

"Hey," he said. "Looks like things are winding down
here. I could use a cup of coffee. How about you?"

"Nice idea," I said. "But I'm grounded, remember?"

"I don't think your mom's going to remember." I
looked in the direction he was pointing. Mom and Kitty
were chatting animatedly, while my dad sat there with a
sleeping Sara in his arms, looking bored.

And when I went up to them and said, "Um, hey. Is it
okay if I go for a coffee with Jason? I swear I'll come
right home afterward," Mom just said, "Call if you're
going to be out after ten," and went right back to chatting.

Wow. It's amazing what a little wedding can do to
improve everyone's spirits.

"Popularity is the easiest
thing in the world to gain,
and the hardest thing to hold."
—Will Rogers

 *Thirty-five*

SATURDAY, SEPTEMBER 2, 11 P.M.

I sort of forgot about the whole rager thing until Jason and I were getting ready to head into the Coffee Pot—feeling nice and happy from the wedding and being so in love with each other and all of that—and we bumped right into Mark Finley and Lauren Moffat, heading toward the ATM.

Alyssa Krueger was with them. So was Sean de Marco, Todd Rubin, and Darlene Staggs.

The whole gang, together again.

Only nobody seemed very happy about it. At least, not about seeing me.

"Well, well, well," Lauren said with a sneer. "If it isn't Steph Landry, world's biggest party *wrecker*."

And the happiness I'd been feeling all day, on account of Jason loving me, sort of dimmed. Just a little.

That's how big a damper Lauren Moffat can be on a

girl. Even a girl newly in love.

"Come on, Lauren," Jason said. "Lay off her. You guys would have trashed the place, and you know it."

"Um, was I talking to you, Big Nose?" Lauren asked.

Which was when something inside of me snapped. Just like that. It was like suddenly I was transported back to Bloomville Middle School and the very first time Lauren ever accused me of Pulling a Steph.

Only instead of being a meek little twelve-year-old who just stood there and took it, I was a strong, independent sixteen-year-old who didn't have time for Lauren and her drama.

"You know what, Lauren?" I said, taking a step toward her.

And I guess she must have sensed that something in me had snapped, because she took a hasty step back, like she thought I was going to hit her, or something. As if she was even worth the lawsuit her dad would've slapped on me.

"I'm sick of you," I went on, my face right up in hers. "You and all your phony B.S." Only I didn't just say the initials. "I made *one* mistake—I spilled a drink on you— for which I apologized profusely AND got you a new skirt, and you *still* had to hold it against me. For FIVE years. Not just hold it against me, but made sure everybody else in school did, too. And now you want to throw down with me again? Fine. But I'm warning you, that this time? You better bring it. Because there are a lot more Steph Landrys in the world—people who've made fools of themselves in public, people who don't have every hair perfectly in place all the time, people who don't have rich parents who'll buy them a new car every year—than there are stuck-up beauty queens like you. And if you don't learn to get along with us, eventually you're going to find yourself leading a very, very lonely existence."

I was staring right up into Lauren's eyes. And so I saw it. It was only there for an instant. But it was definitely there.

A flicker of fear.

Then she tossed her long golden hair and said, "God, get off me, beeyotch. If I'm such a terrible person, how come I'm the one here with so many friends, while you're here with"—her gaze raked Jason up and down—"*that*?"

Okay, now I was going to hit her. For what she'd said about Jason.

But before I could leap at her throat, Darlene stepped between us, saying, "Actually, Steph, I'm glad we ran into each other. There's a new Brittany Murphy in town, and I was wondering if you wanted to see it with me tomorrow."

I stared at Darlene. So did Lauren. So did Alyssa and Mark and Sean and Todd. But then Todd always stares at Darlene, so this wasn't particularly unusual.

"Um," I said, totally confused about what was going on. "Yeah. Sure. I'd be happy to."

"Darlene," Lauren said in an icy voice. "What are you *doing*?"

"Making plans to go see a movie with a friend," Darlene replied. There was nothing ditzy in her tone at all. "Do you mind?"

Lauren's heavily mascara-ed eyes narrowed.

But before Lauren could say anything, Alyssa took a step away from her, until she was standing next to me.

"Hey," Alyssa said. "Is it okay if I come with you guys, too?"

Darlene looked at me. I looked back at Darlene.

And realized this wasn't about going to the movies.

Well, it was. But it sort of wasn't, at the same time.

"Sure," I said to Alyssa. "You can come." Then, remembering the advice from The Book, added, "The more the merrier."

"Great," Alyssa said. And smiled at me. It was the first smile I'd seen on her face in days.

"Okay," Lauren said, sounding impatient. "What's going on here? Have you all been sniffing glue?"

Darlene ignored her. "What are you guys doing now?" she asked me and Jason.

"Um," Jason said, pointing at the door to the Coffee Pot. "We were going to get coffee. . . ."

"Oh, yum," Darlene said. "I could totally use some coffee. How about you, Alyssa?"

"I love coffee," Alyssa said. "Mind if we join you?"

Jason looked at me with his eyebrows raised. I shrugged.

"Um," Jason said. "Sure?"

"Great!" Alyssa pushed open the door to the Coffee

Pot—an establishment she'd surely never set foot inside before in her life—and went in, Darlene following close behind. . . .

Although Darlene turned on the threshold to look back at Sean and Todd.

"Are you coming?" she asked him. "Or not?"

Todd looked from Darlene to Mark, and then back again. Then he said to Mark, with a shrug, "Sorry, man." Then he and Sean followed Darlene inside.

Jason and I looked at each other. Then he opened the door for me and said, "After you."

I went in. Darlene and Alyssa and Sean and Todd had found a table over by the window. They waved at us— like we wouldn't have been able to find them, given that they were the only people in the whole place, besides Kirsten, who said, "Oh, hello! The usual?" to us.

"The usual," Jason said. And then added, "And we're with them," and pointed at the table Darlene had seized.

Kirsten raised her eyebrows. "New friends?" she asked, looking impressed. "And you tried to tell me you are not popular!"

Then she went over to take their order. Just like that.

Just like that, she assumed we were just being modest about not being popular.

Which is when I said to Jason, "Hang on a minute." And ran back outside.

"Hey," I said to Lauren and Mark, who were walking slowly away.

Lauren spun around. And I saw something I'd never

expected to see in my life.

She was crying.

"*What?*" she demanded.

"I was just—" I swallowed. "I just wanted to know if you guys wanted to join us."

"Are you completely retar—"

But before Lauren could finish, Mark put an arm around her shoulders and said, "Thanks, Steph. We'd love to."

"But—" Lauren yelped.

But I guess Mark had given her a really good squeeze, since all she said was, "Whatever."

And they followed me into the Pot.

Which just goes to show, no matter what anybody else says—the advice in The Book?

It really does work.

 *Thirty-six*

SUNDAY, SEPTEMBER 3, 12 A.M.

Later that night, I went into the bathroom and looked out the window—entirely out of force of habit. I was NOT spying on him—to see what Jason was doing.

He had covered his windows with giant strips of butcher paper.

But it was okay. Because on them, he'd written in glow-in-the-dark stick-on stars:

Good night, Crazytop.

AND SOCIAL ENGAGEMENTS ENTHUSIASM IS CONTAGIOUS, AND SOON YOU WILL BE, TOO
ERE IS NO SUCH THING AS HAVING TOO MANY FRIENDS ARRIVE PROMPTLY FOR PARTIE
O HONEST, NOT PHONY OR FAKE HAVE CONFIDENCE EMPATHIZE BE CHEERFUL AND OU
NFIDENCE NOBODY LIKES A KNOW-IT-ALL THERE IS NO SUCH THING AS HAVING TOO MA
Y, DON'T BE A SNOB NOBODY LIKES A KNOW IT-ALL THERE ARRIVE PROMPTLY FOR PARTI
BE RESPECTFUL AND POLITE NEVER GOSSIP OR SAY SPITEFUL THINGS ABOUT OTHERS N
GIOUS, AND SOON YOU WILL BE, TOO! LIVE WITH PURPOSE BE DIRECT AND HONEST, NO
K OTHERS DON'T BE SHY DON'T BE A SNOB NOT PHONY OR FAKE HAVE CONFIDENCE NO
FAKE HAVE CONFIDENCE NEVER TEASE OR MOCK OTHERS DON'T BE SHY DON'T BE A SN
CHEERFUL AND OUTGOING THINK OF THE FEELINGS OF OTHERS FIRST BE RESPECTFUL A
OMPTLY FOR PARTIES AND SOCIAL ENGAGEMENTS ENTHUSIASM IS CONTAGIOUS, AND SO
NFIDENCE EMPATHIZE BE CHEERFUL AND OUTGOING DON'T BE A SNOB THINK OF THE
AS HAVING TOO MANY FRIENDS ARRIVE PROMPTLY FOR PARTIES AND SOCIAL ENGAGEM
VE WITH PURPOSE BE DIRECT AND HONEST, NOT PHONY OR FAKE HAVE CONFIDENCE E
A SNOB WHO DOESN'T LOVE BEING AROUND A GENUINELY HAPPY, CHEERFUL PERSON
SIP OR SAY SPITEFUL THINGS ABOUT OTHERS NEVER SHOW OFF NEVER TEASE OR MOCK
O LISTENER ARRIVE PROMPTLY FOR PARTIES AND SOCIAL ENGAGEMENTS LIVE WITH PU
ERFUL AND OUTGOING DON'T BE SHY NEVER SHOW OFF NEVER TEASE OR MOCK OTHERS
ECTFUL AND POLITE EMPATHIZE THERE IS NO SUCH THING AS HAVING TOO MANY FRIE
AND SOCIAL ENGAGEMENTS ENTHUSIASM IS CONTAGIOUS, AND SOON YOU WILL BE, TOO
G THINK OF THE FEELINGS OF OTHERS FIRST BE RESPECTFUL AND POLITE NEVER GOSS
DS ARRIVE PROMPTLY FOR PARTIES AND SOCIAL ENGAGEMENTS ENTHUSIASM IS CONTA
D SOCIAL ENGAGEMENTS ?NO ONE! ALWAYS SMILE BE A GOOD LISTENER LIVE WITH PU
HOW OFF NEVER TEASE OR MOCK OTHERS DON'T BE SHY DON'T BE A SNOB NOBODY LI
NY OR FAKE HAVE CONFIDENCE EMPATHIZE BE CHEERFUL AND OUTGOING THINK OF T
KES A KNOW-IT-ALL THERE IS NO SUCH THING AS HAVING TOO MANY FRIENDS ARRIVE P
DY LIKES A KNOW-IT-ALL THERE ARRIVE PROMPTLY FOR PARTIES AND SOCIAL ENGAGE
OLITE NEVER GOSSIP OR SAY SPITEFUL THINGS ABOUT OTHERS NEVER SHOW OFF NEVE
WILL BE, TOO! BE RESPECTFUL AND POLITE WHO DOESN'T LOVE BEING AROUND A GEN
NGS OF OTHERS FIRST BE RESPECTFUL AND POLITE NEVER GOSSIP OR SAY SPITEFUL T
IS ENTHUSIASM IS CONTAGIOUS, AND SOON YOU WILL BE, TOO! WHO DOESN'T LOVE BE
E EMPATHIZE BE CHEERFUL AND OUTGOING DON'T BE SHY THINK OF THE FEELINGS OF
NO ONE! ALWAYS SMILE BE A GOOD LISTENER LIVE WITH PURPOSE BE DIRECT AND HO
OFF NEVER TEASE OR MOCK OTHERS DON'T BE SHY DON'T BE A SNOB NOBODY LIKES A
IVE PROMPTLY FOR PARTIES AND SOCIAL ENGAGEMENTS CHEERFUL PERSON NO ONE
OLITE NEVER GOSSIP OR SAY SPITEFUL THINGS ABOUT NEVER SHOW OFF NEVER TEASE
NFIDENCE EMPATHIZE BE CHEERFUL AND OUTGOING THINK OF THE FEELINGS FIRST B
WHO DOESN'T LOVE BEING AROUND A GENUINELY HAPPY, CHEERFUL PERSON NO ONE
NK OF THE FEELINGS OF OTHERS FIRST BE RESPECTFUL AND POLITE NEVER GOSSIP OR
ENDS ARRIVE PROMPTLY FOR PARTIES AND SOCIAL ENGAGEMENTS ENTHUSIASM IS CO
E, TOO! NOBODY LIKES A KNOW-IT-ALL THERE IS NO SUCH THING AS HAVING TOO MAN
E LIVE WITH PURPOSE BE DIRECT AND HONEST, NOT PHONY OR FAKE HAVE CONFIDEN
E A SNOB NOT PHONY OR FAKE HAVE CONFIDENCE NOBODY LIKES A KNOW-IT-ALL THE
R TEASE OR MOCK OTHERS DON'T BE SHY DON'T BE A SNOB NOBODY LIKES A KNOW-IT-A
NK OF THE FEELINGS OF OTHERS FIRST BE RESPECTFUL AND POLITE NEVER GOSSIP OR
L ENGAGEMENTS ENTHUSIASM IS CONTAGIOUS, AND SOON YOU WILL BE, TOO! LIVE WI
ER SHOW OFF NEVER TEASE OR MOCK OTHERS DON'T BE SHY DON'T BE A SNOB NOT PI
RFUL AND OUTGOING NOT PHONY OR FAKE HAVE CONFIDENCE NEVER TEASE OR MOCK
OR FAKE CONFIDENCE EMPATHIZE BE CHEERFUL AND OUTGOING THINK OF THE
S HAVING TOO MANY FRIENDS ARRIVE PROMPTLY FOR PARTIES AND SOCIAL ENGAGEM
WAYS SMILE BE A GOOD LISTENER LIVE WITH PURPOSE BE DIRECT AND HONEST, NOT
E SHY DON'T BE A SNOB NEVER SHOW OFF NEVER TEASE OR MOCK OTHERS NOBODY
ND HONEST, NOT PHONY OR FAKE HAVE CONFIDENCE EMPATHIZE BE CHEERFUL AND